The Kissing Blades

"A soul-deep love story and a wild adventure."

—Catherine Coulter

The Steel Caress

"Sharp romantic suspense . . . action-packed . . . a wonderful romantic thriller." —BookBrowser

The Deepest Edge

"An amazing thriller that is exotic, passionate, and exhilarating. Don't miss this book!"

—*Romantic Times* (4½ Stars, Top Pick)

INTO THE FIRE

Jessica Hall

AN ONYX BOOK

ONYX
Published by New American Library, a division of
Penguin Group (USA) Inc., 375 Hudson Street,
New York, New York 10014, U.S.A.
Penguin Books Ltd, 80 Strand,
London WC2R 0RL, England
Penguin Books Australia Ltd, 250 Camberwell Road,
Camberwell, Victoria 3124, Australia
Penguin Books Canada Ltd, 10 Alcorn Avenue,
Toronto, Ontario, Canada M4V 3B2
Penguin Books (N.Z.) Ltd, Cnr Rosedale and Airborne Roads,
Albany, Auckland 1310, New Zealand

Penguin Books Ltd, Registered Offices:
80 Strand, London WC2R 0RL, England

First published by Onyx, an imprint of New American Library,
a division of Penguin Group (USA), Inc.

First Printing, March 2004
10 9 8 7 6 5 4 3 2 1

Prologue

June 23, 1974

What the hell am I doing here?

Marc LeClare hauled himself up out of the mud and swiped at the front of his clothes. Something that looked like dried spider guts had gotten tangled around his fingers until he shook it off and saw it was only some bedraggled Spanish moss. The stench of marsh scum filled his nose as the last of the sunlight glimmered through the dense canopy of juniper and oak. Soon it would be dark, and he was alone.

Alone, lost, and madder than a stepped-on snake.

Louis Gamble and his fraternity brothers would be parked out on the interstate, all of them laughing at him and drinking the rest of the beer.

Marc wiped his filthy face on the sleeve of his equally filthy jacket. "This time, they die."

Part of it was his own damn fault. His roommate had pulled plenty of stunts like this on him since they'd been at college, and he should have realized something was up when they roared past the city limits sign into the back country. But he'd been pissed at his mother for insisting he set a date for the wedding and at the same time harping at him for quitting the football team. The two beers Louie had helped him chug hadn't helped.

Drink up, drink up. Your mamma and your little girl-friend will never know.

Louis had convinced everyone to pile into his van for a road trip, and then had driven west, into the backwoods, down dirt roads, past truck stops and boat shacks. Marc hadn't cared. Even when the van had died in the middle of nowhere, he hadn't gotten suspicious.

Too much beer, not enough brains.

Damn, I thought I checked the oil last weekend. As always, Louis had kept a perfectly straight face when he'd turned to him. *Get out and pull the stick, Marc. I swear, if there's a speck of black, I'm gonna set this piece of shit on fire.* His friend had waited until Marc had walked to the hood before Louie had slammed it into reverse and gunned the engine, sticking his head out the driver's side window to hoot at him. *Still thick as a damn brick. See you later, LeClare.*

He should have stayed on the road; they'd come back in a few hours. They always did. But tonight he didn't feel like waiting, and then he'd seen a light shining in the swamp. He'd been drunk enough to think a light meant a house, and maybe a telephone that he could use to call Louis—and then he'd lost the light, and couldn't find the way back to the road—

Something crackled behind him. He swung around, fists ready. "Shit, Louie, where have you assholes been? You are in serious fucking trouble, leaving me out here in the middle of—"

It wasn't his roommate, but a young girl, standing on the edge of the shadows. She stared at him with enormous, dark eyes.

Big-eyed because she'd heard every filthy word

he'd just yelled. "Uh, hi. Sorry, I thought you were—I didn't mean to scare you."

The girl stayed where she was, and watched him. Mud stained her small, bare feet, but her shabby dress was clean. Sweat darkened the too-long fringe of dark hair over her eyes; the rest was caught back in a short ponytail. An empty crawfish trap dangled from her right hand.

Marc's gaze went from the trap to the buttons just below her collarbone. Judging by the curves straining the sides of the buttonholes, she could be anywhere from thirteen to sixteen years old. What he couldn't figure out was why he had the sense of knowing her. Almost as if they'd met before, but not quite. It wasn't all that comfortable a feeling, either.

She noticed the direction of his stare and took a wary step backward.

"Wait." Afraid she'd disappear, he started up the bank toward her, slipped, and nearly ended up face-down in the muck again. "Wait, shit! Hold on, I need some help."

"You lost, boy?"

Coach Lewis had called him *boy*. *You ain't no quarterback, boy. Best thing you could do for this team is to take your dainty white Creole ass on out of here.*

He lost his footing and rapped the side of his head against a low-hanging willow bough.

"Goddamn it!" He grabbed his head, which felt like it was ready to split, then glared at her. "What the fuck do you think?"

She tensed, shifting her grip on the trap. "I think your mama needs to use a whole lotta soap on that mouth of yours. 'Bye."

"Hey, don't go." He lifted a hand, then dropped it. "Sorry—I'm sorry. I've had a lousy day."

"Do tell." She studied him, and her frown eased a notch. "Where you come from, boy?"

Her funny, singsong way of talking made him inspect her again. Could she be a Cajun? He'd heard his mother say they were worthless and ignorant and stole whatever wasn't nailed down. But this girl didn't look stupid or criminal, just poor.

"My name's Marc. I'm from the city." Guilt prodded him as he realized how he must seem to her—a big, dark guy covered with mud who used swear words in every other sentence—so he stayed put and tried to sound harmless. "What's your name?"

"Genevieve."

"Nice name." Like a princess from a fairy tale. "You live around here, right?"

"*Oui.*"

Better and better—she knew her way around, then. "Can you show me how to get out of here?"

She thought about it, long enough to make him start itching with fresh sweat. At last she swung a hand toward the trees. "This way."

He followed her through the hip-tall weeds, away from the riverbank and up into the trees. What was she doing, running around out here near dark? Setting crawfish traps? He picked up the pace as she got farther ahead of him, but not knowing the uneven ground the way she did made it impossible to catch up.

"Ginny, wait up—you're going too fast."

She stopped and waited until he caught up. He thought he heard her mutter something about city boys before she asked, "What're you doing out here in the Atchafalaya anyway?"

Feeling and acting like a horse's ass is what. "My

friends thought it would be a good joke to get me drunk and dump me out here."

"That's not funny." She took his arm and tugged, guiding him around a dark-leafed plant. When he glanced back he saw it was a huge clump of poison ivy. "You don't act drunk."

"Takes more than a couple of beers to do that." Her hand seemed so small on his sleeve. All her nails were short and bare, trimmed straight across as if someone had clipped them with a pair of scissors. She smelled faintly of soap and sunshine, and made him realize how bad he must stink. "How old are you?"

"Seventeen next month." She cocked her head to one side. "You go to college in the city, Marc?"

"Yeah, I'm in my sophomore year." He hated it. "I'm nineteen."

"My cousin Darel's nineteen." She made a gesture toward one side of the bayou. "He doesn't go to college, but he never gets lost."

"I've never been in the swamp before." Feeling defensive, he swiped at his jacket again. "You live with your cousin?"

"No." She pointed past a pair of oaks at a faint, glowing light. "That's my house up there."

As they got closer, Marc saw that the house was little more than a clapboard shack. It sat a few yards off a smaller branch of the Atchafalaya, huddled under a pair of ancient, gnarled oak trees. How could a whole family fit in such a tiny place? The utility shed in the back of his house was bigger.

"You live with your parents?"

"*Oui*. Papa traps and fishes, and Mama sells bait for the fishermen who come. So do I." Her expression changed as she watched him. "What, you don't like fish?"

He tried to imagine his elegant mother selling bait. Not even if someone drugged her. "I like it fine." He glanced at the house, and thought of the other few rumors he'd heard about Cajuns on the bayou. Some people said the men shot first and asked questions later. "Is your dad going to be pissed—uh, upset—to find me with you?"

She shook her head. "You haven't done anything wrong. Papa will take you back to the city."

Marc hoped so. He didn't want to get shot. Didn't want his mother getting wind of this mess. He also had to take care of Louie and his frat brothers. Bigtime.

Yet all those troubling thoughts slowly slipped away as the last rays of sunlight touched Genevieve. She had white, flawless skin, the kind that made her eyes seem almost black. And her hair . . . God, her hair was gorgeous.

No girl he'd ever known looked like her. Sounded like her. Smelled like her. She was as exotic and out of place as a butterfly in a garbage dump. That sense of knowing surged inside him again, but this time it came with heat and wanting. If his hands hadn't been so filthy, he would have touched her.

"Will you come with us?"

"Into the city?" She laughed a little. "Why?"

He found a clean spot on the side of his jacket and wiped off his hand before he took hers. She had little calluses on her palm, but her hand was sturdy and strong. That was when he knew, just as surely as if he could see into the future. They were meant to meet. Meant to touch.

She was the one.

I'm going to marry this girl. "I'd like to talk to you some more."

Chapter One

"Wow."

Isabel Duchesne closed the door behind her and walked into the empty warehouse, eyeing the dimensions of the main floor and the two rows of windows on each side of the building. After trying for almost a year to find affordable office space for her community center—and failing—she could hardly believe all this would be hers.

It's the least I can do for you, Sable, Marc LeClare had said after he proposed donating the vacant warehouse property he owned for her project. *Think of how good this will make me look in the polls.*

She remembered returning his infectious grin. *As long as you don't take it back when you're elected governor.*

Marc had mentioned that a cabinetmaker had rented the warehouse for a number of years, which would account for the faint smell of pine that still lingered. The cobwebs, old sawdust, and rows of empty steel shelving would have to go, but the large, open space was truly ideal.

More than ideal—it was perfect. And it was *hers*.

Sable couldn't help laughing with delight as she

turned around, looking at everything. She had been resigned to squeezing everything into whatever tiny
space she could rent, but now she'd have enough room
for reception and intake desks, offices for her and the
volunteer staff she intended to recruit, and perhaps
even a prenatal and pediatric screening area for pregnant mothers and young children.

"Oh, you've definitely got my vote, Marc," she
murmured to herself as she wandered around the
main floor. Overhead were lofted storage rooms which
could also be put to good use. "This is almost too good
to be true."

Just like Marc.

She made a face as she thought of how awkward
she'd felt the last time they'd met. How hard it had
been for her to know what to say and how to act, never
mind dealing with all these new emotions. She hadn't
even been sure if she wanted a relationship with him.

Marc, on the other hand, had been so happy that
nothing seemed to matter except that they were together. He had listened and watched her intently, and
treated her like she was the most precious thing in the
world. As important and busy as his life was, he'd said
she was now his first priority.

I hope I don't disappoint him.

She glanced down at her suit. It was severely tai-
lored, charcoal gray, with a plain white shell. *Dress like
one of them lawyers on Ally McBeal,* her cousin Hilaire
had advised, *and you'll fit right in with that crowd.* She'd
never felt comfortable around wealthy, powerful people, but Marc would help her—he had assured her of
that.

*They're just like everyone else, Isabel. Besides, now
they'll know you're mine.*

Commercial property in the city of New Orleans

was at such a premium these days that the only way to get an affordable space was to tear down something else or build on top of it. Since Sable's program was financed solely through fund-raisers and other private donations, she hadn't been able to afford either option.

You ain't got no business messin' with them folks in the city, her aunt had said when Sable had told her about Marc's offer. *Caine's right—they don't care about what happens to us.*

Her smile faded as she remembered that, and what Caine Gantry had been doing to sabotage her project. Like most of the other Cajuns on the Atchafalaya, he'd come with his whole crew when Sable had held her first planning meeting at St. Mary's Church. The fishermen had stood silent at the back of the sanctuary, listening to her presentation but not once joining in the discussion of the project.

When Sable was finished, Caine had been the first to walk to the front of the church, but he had ignored the sign-up sheet she'd held out to him. He'd loomed over her, then had very calmly taken her roster and torn it up.

We don't need your charity or your friends from the city coming in and snooping round here.

Why, Caine? She looked at him, then his crew. She knew they were fighting with the wardens from the Department of Fish and Game over new licensing and equipment requirements, and half of them were into illegal smuggling and God knew what on the side. *Do you have something to hide?*

He'd leaned over the desk, his black eyes as cold as his voice. *Go back to Shreveport, Isabel. You don't belong here anymore.*

The juxtaposition of her old ties to the Cajun community and her new relationship with Marc LeClare sank in. The future governor of Louisiana seemed willing to face anything for her sake, but Caine Gantry had already proved to be a big obstacle. So would the press, when they found out about her and Marc. It would be open season on both of them.

How many times you got to get burned 'fore you learn, child? her aunt had demanded. *You don't belong in the city.*

It was true that she hadn't been back to New Orleans for years, not since she'd transferred from Tulane to Louisiana State. Not since the night of the Summer Magnolias dance—aka the absolute worst night of her life.

Hey, coon-ass! Where's your boyfriend?
Afraid he'll stand you up for someone with shoes?
Don't forget your corsage!

And the laughter, the cruel laughter that still rang inside her head after all these years . . .

No. She refused to brood over Jean-Del and the humiliation she'd suffered because of him another second. *That is ancient history; everything is different now. Marc makes everything different. I don't have to be afraid of them anymore.*

A sound from overhead tugged her from her thoughts. It sounded like shoes shuffling.

"Hello?" Her voice boomed in the emptiness, and she cringed and lowered it a notch. "Marc, are you up there?"

There was the sound of a cough, then, "Yeah."

"I'll come up." Sable picked up her briefcase and headed up the staircase. The wrought iron squealed under her weight, making her grab the railing. "Whoa. Great building, but I think we need new stairs." When she reached the top all she could see were vague shapes and shadows. "Marc? Can you switch on the lights?"

Something moved, making a scraping sound, but no lights came on.

"Did we blow a fuse?" A faint, unpleasant odor made her wrinkle her nose. "Do you know where the electrical box is?" As her eyes adjusted to the dark, she put down her briefcase and tentatively moved toward the sound. That smell—*gasoline and . . . fish?*—grew thicker.

"Marc? Are you all right? M—"

Her foot slammed into something immobile, and she fell forward. Her arms went out automatically as she landed on her hands and knees in a sticky puddle of liquid, next to something large and solid. A heavier, terrible smell made her stomach clench. Lights overhead flickered on.

She was kneeling in a pool of dark blood. Right next to a man's body.

He lay facedown, and her wide eyes focused on his short silver hair. A wide, deep indentation distorted the back of his head, and the hair around it was black with congealed blood.

"Oh, God." She grabbed him, rolling him over with frantic, bloody hands, shaking her head. "No, not you. Not—" She went still.

Marc LeClare's face was slack, and his kind brown eyes stared blindly up at the ceiling.

Sable wiped the blood from her hand on her blouse before she pressed her fingertips to the side of his neck. His skin was clammy and cool, and she could feel no pulse.

He was dead—had been dead for some time.

"Please, God, no." She scrambled to her feet, but her knees were shaking so much she nearly went down again. Bile rose in her throat and she choked it back down, looking wildly around them.

Did he fall? What did this to him? Who—She glanced up at the lights and slowly backed away toward the stairs. The smell of fish and gasoline grew stronger.

Whoever did this turned on the lights. He called me up here.

Something swung out of the dark at her, glancing off her head, knocking her back down to the floor. She slipped in the blood, trying to push herself up. The stench of fish and gasoline and death smothered her. "Stop it—don't—"

A second blow sent her hurtling into the dark.

This had gone straight to hell in a hurry.

Billy Tibbideau reached down and adjusted his crotch. His balls felt like they were curdling, and sweat made a wide streak down the back of his green Gantry Charters T-shirt. He'd never hit a woman before, and the bad feelings were knotting up his chest.

You don't put your hands on a woman in anger, Billy, Caine had told him, over and over. *You're a man. You're strong. They're weak.*

"I had to do it." Billy Tibbideau paced a circle around the unconscious woman and the dead man. "She ain't got no business comin' here, snoopin' around."

Damn women are God's curse on men. That was what his daddy always said. When he was a boy, his father had about killed himself trying to keep a roof over their heads and food on the table, but had his mother ever appreciated it? Had she ever let the man have a moment of peace? No, sir, she'd harp on him from the minute he stepped foot in the house, whining about his drinking or money or Billy, until his daddy had to give her the back of his hand, just to shut her up.

William Tibbideau Sr. said that was all women were good for anyway—walloping or screwing—and you had to give them plenty of both to keep them in line. Caine might not wallop them, but he screwed plenty.

The tightness in Billy's chest made him want to kick the woman, but he crouched down to look at her face, and saw it clearly for the first time. "Aw, shit."

It was her—Isabel, Remy Duchesne's girl, the one who'd stirred up half the bayou with her do-gooder nonsense. Remy should have beaten some sense into her years ago, but the old man never had been able to control his women.

You don't hit women, Caine's voice echoed inside Billy's skull.

Had she seen his face? Had she recognized him?

Billy tossed aside the culling pole he'd used to knock her out and went to the window to look down into the back alley. No one in sight, but he'd have to get a move on if he was going to finish the job. Not that he had to—he could wash his hands of this and walk away. But that wouldn't get him the rest of his money.

He'd earned that money and then some.

The pint of Jack he kept in his back pocket was half empty; he drained the rest before wiping his mouth on his sleeve. The bad feelings receded an inch or two. First place he was stopping on the way home was a liquor store, get him a couple of fifths. His wife wouldn't like that, but unlike his mother, Cecilia knew better than to open her mouth to him when he was in a mood.

"Nothin' to it. Torch the place, Billy, that's all." He grabbed the box of bottles he'd brought and carried it to the stairs. "That's all, my ass."

The bodies changed things—they'd have to burn along with the building. He wasn't taking a murder rap just because Remy's girl didn't have the sense to keep her nose out of other people's business. He used his lighter to ignite the strip of rag stuffed in the top of three bottles and then threw them into the corners of the loft. The rags ignited the gasoline inside the bottles as soon as they shattered.

Gotta hurry. He hauled the box downstairs and slipped out into the alley, then tossed the remaining bottles through the windows before he looked up to see how the second floor was burning.

He saw bloody fingers appear in a gap between the boards over the windows. They clenched the edge, straining at it.

She was alive. She was trying to get out.

"Playing possum on me, sneaky little bitch." Billy ran around the side, checking the street from the corner before he slipped out to the front of the warehouse. She wouldn't be able to get out the windows, but if she got down the stairs—

Isabel knew Caine. She'd *tell* Caine.

His hands shook as he frantically searched his pockets, then found the key he'd been given. He shoved it into the lock and turned it, but he used too much force and the key snapped in half. "God*damn*." He tried to pull out the broken bit, but it was jammed, along with the lock.

Dumb-ass firemen wouldn't notice it, Billy decided. Heat and smoke were pouring out of the first-floor windows; in a few minutes the whole place would go up. The important thing was, Isabel wouldn't be walking out of there alive. She wouldn't go tattling to Caine on him.

He could almost feel his daddy's big hand clap him

on the shoulder. *One less whining bitch in the world—you done good, son.*

Watching the fire and imagining the woman inside burning made the last of the bad feelings go away. He had a whomping hard-on for some reason, though. That was fine with him; he'd nail Cecilia as soon as he got home. The distant sound of an approaching siren made him dart back around the building and trot down to where he'd parked his truck.

Billy climbed in and started the engine, and rubbed his palm against his crotch. His dick was so hard he might not be able to wait until he got home. He'd just drive down a ways from the building, park, and watch it burn.

Just to be sure.

"Mind telling me why we're responding to a ten-twenty-six?"

J. D. Gamble glanced sideways at his partner, Therese Vincent. "The warehouse belongs to Marc Le-Clare."

"Ah." Terri watched a mother pushing twins in a double stroller cross at the light in front of them. "Cort busy again?"

J. D. nodded. "Fire safety conference in Biloxi."

"He call?"

The light turned green, and he cruised through the intersection. "Yeah."

"So Cort sends us to do his job, as a favor to your dad's college buddy." She shook her head. "That makes perfect sense. Should we stop by the firehouse and fill out his reports for him afterwards?"

"Cort types better than you."

"Monkeys type better than me." J. D.'s partner studied her painfully short fingernails. She kept them that way to avoid biting them. "J. D., have I mentioned lately that your brother is an asshole?"

His mouth hitched. "Several times."

Although it was only eight a.m., and most of the shops remained closed, a few hard-core early birds had already hit the street. As he turned on to Bienville Street, J. D. spotted a couple wearing feathered masks, drinking coffee from Styrofoam cups as they peered through the lacy wrought iron grille guarding an antique store's display windows. Even if the biggest party on the planet weren't in progress, no one would have given the masked tourists a second look. Mardi Gras was a year-round business in the Vieux Carré.

Terri took out a cigarette, but opened the window halfway before she lit it. One of the tourist shops was already playing zydeco, and the zippy little riffs echoed on the nearly empty street. "Your folks throwing the usual soiree next weekend?"

The annual Noir et Blanc Gala, held at his parents' Garden District mansion on the weekend after Mardi Gras started, was as legendary as his father's restaurant. Though tourists flocked daily to the Krewe of Louis to order from the all-French menus, the family party was restricted to five hundred of the most prominent members of New Orleans's first families. Dress was strictly regulated to two colors—black and white—and many of his mother's friends flew to Paris each year to find new styles to wear and wow the society reporters.

"Yeah. Evan and his wife are flying in from Montana on Friday." He eyed his partner. "My mother did send you an invitation, didn't she?"

"Why, no. My goodness." Terri pressed a hand to her cheek. "It must have gotten lost in the mail."

He knew what Elizabet would do if he asked her

about it—flutter her hands and blame one of the maids. "I'm inviting you. Come on by so you can meet Evan's wife, Wendy. You'll like her."

"No, thanks." She ran a hand over her short brown hair, then tugged at her charcoal gray jacket. "My wardrobe simply isn't up to one of your mama's parties."

"Doesn't matter."

"Au contraire, my friend. When you're the only woman wearing permanent press in a room full of white designer silk gowns, it absolutely does matter." The smell of burning wood wafted into the car, and Terri squinted through the windshield at the black smoke still rising in a voluminous column into the sky. "There it is."

After negotiating his way through the police barricades, J. D. parked out of the way, a block behind the pumper truck. Flashing red, blue, and white lights lit the hazy air like dance club strobes. Heat rolled out through the smoke in transparent waves, driving back anyone who strayed too close. Firefighters held hoses on the smoldering building from all sides, but it was only too obvious that the structure was gutted. The stench of wet charred wood and the chemical foam they'd sprayed over a burned-out car parked in the alley next to the building added an unpleasant density to the thickened air.

Terri got out with J. D. and slammed the car door as she surveyed the scene. "I hope that guy has decent insurance," she said, nodding toward the car before scanning the other buildings. "Not a good place for a campfire—the whole block could have gone up."

J. D. walked up to a patrolman who was busy filling out a field report. The uniform recognized him and lowered his clipboard. "Lieutenant?"

J. D. scanned the crowd, looking for particularly avid faces. Mostly there were tourists; some were snapping pictures. "Where are you boys at here?"

"They got the fire mostly out, Lieutenant, but the building's history." The officer grinned. "We got a survivor, though."

"Lucky bastard." Terri peeled off her jacket and draped it over her arm as she plucked at the front of her blouse a few times. "Must have been a hot one."

"Old building, lotta wood," the cop told her. "All it takes is a little gasoline, a match, and whomp, you got yourself a barbecue."

"Officer. Lieutenant." One of the firemen joined them. Water made channels in the black of his soot-streaked gear. "Security guard from down the block claims the place was empty, but we pulled someone out of there. We're going in to have a look around, see if anyone else was caught inside."

J. D. nodded. "Where's the survivor?"

"Still at the unit, getting oxygen." The firefighter jerked his chin to the left.

J. D. saw the fire rescue unit, parked two alleys down. Two men in paramedic jackets were flanking a smaller figure sitting just inside the open back doors. A glimmer of dark red hair made his eyes narrow. "Is that a woman?"

"Yeah. Real looker, too." The uniform cleared his throat when Terri gave him the eye. "Uh, not a local, according to witnesses. She's not carrying any ID and she's not saying much. Couple of minor head injuries."

"Nice that you noticed that," Terri drawled. "Her being such a looker and all."

J. D. didn't laugh. To Terri, he said, "Start canvassing the crowd. I'll talk to the girl."

She huffed in mock disgust. "You always talk to the girls."

J. D.'s attention remained fixed on the woman, who had a plastic oxygen mask covering her nose and mouth. Her hair was red. An unusual red, deep and pure, that glowed like old garnets. He'd only known one woman with that particular color hair.

Can't be her.

He stepped over a double length of wide gray fire hose and headed for the unit. As he drew closer, he saw other, disturbing details—the small, slender build, the pale skin, the elegant, long-fingered hands. Even the shreds of ripped stockings still clinging to her legs couldn't disguise their shapely length. Or the two-inch-long scar running down the front of her right leg.

The memory hit him like an angry fist.

Are you all right? Seeing her white face, the blood running down her leg. She'd fallen in the cafeteria, right next to his table. Lifting her up. *You're bleeding—*

One of the paramedics looked up. "Help you, Lieutenant?"

"No." When he saw the blood on her clothes, J. D. pulled the mask from the woman's face. And even though he was braced for it, the sight of her face nearly drove him to his knees. "Sable."

Wide eyes, as dark as *café brûlot*, stared up at him in shock. She didn't say a word.

He tossed the mask aside, still not convinced she was real. As he reached for her, she moved her head, just enough to avoid his touch—and the stunned look turned to one of anger and disgust.

An answering rage welled up inside him, hot and strong enough to make him want to snatch her up in his arms. He forced himself to study her, but he couldn't see where the blood had come from. "What happened to her? Where is she injured?"

The paramedic retrieved the mask. "She's okay. She just inhaled a little smoke, got some bumps on her head. Probably slipped and fell, trying to get out."

He wanted to strip her down and check her personally. "And the blood?"

"The head wounds didn't break the skin; I don't think it's hers."

J. D. saw fear flicker over her face. "Is she done here?"

The paramedic checked her lungs with a stethoscope, then nodded. "Yeah, but she needs a follow-up. She might have a concussion."

"I'll handle it." He took her by the arms, felt her flinch, felt the contraction of the tense muscles beneath her soft skin. What color remained under her skin abruptly went out of her face at that first touch, the same way it had that day at the cafeteria. Her dark eyes remained fixed on his face.

She's afraid. Why? It wasn't as if he'd never touched her before. He'd touched her plenty. All over. Every inch.

Before he could haul her to her feet, the patrolman appeared at his side. "Lieutenant, you'd better come over here and have a look at this."

He let her go. "What?"

"They just found a body inside." The patrolman handed him a scorched, unfolded wallet in an evidence bag. "ID says Marcus Aurelius LeClare."

Like any man, Billy preferred screwing to jerking off, but he'd oddly enjoyed sitting in his truck and stroking himself as he'd watched the building burn. No one had paid any mind to him, not even the two curious old folks who had parked their big Lincoln Town Car behind his truck and come out to stand and gawk. They were only three feet away from his window, but for all they cared, he could have been invisible.

Yet he'd been the one to give them the show. Him, no-account Billy Tibbideau.

It was a strange thing. Billy liked doing his little side jobs; he'd always been smart enough to get away with them, too. Only this time, knowing Isabel was caught in there and being burned alive, and that he was the one who'd put her there—that made him feel special. Powerful.

He liked the feeling.

"That's right, girl," he muttered as he worked his fist. "I got you this time, didn't I?"

His pleasure didn't last long, though. It dwindled as soon as he saw a firefighter haul Isabel Duchesne out of the burning building. He stopped stroking himself as soon as he saw her emerge, coughing and covered with soot.

Aw, damn. His erection abruptly wilted in his fist. *Why the hell ain't she burned up?*

The old lady standing on the sidewalk turned to stare at him as if she'd heard him.

He scowled back as he tucked his flaccid penis back in his jeans and yanked up his zipper. "Who you looking at, you nosy old bitch?"

She opened her mouth to say something, and then her eyes shifted to the other side of his truck. She grabbed her husband's arm and tugged him back toward their car.

He smirked. "That's right, you better—"

Something drove Billy's head into the steering

wheel, then dragged him across the bench seat and out the passenger door.

The big dark man slammed him into the cab frame. "This your idea of working?"

Billy stared up into Caine Gantry's black eyes. His boss was the only man Billy respected—and feared— more than his own daddy.

"Hey, Caine." He darted a nervous glance at the fire. "I was—I just—"

Caine turned his head and stared at the blazing building for a long moment. When he looked back at Billy, his expression was ferocious. "You dumb son of a bitch."

Billy knew he was in for it then, and did the sensible thing: He kneed his boss in the groin.

Only Caine shifted a moment too soon, and Billy's knee connected with the big man's thigh, which was the same as smacking into a brick wall.

His boss smiled and stepped back. "Thank you."

Caine had a reputation for never hitting first, or more than once.

"It ain't what you're thinking." Billy stumbled back, frantically trying to put space between them. "I didn't do nothing wrong. I'm on the job, Caine, honest."

The big man came after him. "I'm paying you to sit here and jerk off in front of old ladies?"

Shame and rage buzzed in Billy's head as he struck again, this time going for Caine's belly and ribs. The big man only pushed him back and hit him in the face—once.

Pain exploded inside Billy's head, while big dark spots danced in front of his eyes.

A heartbeat later Caine had him pinned against the truck again. He leaned in and sniffed, then shoved a hand into Billy's back pocket and pulled out the empty pint of Jack.

He looked into Billy's eyes. "I told you what I'd do if I found you drinking again, didn't I?"

Sweating and shaking, Billy swallowed, and then nodded once. "It won't happen again. I just slipped up, Caine. Just a little bit."

The bottle went flying and smashed all over the road.

"Aw, come on." Tears welled into Billy's eyes. "You can't do this to me. We're friends. I got a wife—I need the work."

Caine reached into his shirt pocket and pulled out a wad of cash, which he stuffed in Billy's bleeding mouth. "That's all you're getting outta me." He released him and took a step back. "Hit the road."

Billy spit the stained bills into his hand and clutched them. "Ain't got to be this way, Caine. You and me, we can work this out. Things'll be better—"

The big Cajun grabbed him by the hair and rammed his head into the cab frame, then let him drop to the ground. "We're done. Hit the road."

This isn't happening.

As Sable sat in the back of the unmarked police car, she tried to sort out what had happened. Marc was dead, and she had nearly died herself. Someone had knocked her out and then had set fire to the warehouse.

To cover up the murder.

Why would someone want Marc dead? Was it because of his campaign? Was this some kind of assassination? She'd researched him before they'd met, and she knew how popular he was—he'd been favored to win the election easily, and even the press liked him.

The press.

They'd be here soon. They'd want to know what had happened, and she was the only witness. No one knew who she was. To the rest of the world she was nothing, nobody, a charity worker from Shreveport with a project no one had cared about.

She couldn't tell them about her and Marc. Not by herself. No one would believe her.

"Pretty little thing," one of the cops standing outside the car said to another as they both stared at her. "Too young to be the wife—girlfriend, maybe?"

She blocked out the voices and concentrated on what had happened. She remembered walking upstairs, smelling that terrible odor, finding Marc dead. Someone had hit her, then pain, falling, blackness. She'd woken up next to Marc's body, flames all around her. She'd tried to drag him first, but he was too heavy, and the fire was burning out of control. She'd gotten to a window, but she couldn't pry away the boards over it, and then she had groped her way downstairs. The dense, oily smoke and the heat had made it impossible to see the way out. She'd nearly lost consciousness again.

I could have died in there. Right next to Marc.

The rest of her memory was patchy—she'd been so frightened. The last things that had registered were the terrifying sound of the ceiling falling in, and the strong grip of the firefighter who had hauled her out of there.

Oh, thank God, help me—

Are you hurt?

Sable looked down at herself. Marc's blood was all over her blouse and jacket. It was dried and flaking on her skin; it was under her fingernails. For a moment her head swam, and she thought she might have to throw up.

"Ma'am?" One of the patrolmen looked in on her, his expression concerned. "You want me to get Lieutenant Gamble?"

"No, thank you." She took a deep breath and willed her voice to remain steady. "I'm fine."

She wasn't fine. Seeing Jean-Delano had been as much a shock as finding Marc dead. But he wasn't her Jean-Delano anymore; he was Lieutenant J. D. Gamble, a homicide detective. One of the cops had told her that after Jean-Del had left her to go and see Marc's body. Not that it mattered. He could have been mayor of New Orleans and it wouldn't have made a difference. Jean-Del was part of the past, a relic, someone she'd turned her back on and forgotten.

And still the shock of seeing him kept smashing over her, as hard and merciless as the blow that had knocked her unconscious.

Jean-Del, here. Jean-Del, a cop. She hadn't given anyone her name. *How did he know I was here?*

The tall, lanky brunette who had been speaking to J. D. a few yards from the car climbed in the front and looked back over the bench seat. She had a clever, narrow face, shrewd, gray green eyes, and oddly beautiful hands, like an artist's. "I'm Sergeant Vincent. How are you holding up?"

The cool voice slapped Sable out of her daze, but she didn't blink, didn't react. She had spent years learning how to hide behind her own face, and now it was time to take cover. "I'm okay."

"Good. I'd like to ask you some questions, if you feel up to it?" When she nodded, Sergeant Vincent took out a notebook. "What's your full name, ma'am?"

"Isabel Marie Duchesne."

She wrote that down. "Isabel, what's your home address?"

Sable thought of her father, and how he would react to the news that she'd nearly been killed in a fire. She couldn't allow them to contact Remy. "I don't have one."

The cop's dark eyebrows arched. "You're homeless?"

What would be a reasonable excuse? She remembered the paper she'd left lying on the front seat of her car, folded out to the classified section. "I'm looking for an apartment at the moment." That was part of the truth. She had never been a very convincing liar, even under the best of circumstances.

"You weren't looking for an apartment in this part of town, though. Why did you come here this morning, Ms. Duchesne?"

"I'm also looking for office space."

The brunette tapped her pencil against the notebook for a moment. "Why don't you tell me what happened, starting from the time you arrived?"

Something made Sable's hands sting as she grabbed the edge of the seat. *No one knows about us.* Carefully she eased her fingers off the vinyl-covered cushion and put her hands in her lap. She had to stay calm, keep her head straight. She didn't have to talk about Marc. All she had to do was give a statement to the police.

But J. D. is the police, a snide little voice inside her head reminded her. *And your track record with him sucks.*

The woman cop was waiting for her to say something. "I can't remember much."

Sergeant Vincent regarded her for a long moment. "You have amnesia?"

Sable stared back at her, unable to tell if she was joking or serious. "It's just . . . things are a little fuzzy."

"Are they?" Sergeant Vincent glanced down and frowned. "What did you do to your hands?"

Sable examined her palms, both of which had some long, dark splinters embedded in the flesh above each wrist. For the life of her, she didn't know how they had gotten there. "I don't know."

Without warning, Jean-Delano slid in behind the wheel and slammed his door, making Sable jump.

Not Jean Delano. J. D. Lieutenant Gamble. Have to remember that.

He had changed over the years. His hair was shorter, clipped close to his head on the sides, probably to keep it from curling. There were a few silver strands at his temples. He wasn't as lean as he'd been in college; his shoulders seemed wider, his chest deeper. A thin scar flagged one of his cheekbones and, along with the lines etching his temples, made him appear tougher, harder.

"We'll do this at the station." J. D. started the engine and looked at the brunette. "You ready to go?"

The way Sable's heart skipped at the sound of his voice annoyed her. *Forget about his voice, his face. He's just a cop.*

"Yeah." Sergeant Vincent flipped the notepad closed as J. D. shifted into drive and pulled out from the curb. "In a hurry, are we?" He didn't answer her, and she clipped on her seat belt. "Ho. Kay."

Sable dragged her thoughts away from J. D. and concentrated on what she had to do first. Remy—the news of what had happened would be too much of a shock. Her father was on heart medication now, and his doctor had warned her about the dangers of any additional stress. That meant keeping him away from the city and out of this. "I have to get to a phone as soon as possible."

"No problem, Ms. Duchesne." J. D.'s partner lit a cigarette. "You can make your call from the station."

J. D.'s gaze met hers in the rearview mirror for a moment. That was one thing that hadn't changed—the startling blue of his eyes. They went dark when he was angry, and right now they looked as black as the depths of hell.

I'm not letting him take me there again.

Terri Vincent loved being a cop, but she wasn't too crazy about the paperwork.

As J. D. drove them back to headquarters, she made a mental list of the reports and the forms she would have to fill out. There were a lot. Finding a dead body at the scene of an arson was serious business.

The New Orleans Police Department had relocated the year before into the new, state-of-the-art facility built for them by the city as part of an ongoing campaign to improve local law enforcement. The new headquarters housed everything required for the day-to-day control of the eight police districts under NOPD command, along with computerized infrastructures that automated everything from ballistics identification to evidence tracking. Community policing and investigation units were integrated with special teams to coordinate local, state, and federal investigations, as well as supervise major annual events like Mardi Gras and the Sugar Bowl.

Yet as with most metropolitan law enforcement agencies, it already looked like the force had been entrenched in the new building for decades. Overcrowded work space, rows of dilapidated filing cabinets, and endless stacks of paperwork formed a labyrinth on every floor. The new computer systems took up precious space and generated reams of reports to add to the clutter.

Terri noticed a group of college students sitting quiet and sullen on the hard wooden benches in front of the big desk that was the first stop on their way to processing. Someone's Mardi Gras party had gotten out of hand, judging from the bruised, sweaty faces and the plastic barf bags the desk sergeant had distributed.

J. D. walked their witness straight past check-in and went for the elevator. Terri stayed behind long enough to send a couple of uniforms to Marc LeClare's house, to collect the widow and bring her down to the morgue to confirm the ID.

"You going to call your dad?" Terri said as she caught up, grabbing the elevator door before it closed.

"Later." He punched the second-floor button.

She didn't like the expression on her partner's face. It was starting to look permanent. "You want to do the prelim report first?" She was hopeful; J. D. was a much better typist than she was—plus their witness probably needed a few minutes to compose herself.

"No." When the doors opened, J. D. steered Sable to the left, toward the corridor of interrogation rooms, offices, and cubicles that made up the Division of Homicide.

So he wanted to get right to the interview. Not a bad idea, considering the feeding frenzy the press would descend to as soon as they heard Marc LeClare was dead. "Want to run this by the captain first, in case this turns out to be a murder?"

J. D. paused, long enough to make Terri realize something was definitely wrong.

"No." He went toward the first available room.

She'd known something was up, back in the Quarter, but J. D. was too good a cop to ignore procedure. She caught his arm. "Hey. Why don't we ask Hazenel and Garcia to take this one? I got that vacation time coming up, and they still owe us for catching that leather-bar shooting last month."

He didn't bat an eyelash. "No."

Sable watched their exchange, tensed but silent.

Terri swung a hand toward the room. "Go in and sit down, Ms. Duchesne. We'll be with you in a minute." As soon as the witness had crossed the threshold, Terri shut the door and got between it and her partner. "You want to tell me exactly what is going on here?"

"I know her."

"Oh, yeah, I figured out that much. Who is she?"

"Someone I knew back in college." He stared through the frosted glass panel, his dark eyes tracking the movements of Sable's shadow.

Terri took out a cigarette, and then remembered that the building had a strict no-smoking policy and scowled. "Okay. Here's the deal: The victim was your father's best friend, and you went to school with the only witness we've got. That spells conflict of interest in large capital letters underlined three times." When he didn't respond to the joke, she got serious. "We have to give it over to Hazenel and Garcia. Let them handle it."

"No."

"She's young and beautiful; Marc LeClare was old and rich. Doesn't take a genius to figure out that equation—are you listening to me?" She prodded his chest with a finger. "You can*not* screw around with this girl, J. D. The captain will have your testicles for breakfast."

"I'm not screwing—" A passing detective gave them a curious look, so J. D. leaned in and lowered his voice. "I'm not screwing her, and she wasn't screwing Marc."

"And you know this how? Through your secret psychic powers?" Terri sighed. "Jesus, for all we know, *she* could have done LeClare and set fire to the place."

"Before or after she conked herself in the head?"

She shrugged. "Maybe trying to find parking pissed her off. I've been tempted to slam my head into the windshield a few times, looking for a space."

He didn't laugh, the way he normally would. "Someone tried to kill her, Ter. I'm not letting her out of my sight. Got it?"

She'd never seen him like this. Not even around Cort when both of them were having a crappy day. "Sure. I got it." She stepped to the side and swung a hand at the door. "But I'm doing the interview with you."

He dragged a hand through his short black hair, spiking it. "Terri—"

"Don't even go there, J. D." If he was going to make a damn fool of himself, she'd be there to cover his ass. "I don't care how cozy you two were back at Tulane. She's a witness to an arson and possibly the murder of our future governor. Her face will be on the front page of every newspaper in the state by morning. You want to be listed as the detective in charge of the case, or the embittered ex-boyfriend?"

He grabbed the knob and nearly yanked the door off its hinges. "I question her."

"Knock yourself out, pal." Terri stalked past him.

Chapter Two

Their witness had seated herself at the conference table inside the interview room. It felt a little stuffy, so Terri opened a window before asking Sable if she wanted anything to drink.

"May I have some water, please?" Her voice sounded raspy and strained, but that might have been from the smoke.

As Terri got a cup from the cooler and filled it, she kept an eye on her partner. J. D.'s usual method with witnesses was to sit down, put them at ease, and charm all the details out of them. He was good at it, too. Her partner never had a problem making anyone feel as if they could tell him anything. She'd probably told him way too much about herself over the years.

Not this time, though. J. D. didn't open the interview by consoling the victim, didn't establish rapport, didn't do anything the way he usually did. He didn't even sit down, but slowly walked the length of the room, watching Sable with the single-minded intensity of a starved junkyard dog presented with a wounded rabbit.

Or a rejected lover, looking for a little revenge.

It didn't make sense to Terri. Sable Duchesne was a very pretty woman, but hardly J. D.'s type. He stuck to high-maintenance Garden District debutantes who never wore white after Labor Day and had their names plastered all over the society pages. Lately he'd been spending a lot of time with one particularly obnoxious Creole debutante, Moriah Navarre, and if his mama had her way, he would be married to her as soon as possible.

Marc LeClare's death would definitely upset J. D.'s father, and possibly put Elizabet Gamble's wedding plans on the back burner. That worked for Terri—any excuse to keep from shopping for a dress was okay by her, and she'd never been too crazy about the idea of J. D. marrying The Deb.

"Here you go." She handed Sable the water, and noticed the wounds on her palms again when she accepted the cup. "You sure you don't remember how you got those splinters, Ms. Duchesne?"

Sable examined her hands. "I think I tried to get out through a window."

As Terri sat down, J. D. came to stand over Sable, not touching her but getting a little too close. The witness ignored him completely.

Terri cleared her throat and gave her partner a direct look. *Get on with it*, she mouthed.

"Are you living in New Orleans now?" he asked.

Sable drank some of the water before she answered. "No."

He circled around her chair, as if trying to draw her attention to him. "Why were you at that warehouse this morning?"

"I was looking at it as office space." She stared down at the cup. "I think I should speak to an attorney."

"You'll speak to me now," J. D. told her.

After a minute of silence, Terri decided to give her a

gentle prod. "Ms. Duchesne, you're not being charged with anything. We only want to know what happened."

Sable's shoulders hunched. "I don't remember much." She sounded scared and defensive.

Now J. D. will play her. Terri had seen him soothe any number of other shaken witnesses, reassuring them while coaxing the information from them.

J. D. clamped one hand on the back of Sable's chair and grabbed the hair at the back of her head. "Who hit you?"

"J. D." Alarmed, Terri got to her feet.

He didn't pull Sable's hair, but pushed it out of the way and examined her scalp. There was a large swollen knot under her hair. "Did you see who did this?"

Dark red hair flew as Sable jerked her head to one side, away from his touch. "No. I didn't see anyone."

"Bullshit." He jerked her chair around so that she was facing him. "What happened in that warehouse? Who hit you? *Answer me.*"

"I don't know." Sable turned her head to look at Terri, anger glittering in her eyes. "You said I could make a phone call. I want to make it now, please."

"J. D.," Terri repeated, with a warning note this time. "You can make your call in a minute, Ms. Duchesne."

Her partner used his hand to grab Sable's jaw and turn her face back toward his. "Where did all this blood come from? How did you know Marc LeClare? Why were you there? Who set the fire? Did you see who hit you?"

They were almost close enough to be kissing, Terri thought, but J. D.'s voice hovered just below a shout.

"I *don't* remember." Sable had her hands folded in

her lap, so tightly that all her tendons stood out like cables ready to snap. "Get your hands off me."

Terri suppressed a sigh. "I think we need a break. J. D.?"

He ignored her and clamped his other hand around the base of Sable's throat. "*Vous me répondrez!*"

"*Je ne peux pas vous aider,*" she hissed back. "*Laissez-moi seule.*"

Terri knew a lot more about Sable Duchesne then, and it only added to the problem. Since her partner wasn't hearing a word she said, she went around the table and kicked him in the shin. "Hey. Back off."

He straightened and let his hands fall away. Under his jacket, the muscles in his arms and shoulders bunched. "I'm not going to hurt her."

"I don't care." She pointed to the door. "Take a walk—cool off. Do a few laps around the building. *Now.*"

J. D. gave Sable one last look, then left.

Terri's partner simply didn't lose his temper. Ever. Seeing it happen scared her, enough to make her drop her own guard for a moment. "What is it with you two?"

Sable averted her dark brown eyes, but not before Terri saw a suspicious shimmer. "Nothing."

Terri swore under her breath. "Here." She found a box of tissues, and put it down on the table. "You'd better pull yourself together, lady. That dead man was going to be our next governor. You are in for a full course of trouble, and J. D. is only the appetizer."

Sable lifted her chin. "I'm not afraid of J. D."

"Yeah?" Slipping easily into the patois of her youth, Terri added, "You think again. This ain't no chinka-chinka dance, *chère.*" She nodded as their witness gave her a shocked look. "That's right. You ain't on the bayou listening to no Dutch nightingales now. This for real bad—you think about that, eh?"

When Terri stepped outside the interview room, she found J. D. leaning against the wall, staring at the ceiling tiles. How did a wealthy Creole society son like him get involved with a backwater Cajun girl? Terri wasn't sure she wanted to know. "Want to take a shot at me now?"

J. D. thrust his hands in his pockets. "Maybe."

Anger wasn't something she was used to feeling around her partner. She trusted J. D. with her life, and she wasn't about to let him screw up his. "I'm glad you're getting a laugh out of this, because I'm not."

"You're crowding me."

"Gee, I'm all broken up about that. Maybe you forgot—we don't do the bad cop/worse cop routine, and she's not even a damn suspect." She shoved at his shoulder. "What were you thinking, putting your hands on her?"

He muttered something vile under his breath. "She won't talk to me in front of you. Give me five minutes alone with her. I'll get the answers."

Her jaw sagged. "Do I really look *that* stupid to you? You want to blow this whole case because you got a hard-on for her?"

"It's not that and you know it." J. D. looked up at the ceiling, then back at her. "Christ, Ter, I know her. She's just scared."

"Really. That woman is a witness—the only witness so far—to a felony arson, and maybe a murder. The DA isn't going to put up with her little amnesia act for a second. Not even if she was your *wife*." Then it hit Terri, and she smacked her palm on her forehead. "That's it, isn't it? You and her?"

"It was a long time ago." J. D.'s gaze never wavered. "I need time alone with her. I wouldn't ask if it wasn't important."

"Shit." Terri rubbed her eyes. In the five years they'd worked together, J. D. had never asked her to bend the rules. The fact that he wanted to now only made things worse. But he was her partner. "All right, I'm going to get some forms and bring her a phone. You've got ten minutes to kiss and make up with your sweetheart." When he would have gone back into the room, she grabbed his sleeve. "And when I get back, I'm dusting her for prints, so keep your hands in your pockets."

He nodded and went in. Terri walked down the corridor, glancing back once to see him closing the blinds.

J. D. Gamble in love with a Cajun girl. His mama must have had a stroke. Well, at least things can't get any worse. Terri saw J. D.'s girlfriend standing at her desk, and groaned. *Oh yes, they can.*

"Detective Vincent." Moriah Navarre sat down in J. D.'s chair and crossed her thin, tanned legs. She wore a tan silk blouse with khaki shorts and had tucked her golden hair up into a trendy little fedora. Chunky gold and diamond jewelry glinted at her throat and ears. The blouse clung just enough to show off every curve of her natural assets. "Is Jean-Del available?"

Every male in the detective squad room appeared mesmerized by Moriah's chest, or legs. Terri could almost hear the drool starting to drip. "Just a minute, Ms. Navarre." She picked up the phone and dialed the number for the current time and weather conditions. She listened to the entire prerecorded message while the elegant blonde frowned at her. To appear busy, Terri wrote out what she needed to pick up from the grocery store, then set the receiver down before reaching for a file she'd closed out a week ago.

The young socialite shifted her weight and sighed a few times. Once she looked pointedly at her wristwatch, which naturally matched her jewelry.

Terri let another five minutes pass, but she needed to get back to check on J. D. She glanced up and smiled. "Sorry, we're a little busy today. You're looking for J. D.?"

The diamonds in Moriah's earlobes sparkled as she lifted her chin. "Yes. He's going to take me to lunch."

Terri wondered if she knew about Sable, but figured she'd hear it from J. D. soon enough. Probably would be best to get her out of here for now. "He's interviewing a witness to an arson," she finally said. "Getting a statement usually takes a while."

"You should have mentioned that before." Moriah slowly rose. "Perhaps Cort will join me instead."

Despite the sympathy she felt for the girl, Terri heard her own voice go flat. "Cort's in Biloxi, at a conference. His brother Evan's flying in this week, but oh, that's right, he's bringing his wife." She smiled. "Looks like you've run out of Gambles."

"Aren't you up-to-date on everyone's whereabouts?" J. D.'s girlfriend produced a pretty laugh. "Part of your work, I suppose."

Terri seriously doubted Moriah Navarre knew anything about work. The Deb had gone to the best schools in Europe, served as her father's hostess when her mother was "on the Continent," and otherwise devoted herself to not breaking a sweat. She'd dated all three Gamble brothers, vacillating between Cort, Evan, and J. D. for some time before settling on Terri's partner.

Like comparison shopping, only for men instead of hand-made Italian pumps.

Moriah's flirtatious wave at one of the younger detectives made Terri decide to end things before she snapped out something she'd enjoy. "Any message for J. D.?"

"Yes. Tell him to call me as soon as he's free. Oh, and remind him that he needs to get the final fitting for his tux for Saturday night." She gave Terri a small smile of insincere commiseration. "Sorry we won't be seeing you there."

Terri imagined lepers would be more welcome than she was. "J. D. invited me, but I already had plans."

"What a pity. I think you'd look marvelous in white, myself. Something simple, with a few flounces here and there to de-emphasize those narrow hips and shoulders." She studied Terri's face. "Perhaps more cream than white, with your skin tone. You are so very dark, aren't you?"

Moriah's family lineage stretched back to the influx of refugees seeking asylum after Napoleon fell at Waterloo. Terri wasn't too sure who her grandparents were. "I'll give J. D. your message." She said it the same way she would *nice shot, bitch.*

"Thank you so much, Detective."

She watched J. D.'s girlfriend saunter out, then listened to the other cops mutter in low voices about Gamble's great luck with the ladies.

If he marries her, I'll have to put in a transfer request. No way am I putting up with The Deb calling here every day wanting J. D. to come home and help her count the family silver.

Sable closed her eyes and rested her head on her folded arms. She could have wept, but the tears had retreated as swiftly as J. D. had. Now she only felt numb. The same way she had that night, ten years ago.

"You don't talk much, do you?"

She glanced at the friendly face of the trucker beside her. He'd picked her up just outside campus and, after giving her a good scolding for hitchhiking, agreed to give her a ride back to the bayou. He seemed like a nice man, and he'd accepted her story about her nonexistent car breaking down in a ditch. Considering how she looked—and smelled—it was a small wonder he didn't make her ride in the back with the frozen shrimp he was hauling north to Baton Rouge.

All she had to do was hold on a few more minutes. A few more minutes, and she'd be home. She'd be safe. She'd never have to go back again.

"Not much to say." She felt certain that she could shriek with rage until her lungs collapsed, but that wouldn't solve anything. Plus it would scare the daylights out of the trucker, and likely then she'd have to walk home.

"You sure you don't want me to stop somewhere, honey, so you can get cleaned up and call a tow truck?" the man offered as they headed out of New Orleans. "Look like you could use a cup of coffee, too."

If he stopped, she'd explode. She should know—she'd already done it once that evening. "No, sir, but thank you," she said. "My dad will take care of it. I just want to go home."

"All right, then." He turned on his radio, and Waylon Jennings and Willie Nelson started singing in duet about a good-hearted woman in love with a good-timing man. "Now, that's some real music," he said to her, tapping the wheel with his thumb in time with the song. "You can keep your Reba and your Garth Brooks—just gimme Waylon and Willie."

The sound of a car screeching to a halt outside brought Sable back to the present. Terri Vincent had opened the only window, but it was covered with a thick steel mesh bolted on all sides to the frame. From the shadows on the door panel, it looked as though J. D. and his partner were standing right outside. Sable lifted a hand and rubbed the large bump on the back of her head.

Maybe I can pretend to be sick, or faint.

That was stupid, and it would never work—it never did on any of the cop dramas she'd watched on television. No, they would keep her here until she told them what they wanted to know, God help her. Her fingers slid down her neck, then up to the still-sensitive place on her jaw where J. D. had held her. She bruised easily and he'd probably left some marks. Her skin still tingled and ached from his touch.

He's so angry.

So was she. The moment he'd touched her, it had all come back—everything she had spent years trying to forget. The feel of his skin on hers, the way he used to touch her, as if he were an addict and her body were his drug of choice.

But it hadn't been all sex. That night, outside his parents' magnificent home. Sitting on the porch swing holding hands, watching the stars come out. He'd teased her about not eating enough of his father's excellent food, and she'd confessed her confusion over the bewildering amount of utensils. He'd laughed and told her that he always mixed up the salad and dessert forks himself.

She hadn't meant to say it, but it just burst out of her. *Jean-Delano, I love you.*

He hadn't laughed. He'd lifted her onto his lap and held her, and he'd looked at her for a long time, like she was something rare and precious. *Do you mean that? Really, you do?*

Sable lifted her head as the door opened. J. D. walked inside, this time without his partner. He wasn't the boy she loved back in school anymore. He was all business, a homicide detective intent on questioning a witness.

Questioning her.

Nausea rolled in her stomach as she thought of how she had stumbled over Marc's body, and the blood. How could she tell Jean-Del about that without revealing everything about her and Marc? Would J. D. believe her, even if she did confide in him?

Ten years ago he'd been all too ready to condemn her. *Have you lost your mind? How could you do that to my friends?*

No, she couldn't trust him. Not with this.

"It's just you and me now." He came over and sat across from her, in the seat Sergeant Vincent had occupied. He sounded calm and professional, but an aura of something dark and violent radiated from him. "I want you to tell me everything that happened, from the time you arrived at the warehouse to when you escaped the fire."

She avoided his gaze. "I went there to see the property. When I went inside, someone hit me from behind. That's all I remember."

Frustration and anger flickered across his face; then his voice changed and softened a few degrees. "Did you see his face?"

He still had a wonderful voice—smooth and deep, with the kind of warmth that stroked her like a gentle hand. For a moment, she was almost tempted to confide in him. Almost. "No."

J. D. sat back, studying her for a minute. "You haven't been back to New Orleans since you left school. I would have heard about it."

She stared at him. They hadn't seen each other in a decade; why would he care whether she'd come back to the city? Then she thought of Marc, and realized he must have known the Gambles—the LeClares and the Gambles were both old Creole families, and between them had more money than God.

Her stomach, already knotted, clenched even tighter. They were going to crucify her for her relationship with Marc—and they'd make J. D. pound in the nails personally.

He tried again. "How did you meet Marc LeClare?"

"How did you know I was there?" she countered, stalling for time.

"Fate. Dumb luck. Take your pick." He looked down at her hands. "Sable, whatever you're hiding, you can tell me. I can protect you."

The way he had in college? She'd be better off dancing naked in front of a news camera. "I'm sorry, I don't remember anything else." The splinters in her palms shifted and stung as she curled her hands. "Can I go now?"

"Let me see your hands." When she wouldn't, he reached across the table and took one gently but firmly by the wrist. "Open your fingers." He bent closer and turned her palm from right to left. "These look like wood splinters—are they?"

"I guess." If he didn't stop touching her, she was going to climb straight up the walls.

He went over to a cabinet, took out a small first aid kit, and brought it to the table. "Your palms aren't bruised. Did you grab some old wood inside the warehouse when you were trying to get out?" He pulled up a chair next to hers.

She had been so desperate to get away from the fire

that no pain and few details had registered at the time. "I think so. I remember some boards over a window."

He took out a pair of tweezers, wiped the slanted ends with an alcohol swab, then took hold of her wrist again. She jerked a little as he tugged at the first sliver. "Hold still."

"It hurts." No, it didn't. It was his hand, his fingers against her skin. His body, so close she could feel the heat coming through his clothes and hers. She could see the faint dark shadow along his jaw and his upper lip, the marked grooves of tension on either side of his mouth. She wanted to touch his skin to feel the rasp of his beard.

He still has to shave twice a day.

"You left Tulane, and you moved out of the city," he murmured as he extracted the first splinter and placed it in a little clear plastic bag. "Where did you go?"

"Away." She'd lost her scholarship, of course, and it had taken another year before she'd managed to save enough from guiding swamp tours to go back to school. It had been different at L.S.U.; no one had known her, and no one had cared where she came from. In many ways it had been like being able to breathe for the first time in years—except that she had missed him terribly, even after a year of being apart.

The same way she'd missed him every day since.

He met her gaze. "Why?"

Because I loved you too much. "I found a better school." She bit her lip as he drew another sliver of wood from her palm. His breath smelled like coffee and mint. "Why did you become a police officer? I thought you'd be in politics by now." That had been his mother's most fervent hope, according to what Sable recalled.

"I did, too." His mouth curled on one side. "Evan's

training horses up in Montana now." He switched hands and started on her other palm. "Cort's the city fire marshal."

She'd never met Evan, but Cort and his mother had never approved of their relationship. Only J. D.'s father, Louis, had made an effort to be kind to her, and she had liked him a lot. "How is your dad?"

"Older." He finished removing the last splinter and set the tweezers aside. "My mother wants him to retire and let one of my cousins run the restaurant, but Dad still goes in every day." He swabbed her palms again. "Why did you leave me?"

The alcohol stung, but not as much as the question. She took in a sharp breath. "That's ancient history, J. D."

"I was on my way to pick you up that night when I ran into my friends. I couldn't believe what they said you'd done to them. I went after you, and saw you get into that truck." When she tried to stand, he latched on to both of her wrists. "I know you heard me when I caught up with you. Why did you hide from me?"

Because your friends had tortured and humiliated me. Because I was eighteen years old and scared and stupid in love with you. "It was a long time ago, Jean-Del." She hadn't meant to use his name, but it hung between them, a ghost from that other time. His eyes narrowed and focused on her mouth. "Let it go. Let *me* go."

"No." He shifted closer. "Not this time."

Terri Vincent came in, carrying a phone, and plugged it into an empty wall jack before setting it in front of Sable. "You can make your phone call, Ms. Duchesne." She looked at J. D. "Let's get some coffee and give the lady some privacy."

J. D. cursed under his breath as he stalked out of the room.

Sable waited until Terri left and locked the door before she dialed the number to Martin's Country Store with trembling fingers.

"*Allô*, Martin's?" It was one of Hilaire's cashiers.

"*Je voudrais parler à* Hilaire," Sable said. *Please, please, Hil, be there.*

The girl was new and didn't recognize her voice. "*C'est de la part de qui?*"

"Sable Duchesne, her cousin—*je suis la cousine de Hilaire.*"

"*Ah, oui—un instant, s'il vous plaît.*"

A moment later Hilaire Martin's cheerful voice came over the line. "So, how did it go? Is the place big enough? He take you somewhere ritzy for lunch?"

Sable's hand tightened on the receiver. "Hil, listen to me. I'm in trouble."

She gave her cousin the bare details of what had happened. The other end of the line went completely silent until she reached the part about Jean-Delano being the detective in charge of the case.

"*C'est rien que de la merde!*" Hilaire, who knew every detail about what had happened to Sable in college, was outraged.

"This is not bullshit, Hil. It's real." Tears welled up again, but she blinked them back. "Marc's dead."

"Ah, *chère*. I'm so sorry." Her cousin's sweet voice hardened as she added, "You just tell them keep that no-good stuck-up *fils de pute* away from you!"

Sable rubbed her fingertips against the growing ache in her temple. "I can't do that. He's in charge of the case and I'm the only witness."

"What difference does that make?" Hilaire made a rude sound. "Jean-Del, working for the poh-lice. Now I heard everything."

Sable knew J. D. and his partner would be back any

minute, so she hurried out the rest. "My car got burned; I need someone to come and get me. And don't tell my father a word about this."

"He listen to that news radio station all the time on the boat, you know," Hil reminded her. "He hear about this, he will go crazy."

That was true enough—if he heard Isabel had been in a fire on the radio, nothing would keep Remy Duchesne from coming after her.

"You're right. Check and see that he's taken his pills before you tell him. Make sure he understands that I'm not hurt." Her head was really throbbing now. "And hurry, please, Hil." She hung up the phone.

I want to go home. Home, where she would be safe—the only place she'd thought she'd be safe after what happened at Tulane.

Sitting in the truck, listening to the music. Trying not to feel the duckweed and the mud that were slowly drying into the delicate layer of creamy lace covering the front of her dress—her mama's best dress, that Sable had stayed up every night for the last week altering so she could wear it to the Summer Magnolias Graduation Dance. It kept her from thinking about the pretty faces of the other girls.

What they'd shouted at her, however, kept ringing in her ears, sending surges of heat up her throat and into her face.

"Hey, coon-ass! Where's your boyfriend?"

Sable had never suspected that they would be waiting for her outside the dorm. Jean-Delano always picked her up for their dates, but he'd left a message at the desk saying he would be late and asking her to meet him in back of Smith Hall. Maybe if she hadn't been so nervous about going to the dance with him she would have realized that something was wrong.

Jean-Del had never left messages, because he'd never been late before. If anything, he'd shown up early.

She'd hurried out of the dorm, worried that someone had tried to talk him out of taking her as his date, and had walked straight into them. Sixteen football players and their sorority girlfriends, standing in the shadows behind the old dormitory, waiting. All of them were dressed up just like her—only better. She'd stopped and stared at them in disbelief. J. D. wouldn't bring his friends with him, not to pick her up.

But J. D. wasn't there.

"Going somewhere, fish bait?"

The boys wore fine black tuxes, eerily identical, like their game uniforms. They wore them with the confidence of boys who didn't have to rent their formal wear.

It was their dates who were truly breathtaking. All the girls wore dazzling pastel-colored silk gowns, with fancy trims and beads that made them appear like young, chic brides. Sable's ecru lace dress, which had seemed so feminine and classic in her dorm room, appeared dingy by comparison. The expensive diamond and gold jewelry they wore made her only necklace—a single strand of faux pearls—look painfully cheap.

One thing was clear—from the looks on their faces, they hadn't come to walk her over to the dance for Jean-Delano.

She'd tried to move around them, but they'd formed a tight circle, closing her in an envelope of designer perfume. "Where did you get that little rag? Kmart? The Salvation Army?"

She knew what they were like from six months of similar torment, and although her heart rabbited in her chest, she kept her voice calm and asked them to leave her alone. The girls had laughed at her. They were a tight-knit, arrogant group, all pledged to the same sorority, all dating jocks, all children of old, established Creole families. Just like their boyfriends.

Sable was none of those things. She had never been in-

vited to join their clubs and social circles. Her scholarship only covered her tuition, so after classes she worked serving and busing tables in the school cafeteria, and even then she had to count her pennies. The awful uniform and hairnet the administration insisted that the cafeteria staff wear made her an easy target for the wealthier, privileged girls whose parents paid for everything. When she'd started dating one of the best-looking guys on campus, that only compounded the problem.

It wasn't just her poverty and her lack of pedigree that made the girls hate her, though. It was the way their boyfriends looked at her when Jean-Del wasn't around to see.

She'd given up on reasoning with the group and had tried to break through the circle. One of the boys had pushed her back, and she'd nearly fallen in the mud, only just stopping herself with one hand.

Sable shifted in her seat and wrapped her arms around herself.

Before she'd left the dorm, she'd tucked her new gloves in her purse so they wouldn't get dirty. Having saved up her tips, she'd taken the long bus ride to the city to buy them. All the other girls wore white gloves to the senior dances, and Sable hadn't wanted to embarrass Jean-Del by showing up with bare hands. Bad enough she'd had to make over one of her mother's dresses to have something decent to wear.

Thank goodness she hadn't put them on; they would have been ruined by the mud.

"Euuww." One of the girls pointed at Sable's mud-smeared fingers. "If she's serving the punch, I'm not touching it!"

"I don't want to do this," one of the other girls said, sounding a little frightened. She was a petite blonde, the quietest one of the group. "Let's go now."

The boy with her had scoffed. "What are you, afraid of a coon-ass?"

Sable hadn't been foolish and shouted at them. That would have only made things worse. Besides, she could always wash her hands. She looked at the girl who had tried to stop them, saw the pity in her eyes. She tried making an appeal to her. "Please, I have to go. I don't want to be late."

The girl looked as scared as she felt, but Sable's plea made no difference to the others. "What's the matter," another girl had cooed. "Afraid he'll stand you up for someone with shoes?"

Trying to run only got her shoved back again, and this time she went down, face first. Mud splattered her face, her hair, and the front of her dress. While the others laughed, she stayed down, knowing it was over then, wishing she were dead. This wouldn't wash off. She couldn't go to the dance; she couldn't be with Jean-Del.

They would never let them be together. "I promised him I wouldn't be late," was all she could think. "He's going to be so upset."

Everyone laughed as she got up on her hands and knees.

"I think she needs a little bath," one of the girls drawled.

The one girl who had protested tried to stop them. "Don't do this, she's had enough!"

The boy carrying the bucket shrugged the girl off and then tossed the contents of the bucket at Sable.

She didn't know where they'd gotten the duckweed—they were twenty miles from the nearest bayou. But suddenly she was covered with the slimy green stuff, and soaked with the cold, brackish brown water it had grown in. All she could do was shield her head with her arms and keep her eyes and mouth closed until it was over.

Like now.

Sable knew what she had to do. She had to protect

herself until she could get away. Then she would run—run as fast and as far away as she could.

J. D. didn't want coffee. He wanted to grab Sable, march her out of the station, and take her somewhere quiet. Then he wanted to shake the truth out of her. She was hiding something; he could see it in her eyes—but what? What possible connection could she have with Marc LeClare? She was dressed like a businesswoman; it might be just as she'd said—she'd been looking to rent some property and she'd gone to the warehouse for business reasons only.

But why did his gut tell him there was more to it than that?

She's young and beautiful; Marc LeClare was old and rich. Doesn't take a genius to figure out that equation.

The thought of Marc putting his hands on Sable made J. D.'s hands curl over into fists. *It had better damn sight be business only.*

"I don't like that look on your face," Terri said as she walked up and handed him his mug, then sipped from her own. "That look says 'I'm thinking with the little head. I'm going to do something macho and idiotic and get myself suspended.'"

He swallowed the boiling-hot coffee without feeling the burn. "I'm not thinking with my dick."

"A rare and valuable trait not often found in the male of the species. I'll have to alert the media." Terri gestured toward the interview room where he'd left Sable. "Does she know that?"

"She's just shaken up."

"I imagine nearly being burned to death creates something of a shock to the system. So does being questioned by your ex-boyfriend. You break up with a guy; you just never want to see his ugly face again."

Terri took a sip from her mug. "By the way, your current girlfriend stopped in. You were supposed to take her to lunch. Do call her."

Moriah. He hadn't given her a single thought.

"I told her you were tied up taking a statement from our witness," his partner said. "And Laure LeClare will be here in a few minutes. I don't think she'll be too happy to hear you used to be sweethearts with the girl her hubby was likely bopping on the side, do you?"

Before he could snap her head off, a uniform from the front desk approached them. "Uh, Lieutenant Gamble? Captain wants you and Sergeant Vincent downstairs now. Press is swarming."

"Thanks," Terri said, and waited until the officer retreated before hunching her shoulders. "Damn it, I knew I should have taken that vacation time this week."

"You go," J. D. told Terri. He was in no mood to deal with the media. "Tell Cap I'm showing Sable some mug shots."

"That had better be the only thing you show her," his partner warned as she tugged on her jacket and headed for the stairs.

He filled a Styrofoam cup with coffee and added a spoon of sugar, then took it with him to the interview room. Sable looked up as he came in and then down at the phone.

"Did you get in touch with your family?" he asked as he set the cup in front of her. She didn't touch it or answer him. "Black, one sugar, the way you like it."

She shook her head a little and glanced at the window.

Dark thoughts had been humming inside his head since he'd seen her at the fire rescue unit, but now they bloomed into something primal and violent. She wouldn't speak to him; she wouldn't touch the coffee. She rejected him now as completely as she had ten years ago.

J. D. didn't like it any more than he had then, but now it wasn't about a stupid dance or slinging mud at some of his friends. Now her life was on the line.

"Listen to me," he said, keeping his voice low and even. "You hate me—that's fine. I'm not real fond of you, either. But I'm the only friend you have here. Talk to me."

She met his gaze. Something had changed—the fear in her eyes was gone, replaced by something darker and angrier. "I don't need your help." Each word dripped with contempt.

She wasn't going to play him this way. Not this time.

"Wrong. There's nowhere for you to run. No place to hide." His vision sharpened as he focused on her face and smiled. "I've got you, baby, and you're not going anywhere."

She shoved back away from the table, out of reach. "Don't touch me. I swear to God, I'll scream my head off."

His mouth thinned. "Then I'd have to shut you up." He came around the table, pausing only to wedge a chair against the doorknob. "Which I would enjoy. Please, be my guest."

Sable stumbled out of the chair, knocking it over as she frantically looked for an avenue of escape. "I'll talk to the other cop—that woman, your partner." Her teeth were almost chattering. "Not you."

He hesitated, tilting his head to one side as he regarded her. Yes, she was angry, and frightened of him—which was smart; he hadn't felt this furious in years. But why would she choose Terri over him? Terri didn't know her. He wanted to shake her; he wanted to hold her in his arms and comfort her. "Why are you doing this?" He made his tone gentle and soothing. "Let me help you."

"I don't need your help." She jammed herself between the watercooler and the wall. "I don't need anything from you."

"Maybe you're right." He started advancing again. "Marc LeClare and my family have been friends for years. He was a good, decent man who wanted to make things better for everyone. You're just some girl I dated in college." Which was a lie. She was the girl he'd loved, the only girl he'd ever loved. He'd planned to ask her to marry him at the dance, the night she'd run away from him. "Something happened in that warehouse, and you're going to tell me—if I have to beat it out of you."

Somehow that got to her, because color flooded back into her face from the neck up. She started moving her head from side to side, slowly, like a dreamer in denial.

"Yeah," he said softly. "You will." It gave him deep, fierce satisfaction to have her under his total control. She couldn't escape him this time, and once he straightened out this mess, he'd make sure she'd never run away from him again.

Before he could touch her, she shoved at the heavy watercooler, and knocked it over.

Chapter Three

Terri wanted nothing more than to ditch the impromptu press conference and get back upstairs before J. D. did something unforgivable—or worse, prosecutable. But Captain Pellerin was in a lousy mood, and the reporters smelled blood. Someone had leaked the news that gubernatorial candidate Marc LeClare had been found burned to death in one of his own warehouses, and aside from Mardi Gras, there was no bigger news than that.

She stood at Pellerin's side as he issued a terse, no-frills, no-details statement, refusing to identify the victim until the next of kin were notified; then he parried a few pointed questions before dismissing the media. The reporters tried to suck her into spilling something, but Terri knew better than to open her mouth.

"I want you and Gamble in my office," Pellerin told her as they went back upstairs. He was a short, heavy-set man who looked like a rabid bulldog on his *good* days. "As soon as he's done with the witness."

"Yes, sir." She kept her expression blank, but her stomach knotted. Pellerin didn't get steamed without good reason—and it wasn't just the media sharks. Every friend Marc LeClare had—and he had them all the way up to the White House—would be calling and demanding answers.

And when they found out about the girl? All hell would break loose.

She went to her desk to pull the necessary report forms for Laure LeClare to fill out, when her phone rang. "Detective Vincent."

"It's me," a familiar deep voice, almost identical to J. D.'s, said. "What's going on down there?"

Every one of her muscles tightened; Terri could think of no one she'd rather speak to less. The voice belonged to Chief Fire Marshal Cortland Gamble, another person her partner should have dealt with himself. Unlike his brother, Cort was rigid and serious, and devoted himself utterly to the job. He was universally respected and the best fire marshal the city had had in years.

None of which explained why she'd fallen for him years ago.

Terri was still so ridiculously infatuated with Cort Gamble that she didn't trust herself around him. One kind word from him would have punched through the fortress she'd built around her heart and wrecked her forever, and she couldn't allow that. *Wouldn't* allow him to do that to her. So she avoided him, and hoped in time that she could starve her stupid female feelings to death.

It hadn't worked so far, but there was nothing else she could do. Like J. D., Cort liked high-maintenance, low-IQ women who looked good on his arm. Terri Vincent was as far from that as a woman could get and still qualify as a member of the female gender. "Arson, murder, mayhem, the usual." She kept her tone light and happy. Cort hated light and happy. "How's the weather in Biloxi, Chief? You working on your tan?"

"I just got word from my department," he said, his voice dropping from chilly to flash frozen. "Who killed Marc LeClare?"

"We're investigating that." She wasn't going to tell him that his brother's ex-girlfriend was mixed up with his father's best friend; the phone lines couldn't handle that kind of volume. "Maybe you should come on home; I think J. D.'s going to need some help on this one." Though what Cort could do for him, she didn't know. Cortland Gamble was as by-the-book as a Supreme Court judge.

"I'll catch the first flight I can get. You tell J. D."

Am I his partner or his answering service? That was when Terri heard the crash from the direction of the interview rooms. "Gotta go. See you around, Marshal."

She slammed down the phone and sprinted across the squad room toward the corridor. Water was gushing out from under the door—had J. D. punched out the watercooler? She should have listened to her gut and never have left him alone with Sable Duchesne.

She grabbed the door, but it was jammed from the inside. "J. D.?"

The crash was so loud it seemed to rattle the walls. The five-gallon container atop the refrigeration unit broke free and began gushing water all over the floor.

J. D. ignored it, and caught Sable as she darted for the door. "Damn it, Sable, no."

The water made her flat-soled shoes slide, and she had to clutch at his jacket to regain her balance. That brought her body up against his from thigh to chest.

"Let go of me," she said, arching away.

"So you can fall on your ass and get wet? Hold still." He controlled her with his hands and arms, keeping her pressed up against him as the water jug emptied out. His breath touched her face. "Every reporter in town is downstairs. Did you think you could just walk out of here?"

"I wouldn't have walked." She looked down at the floor and felt suddenly ashamed. "*Dieu*, what a mess."

"Floor needed mopping anyway." He brushed her dirty hair away from her face. "Someone will deal with it later."

Just like the rich Creole boy he'd been, always assuming someone else would clean up after him. "But not you." She twisted, jerking within his grasp, but he wouldn't let her go.

J. D. locked his arms around her, forcing her up against his rigid frame. She felt her breasts swell as they pressed into his chest, felt the shocking ridge of his erection burning into her hip. Liquid heat started to pool between her thighs as her body responded to what her mind could not accept.

Dear God, no. I was over this; I was over him.

"Shit." He hissed in a quick breath when she moved, trying to put space between them but only rubbing the curve of her hip against him. "Stop doing that."

Something heavy slammed into the door, and the chair jamming it slid away from the knob. Terri Vincent charged in, sized up the situation, and quickly slammed the door shut behind her.

She looked from the water to Sable to J. D. "Unbelievable. Do I have to get a hose?"

J. D. kept Sable in his arms as he turned to his partner. "What do you want?"

"Besides a mop? A new partner. One with a functioning brain." Before J. D. could reply, Terri held up a hand. "No, no, don't tell me. I really don't want to know, and we've got other problems to deal with besides the flood here."

He slowly released Sable, but as she tried to step away, curled his fingers around her right wrist. "Stay put," he said to her, then looked at Terri. "Like what?"

She told him, ticking points off her fingers as she did. "Someone leaked crime scene info to the press, so they already know the vic was Marc LeClare. Captain Pellerin wants us in his office so he can chew both our asses up one wall and down the other. LeClare's widow will be here any minute—she's coming from IDing the body at the morgue—and we need to interview her. Oh, and your brother's flying back from Biloxi to help you with our case. Won't that be fun?"

He dragged a hand through his hair. "This is turning into a circus."

"They're already lining up downstairs to sell popcorn and peanuts." She nodded toward Sable. "No more time to play fond memories, J. D. We've got to get her out of here, right now."

Moriah Navarre heard the low, appreciative male whistles behind her as she came out of the dress shop, but didn't react to them. She was too angry. She'd driven all the way downtown so J. D. could take her to lunch, and he'd stood her up—again. She couldn't make him jealous by seeing his brother, because Cort was out of town—again. And J. D.'s partner had scored points off her by informing her on both accounts—again.

She hated Terri Vincent almost as much as the wolf whistles.

It wasn't just because J. D.'s partner was smart, funny, and attractive—although she was, enough to make Moriah wish she'd transfer to another division.

In Alaska. And while it grated that J. D. spent all day with Terri while barely remembering to call Moriah twice a week, she understood that his job had to come first—for now.

No, what really bugged her was the way Terri Vincent treated her. Most of the time she showed nothing but contempt, but now and then, she came across with this completely inappropriate pity. As if Moriah Navarre of the New Orleans Navarres, who had the money and looks and friends the female cop would never have, needed sympathy.

She took out her cell phone and tried calling Laure LeClare. As president of the Garden District Historical Society, Laure supervised several committees, and Moriah had volunteered to help out with a society tea. The housekeeper answered, and told her that Laure had had to go downtown. As Moriah hung up, she frowned. She'd promised to stop by the LeClares' house after lunch to discuss the catering for the tea, but perhaps Laure had forgotten.

"Hey, baby, how 'bout you strut that fine little ass of yours this way?"

She turned around to see a trio of city workers loitering around an open manhole. The biggest one, a minimountain of muscle with a bristly black goatee and a gleaming shaved head, was grinning at her like an ape in heat.

When you look at some men, her mother maintained, *you just know Darwin was right*.

Moriah was in no mood for infatuated primates. If she were Terri Vincent, she could just flash her badge or her gun and they'd shut right up. But Terri commanded respect—Moriah didn't.

Maybe it was time that changed. "Are you speaking to me?"

"Yeah, sugar, come on over." He patted the top of one of his log-shaped thighs. "You can park yourself right here. I'll give you something to talk about."

His companions erupted into laughter.

She put away her phone, changed direction, and walked right up to them. The workers hooted as she took a stand in front of her oversized heckler.

"You know, women really don't like being ogled," she told him, keeping her tone calm and cool. "Or being subjected to that kind of language."

"You're no fun." He leered at the front of her blouse. "What's the matter, honey? Am I scaring you?"

"Scaring me? Hardly." Moriah glanced at the wheelbarrow by the manhole cover, and remembered a trick her brother, James, had showed her once. Deliberately she reached out and squeezed his bulging, sweaty bicep. "Let me guess—you're the biggest, strongest guy on this crew, right?"

"Damn straight." And proud of it, from the way he flexed his arm under her fingers. "I can go all night long, sugar. *All* night long."

"How about twenty yards?" She pointed to the wheelbarrow. "I bet you that I can push something in that wheelbarrow across the street, but you won't be able to push it back."

He sized up her spare, petite frame and shook his head sadly. "Oh, darlin', wake up. You're dreaming."

"Maybe. Maybe not." She tilted her head to one side, looking at him from under her lashes. "Tell you what—if you win, I'll go out on a date with you."

As his buddies produced sounds of lewd approval, the minimountain's goatee stretched until it nearly met his ears.

"But if I win," she added, "you have to promise to stop harassing women on the street."

"Hot damn, then I've already won." He hitched up his belt as he stood. "Let's go."

"Great." She went over, grabbed the wheelbarrow, and brought it to him. "Okay, climb in."

"What the—" His mouth flattened and his face reddened as he got the joke.

The other men started laughing again, this time at their friend, until they were gasping for breath and grabbing their sides.

The infatuation faded from the minimountain's eyes. "Hell, lady, that ain't fair."

"I never said it would be." She patted his cheek. "Now remember your promise."

On the way back to her car, her cell phone rang, and she took it out of her purse, hoping it was J. D. "Hello?"

"Moriah." It was Laure LeClare, and she was sobbing. "I'm at the police station. . . . can you come here?"

"Lord, I was just there—are you all right?" Alarmed, Moriah searched in her purse for her keys. "What's wrong? What's happened?"

"It's Marc. . . ." Laure broke off for a moment, then managed to get out a few more words. "He was caught in a fire, Moriah—he's dead. My husband's dead."

"I'll take her out through the back," Terri offered as she, J. D., and Sable left the interview room and headed for the elevators. "You'd better talk to the wife."

J. D. knew Marc's wife from the many social occasions that the Gambles attended. Laure LeClare was an elegant, soft-spoken woman who had been a devoted wife and a staunch supporter of her husband's election campaign. J. D. knew she was going to be devastated, and as a friend of the family he felt obligated to take her statement and make sure she returned home safely—especially with the media still lurking around. At the same time, he didn't want to leave Sable.

Terri intercepted his gaze. "Go. I'll look after her."

As soon as the elevator doors opened to the main floor, a young woman in a bright orange tank top and an older man in shabby clothes waiting in the lobby stood up. Before Terri could stop her, Sable hurried out of the elevator.

"*Elle voilà*—there she is!" the generously endowed blonde cried out, hurrying over. "*Êtes-vous bien?* Are you all right, *chère?*"

J. D. didn't recognize either one of them, but from the look on Sable's face and the dialect of French the girl spoke, he assumed they were relatives. Something twisted inside him. Back in college, she had never introduced him to her family.

"*Non, non.*" The man approached, shaking his head. He wore sun-faded work clothes, and his hands were heavily callused. "*Comment est-ce que ceci s'est produit? Qui a fait ceci à vous?*"

"*Je suis très bien*—I'm fine. The police are still checking into things, Uncle." Sable ignored Terri, who was trying to steer her away from the lobby. "Did you speak to Remy?"

"*Oui.*" Hilaire shot an ugly look at J. D. "Your Papa, he had to take some of his pills, but he is well, *chère.*"

"Ms. Duchesne, we need to leave," Terri said, her voice low. She caught J. D.'s gaze, and nodded toward the reporters on the other side of the lobby, who were watching them with intense interest.

"This is my cousin Hilaire Martin and her father, my uncle August," Sable said. "I'm going home with them."

"You can't." J. D. put a hand on her cheek and made her look at him. "It isn't safe."

A reporter approached them, followed by a cameraman. "Excuse me, is this the lady they rescued from the warehouse fire?"

"Get lost," J. D. said.

Terri stepped between them."Nothing happening here, friend. Move along."

The reporter ignored both of them and craned his neck to look at Sable. "Ma'am? May I have your name? Were you friends with Marc LeClare?"

Hilaire snorted. "She was more than friends."

Another reporter focused his attention on Sable's cousin. "What sort of relationship did they have?"

Sable stared at her cousin. "Hilaire, shut up."

The other girl winced. "Right, uh, no comment."

"J. D.?"

Terri swore softly under her breath.

J. D. swiveled around to see Moriah Navarre walking toward them. Beside her was Laure LeClare, ashen-faced and leaning heavily against Moriah while staring at Sable with wide, disbelieving eyes. Moriah also regarded Sable as if she were some kind of ax murderess.

They'd obviously heard every word. As awkward situations went, it didn't get worse—and then it did.

More cameras encircled them as reporters converged around them, calling out questions to J. D., Sable, and the widow.

"Mrs. LeClare, can you confirm that your husband was the victim found burned to death this morning in the French Quarter?"

"Was he murdered? Could the murder be politically motivated?"

"Lieutenant Gamble, who's the redhead?"

* * *

Sable cringed as the media pressed in. Terri Vincent started calling out loudly for everyone to step back, but they weren't listening to her. The same way it had been that night before the dance.

She was covered in filth, her dress ruined, everything she'd done for nothing. She was on her hands and knees in the mud, where they said she belonged.

But she didn't belong there. She'd done nothing wrong.

The biggest boy pulled her up and shoved a huge handful of gray Spanish moss down the front of her ruined dress. "Don't forget your corsage!" He kept his hand in long enough to squeeze her breast.

That was when all the feelings she had been holding back for months erupted, and she snapped.

She wrenched out the boy's hand and the moss, and flung it in his face. Then she bent down, filled her hands with mud, and started throwing it at anything that moved.

"Don't you like my perfume?" She pelted the girls' fine white dresses and the boys' immaculate tuxes. "Come on, try some on!"

The girls ran away screaming, and their boyfriends followed. Like the cowards they were.

Other girls came out of the dorm and shrieked at Sable to stop. She threw mud at them, too. She threw mud at anyone who came near her. It felt wonderful. She stopped only when she heard someone shouting to call the police. Then she walked away from the dorm and out to the highway, never stopping or looking back. She paused to get most of the filth off her face, using her pretty new gloves to wipe it away. As she waved down the truck, she dropped her gloves by the roadside before climbing up and asking for a ride out to the Atchafalaya.

She'd go home, and she'd stay there, where she belonged. And God help anyone who came after her.

A heavyset man grabbed Sable from the side. "What is your name? Are you Marc LeClare's mistress?" He shoved a microphone in her face.

"Get away from me." Sable slapped the microphone away, but the reporter pushed back. "Leave me alone!"

Someone else pushed from the other side, and Sable lost her balance and fell backward, arms flailing.

Terri shouted for assistance while J. D. made the grab to catch Sable, but her head struck the corner of the elevator door frame with a loud rap. He got his arms between her and the floor before she could hit it, but she went limp. Blood trickled from the corner of her mouth.

J. D. knelt and supported her head. "Sable?"

"Is that a first name, or last?" One of the reporters pushed forward eagerly.

Terri elbowed him aside, crouched down next to J. D., and leaned in. "Get her out of here; take her to the hospital."

J. D. gathered her up in his arms, stood, and used his shoulder to ram his way through the throng of reporters. He strode past the gaping Moriah and Laure, proceeded behind the reception desk, and pulled the keys for an unmarked car from the vehicle board.

"I'm taking her over to Mercy," he told the desk sergeant in a low, furious voice. "Tell these fucking piranhas she'll be at Charity."

The uniformed officer started to say something, then looked at J. D.'s face and nodded. "You got it, Lieutenant."

When Caine got back from the city, his men were already out on the water. Only John had stayed behind, and after one look at Caine's face he got busy repairing some traps.

Caine called Billy's wife, Cecilia, who began crying as soon as he told her that he'd fired Billy. He offered to have someone take her in until her husband got over his latest binge, but she only hung up on him.

Someone would look after Cecilia anyway. Bayou people took care of their own.

Caine kept the radio on while he worked on patching a hull, and stopped only to listen to the latest update on the warehouse fire. It hadn't been confirmed, but a source was quoted as identifying the body found at the scene as gubernatorial candidate Marc LeClare. The reporters didn't have the name of the young, red-headed woman who had survived the fire, or why she'd been in the warehouse with LeClare.

Caine knew. He'd always known everything about her. But Isabel had made her choices ten years ago, and so had he.

"Gantry."

Remy Duchesne's rasping voice echoed in the boathouse, but Caine didn't look up from the hole he was patching on the port side of his fishing boat. He'd been expecting a visit from his old boss all morning. "Here."

The old man walked across to join him, and studied the work in progress. "You run into something with that?" He nodded not at the boat but at Caine's right hand, which was swollen and gashed across three knuckles.

Caine thought about telling Remy about Billy, then looked up into his ruined face and felt the old rage and shame crushing down on him, just as heavy and immovable as ever. "Trap got wedged." He dropped the brush back into the can of liquid sealant he was using to waterproof the patch and stood up.

Caine was bigger than anyone on the Atchafalaya, thanks to his bad blood, and he had at least a foot and a half on Remy, who was short and wire-thin. Still, when Caine looked at the twisted, raddled skin of his old boss's face, he felt about six inches tall.

Caine's father, Bud Gantry, had been the one who put those scars on Remy Duchesne's face.

"I need to talk to you," Remy said. "Just a minute." Caine went down into the cabin and stepped into the tiny head, then shut the door and leaned back against the wall.

After Bud went to prison, Caine's mother, Dodie, had been free to devote herself fully to the two things she had loved more than Bud—drinking and screwing whoever bought her a drink. Dodie had died of liver failure a few years later, leaving sixteen-year-old Caine an orphan.

Even back then, everyone tried to look out for each other, but the belligerent son of a bragging brute and a drunken whore didn't rate much attention.

It had been Remy Duchesne who had helped Caine bury his mother, and then had offered him a job checking traps and taking tourists out. Maybe it was because Caine had always lived like a wild thing, or that Remy had noticed him hanging around the bait shop. Caine had been proud, and wanted to refuse, but the opportunity to be closer to Sable had been irresistible.

That had been all Caine had lived for—being close to Isabel Duchesne. From the time she was a baby, he'd been spellbound by her. She was, quite simply, the loveliest thing he'd ever seen.

Caine had stayed with Remy and watched the old man's little girl grow into a beautiful woman. He'd watched her win her scholarship and head off to college, and had never said a word to her about how he felt. Caine knew he'd never be good enough for her, but there was always a little hope in his heart that someday she'd notice him. If he worked hard, and lived right, maybe one day he could earn the right to take her out dancing under the stars. It wasn't until the night that Sable ran away from Tulane that he discovered how she truly felt about him.

He saw Isabel run across the old weathered boards of the pier, stopping only to grab a small empty crate. When she got to the boathouse, she stood on the crate, opened the window, and hoisted herself through, then closed it behind her.

"Sable!" an angry voice called. "Where the hell are you?"

Caine watched from the shadows as Sable pressed back against the wall. She was shaking, tears streaming down her face, and her hair and skin and delicate lace dress—her mother's dress—were dripping with filth.

He came up behind her, and put his big, bony hand over her mouth, stifling the cry he knew she would make. "Shhh." He moved around her until he stepped into the light from the window. "Just me."

Sable closed her eyes and slumped against him.

Caine had never held her in his arms before. It didn't matter that she was covered from head to toe with muck. He was holding her, the girl he'd loved for so long that he couldn't breathe without thinking of her. He held on as long as he dared, then gently set her back to arm's length. "He do this to you, chère?"

"No." She glanced at the window. "I slipped and fell."

His black eyes narrowed. "You never fell in your life."

As the voice calling her name grew closer, a wrenching sob exploded from her throat. "I can't face him, not like this." She clutched at him, her small hands frantic. "Help me, please, Caine."

He wanted to go and rearrange Jean-Delano Gamble's pretty face, but he settled for pulling her back into the shadows with him. He kept an arm around her waist as he watched the window. As long as Jean-Del stayed away from Sable, Caine wouldn't interfere. If Gamble came in after her, well, then all bets were off.

Outside, footsteps pounded along the pier and then stopped just outside of the shack. "Goddamn it, Sable! Have you lost your mind? How could you do that to my friends?"

Caine pulled her closer, wanting the college boy to come in the boathouse, willing him to go away for her sake.

"Last chance, Sable," Gamble shouted on the other side of the shack's wall. "Do you hear me? You come on out here now and talk to me, or we're finished."

Caine felt the change in her, how her shaking stopped, the way she tensed her shoulders. She carefully eased away from his arm and stepped toward the window.

He couldn't let her do it. He'd heard stories from her cousin on what Gamble and his friends had done to her at that fancy college. She might love him, but he didn't deserve her. No one did.

Before she could answer him, Caine grabbed her, clamped his hand over her mouth, and hauled her back. She struggled, but he held her easily. "No more of this, Isabel," he murmured next to her ear. "You let him go now."

Outside Gamble kicked something, and wood cracked. "Look at this pissant place. This is what you want? The swamp and the gators and chopping fish bait all day? Is that why you threw mud at my friends? Because we don't have to live like this?"

She stopped struggling.

"Fine." Another kick, and something hit the water with a splash. "I'll go back and clean up your mess. You just stay the hell away from me."

When his footsteps died away, Caine took his hand from

her mouth. "There, now." He went to check the window. "He's gone."

"Why did you do that?" she asked him, her voice remote.

He'd done it because he loved her, more and harder and deeper than Jean-Delano Gamble ever would. But he could never tell her that. He was just a swamp rat who worked for her father. "Look at yourself. Look what he's done to you." He gestured at her dress. "Your daddy told you how it would be."

She didn't say anything. She simply stared at him.

Awkwardly Caine touched her cheek. "He ain't good enough for you, chère."

She caught his hand and pulled it away from her face. "You're wrong. I'm not good enough for him."

Caine almost laughed. "How do you figure that?"

"It doesn't matter how smart I am, or how hard I work, or how many scholarships I get. I'm trash. I can buy a dozen pair of white gloves and they'll still know." She tore at her dress with angry hands. "I can't get the stink of the bayou off of me."

Something pierced his heart like an invisible dagger. "It ain't nothing to be ashamed of."

She held up a fold of her dress. "Does this look proud to you, Caine? I wanted to dress like those other girls at school. I wanted to be like them. I hate what I am." She let go of the ruined material and rested her brow against the window, staring out at where Jean-Delano had been. "Now he does, too."

The next day Caine had quit working for Remy and had gone deep into the bayou to fish and trap alone. He'd built himself a shack, and then a boat, and then a living. Those hard, lean years had been the making of Caine Gantry, and when he had saved enough, he'd returned to start his own outfit on the fringe of the

Atchafalaya. He'd managed to forget about Sable and that night.

Until she'd come back, too.

Her plans for her fancy community project had infuriated Caine. She didn't care about the people of the bayou; she just wanted to hand out charity and run their lives so that she could feel above the rest of them. This was his home, his people, and he'd earned the right to live here.

She'd given up hers. She didn't belong here anymore.

He went over to the sink and washed his hands before he went back up to deal with the old man. "What do you need?"

"You heard the news." It wasn't a question. "My Isabel is in trouble."

Caine wiped his hands off on a rag. "What about it?"

"Somebody tried to kill her."

"I heard." Caine thought of Billy, and then moved his shoulders. "Likely they were after LeClare, and she got in the way."

Remy grabbed the front of his shirt. "You know something about this?"

"Just what's on the radio." He gave the old man a mild look. "You gonna work yourself into another heart attack, *cher.*"

"This is my girl I'm talking about, Caine." Remy eased his hand away. "You know what they're gonna do to her. I need your help."

"She knew what she was getting into." His mouth curled. "She should love being in the papers. All that free publicity."

His head snapped back as Remy backhanded him. It wasn't much of a punch, but it seemed to settle things. "You best look for your help somewhere else, Remy."

"I took you in when no one would've as much as spit on you, Caine Gantry. After what your papa did to me and mine, folks round here said I was crazy. I guess I was." Trembling with rage, the old man turned his back on him and walked away.

Sable regained consciousness slowly, but kept her eyes closed and didn't move. Her head pounded something fierce, but she didn't dare reach up to check the spot where she'd hit it. Not when she realized she was alone with J. D., curled up beside him on the front seat of a strange car.

If only he would stop touching her.

He had his hand on her head, his fingers brushing the hair back from the side of her face. "This hasn't been your day, has it, baby?" He made a turn, which shifted her a little, and he put his right arm across her to keep her from tumbling to the floor. "Mine, either. Shit, what else can go wrong?"

The tenderness in his voice made her want to snarl at him, but she bit down on her tongue and rode the waves of fury along with the painful throbbing in her head. A few more minutes, and she'd be at the hospital. He had to be taking her to a hospital.

He wouldn't take her anywhere else, would he?

She started counting the number of times he stopped the car at red lights, willing herself not to jerk when he rested his hand at the base of her throat. His fingertips absently traced the line of her collarbones, leaving trails of fire over the delicate skin and bones. Gooseflesh rose on her arms as she recalled how he would do the same thing when he kissed her. A flood of heat and delight drenched her insides as those old sensations rushed through her, just as powerful and intense as they had been ten years ago.

Oh, God, when were they going to get there?

Just as she opened her eyes, he pulled in over a speed bump and stopped the car. Immediately she closed them and refocused on maintaining her ruse.

"I've got her," she heard J. D. say, then felt him lifting her carefully from the seat. He had her out and in his arms, and carried her as though she weighed no more than an infant.

He didn't let go of her until a nurse hurried up to them and began asking questions. When a gurney was brought and he laid her down gently on it, someone draped her with a sheet.

Now he'll go away, she told herself, relaxing.

He laced her fingers with his. "I'm going in with her."

No, no, leave me alone, J. D., she pleaded silently as the nurse took her pulse and snapped out some orders to call radiology and have the on-call neurosurgeon notified. *Please, just go away.*

"I'm Dr. Mason," a crisp female voice said, close to Sable's left ear. "You know what happened to her?"

"She was hit in the front and the back of her head this morning, then fell about thirty minutes ago and struck the temple on the left side."

Someone was snipping away at her clothes. The cool wash of air against her bare skin made her want to cringe—was he watching them strip her? "Did you do this to her, sir?" the doctor asked, her voice chilling over as her fingers searched through Sable's scalp.

J. D.'s voice took on an equally frigid edge. "No, I didn't."

"What about these burn marks on her clothes?"

"She was caught in a fire this morning," he told her.

"That's when she hit her head the first time. The para-medics said she might have a mild concussion."

"Why wasn't she brought in before?" The doctor's hands moved carefully along her body, halting at her wrists. "These look like defensive wounds. Nancy, call security."

"Hang on, Doc." There was a rustle of cloth and the snap of a wallet. "I'm Lieutenant Gamble from NOPD, Homicide. This lady is a witness to a crime."

"Well, she's a patient now. I want a head and chest on this one, right away." The doctor's voice thawed a few degrees as she quickly finished the exam. "You can go and wait out in the lobby, Lieutenant."

"She's under police protection; I'm staying with her."

He wasn't going to leave her. *Please, no, tell him no.*

"No, you will not," the doctor snapped, as if hearing her thoughts.

"Sorry, Lieutenant, but it's hospital policy," the nurse said. "Don't worry—you'll be able to see her after she's in a room."

"Keep her name off the patient lists—I don't want anyone to know she's been admitted." J. D. was suddenly very close to her, and she felt his hand on her face again. He rubbed his thumb along the curve of her cheek. *"Je vous attendrai."*

I'll be waiting for you.

"Yeah, I know she's at Mercy," Billy snarled into the pay phone. "I'll go in and do her, but it's gonna cost you another fifty grand."

The voice on the other end of the line grew ugly.

"You don't want to be shortchanging me," Billy said, switching the phone from his left to his right ear as he turned and looked at the hospital's ER entrance. "Not when I got proof of what you done."

The line fell silent.

He smiled. "I guess we understand each other. You bring the rest of my money tomorrow night. Don't be late." He slammed the receiver down and walked over to the gas station's minimart.

The clerk, a young black man sitting on a stool behind the counter, put aside the latest issue of *Hustler* to ring up Billy's six-pack of beer. He looked at the money Billy held out like it was a dead rat. "There's blood on that, man. I can't take it."

"Wash it off." Billy threw the stained bills on the counter.

The clerk started to shake his head, then thought better of it and stuffed the money in his till. "Whatever you say, man."

Billy drove over to the visitors' parking lot at the hospital, parked in the front row, and popped open a beer. As he drank, he watched how people came in and went out. The visitors all shuffled through the glassed-in front entrance, where a guard made them sign in and handed them a tag. The staff went in through a side door, but Billy couldn't see what was inside. On the south side of the hospital, a construction crew was working on a fenced-in skeletal extension of the building. Double doors leading into the hospital had been propped open, and there was a rack of hard hats outside the fence. Everyone came and went as they pleased.

He finished his beer and crumpled the can in his fist. Smothering the bitch with a pillow wouldn't be as nice as watching her burn, but sometimes a man had to make compromises.

Chapter Four

"Did you enjoy your flight, Mr. Gamble?"

Cort would have settled for a nod, but the line of disembarking passengers ahead of him had stopped for a handicapped passenger having trouble with his courtesy wheelchair. "Yes, thank you."

"I'm glad we could find you a seat at the last moment." The friendly flight attendant let her gaze drift down, then back up as her practiced smile became more genuine. "Are you visiting New Orleans for Mardi Gras, or are you a local?"

"I'm a native." He checked the line again, then his watch. He'd tried calling J. D. three times while changing planes in Atlanta, but kept getting his voice mail. He wasn't going to call home until he got the facts on the arson and Marc's death straight. He already knew what his mother would have to say.

"I'll be back next week for a two-day layover," the attendant confided, and reached out to rest the tips of her manicured fingers on his sleeve. "Would be great if I had someone to show me around, maybe take me to dinner? . . ."

The coy invitation fishing made him take a good look at her. The blond hair, white teeth, and high breasts were too perfect to be real, but she had a pleasant voice and a nice tan. She was petite, too, which he preferred. From the way she was eyeing his crotch she'd probably be eager to skip the sights and dinner and head straight for the nearest bed.

Cort never had a problem finding eager women, though, and lately he'd been getting pretty bored with them.

"There will be a half million men in the city next week," he told her as the line started moving again and he picked up his carry-on. "You'll find a date."

As he went downstairs to retrieve his garment bag from baggage claim, Cort passed by one of the terminal's courtesy television monitors and caught the tail end of a breaking news broadcast from one of the local city stations.

"—have finally confirmed that the victim is forty-seven-year-old Democratic gubernatorial candidate Marc LeClare. Mr. LeClare, who was a well-known local businessman and community figure, had been favored to win the election by a two-to-one margin." The anchorman produced a sympathetic frown before he went on. "The survivor and apparent witness to the murder, a young woman"—a small, blurry inset photo appeared on the screen beside the anchorman—"has not yet been identified by authorities. News Nine will be bringing you live updates as they come in."

It can't be her. Cort went over and flipped the channel to another local station, and watched another report about the murder. This time the broadcast showed his brother and his partner leading the pale-faced redhead out of an elevator at police headquarters. J. D. looked grim, as did Terri Vincent, which set off the first alarm in Cort's head. When the witness lifted her head and looked up blindly into the camera, Cort began to swear under his breath.

It *was* her—Sable Duchesne, J. D.'s old college girl-friend. *How the hell did she get involved in this?* He kept watching as Sable got into a shoving match with a re-porter and fell, hitting her head on the way down. The ferocious look on his brother's face as he lifted her from the floor made Cort grab his bag and head for the nearest phone—only this time, he called his own de-partment.

"Hell of a mess," his senior investigator told him as he went over what he knew about the arson case. "We're waiting for the medical examiner's report on LeClare. The redhead barely got out before the build-ing went up."

Terri Vincent hadn't breathed a word about the wit-ness being J. D.'s ex. She would have known, too. J. D. wasn't one to keep something like that from his part-ner. Why she hadn't told Cort would be one of the first things he'd take up with her when he got downtown. "What was used to torch the building?"

"Amoco cocktails," his investigator said, referring to a very specific type of homemade gasoline bomb. "We recovered one partially intact, and it's exactly like the ones used to torch that marina last month, and the processing plant in December."

Cort thought of the serial arsonist who had been plaguing LeClare's commercial-fishing industries. From the threats LeClare had received, Cort's depart-ment was fairly sure it was a group of disgruntled in-dependent fishermen torching the businessman's property—fishermen who were Cajuns, just like Sable Duchesne.

It might be a coincidence, or maybe Sable had an-other reason for being there.

"Send someone to pick up my bags at the airport. I'll leave the claim checks at the information counter."

Cort pulled the long-term parking ticket from his wallet.

"Where you headed, Chief?"

"Downtown."

Sable knew the moment J. D. left the examination room, and unconsciously relaxed for a moment before concentrating on keeping the ER staff convinced that she was not going to regain consciousness. Her stretcher was wheeled out of the exam room into a hallway. From the conversation between the nurse and the orderly, they were moving her to radiology and from there would take her to a room.

"So what's her story?" she heard a young male voice ask after she was pushed into a very cold room.

"Not sure. Head injury, I think." The orderly who had taken her from the ER had only received instructions to transport her to radiology. "You want her chart?"

"No, leave it there. I've got a portable pelvis in ten minutes. I've got to get this one done fast." Something soft but stiff encircled her neck. "Help me move her?"

She remained limp as they lifted and maneuvered her onto the exam table, and she kept her eyes closed as the radiology machines and film plates were arranged around her. Only when the volunteer stepped outside did she open her eyes to slits, to see the layout of the room. There was a protective panel behind which a young male technician stood over a complicated-looking console. The orderly was gone, and there was no sign of J. D. anywhere.

I can stop pretending now.

She watched the young male technician as he worked. He turned knobs and punched buttons, and the equipment buzzed. He came out to change plates and smiled down at her.

"Hey, there. How are you feeling?"

"My head hurts," she admitted.

"I imagine it does." His pager went off, and he checked it and sighed. "Listen, sweetheart, I've got an emergency right down the hall here that can't wait. You just relax, and I'll be right back, okay?" When she nodded, he grinned again and wheeled one of the smaller machines out of the room.

Sable rolled onto her side and tugged the thin sheet around her. That and the patient gown she wore were so thin that they didn't keep her from shivering. The minutes ticked by, and when the technician didn't return she grew restless.

Did he forget about me?

At last she sat up, climbed down from the table, and went to see what was holding up the technician. She reached the door just as it swung open, and stepped back behind it.

A short, wiry-looking man in a yellow hard hat came in and walked toward the table. She couldn't see his face, but he left a strangely familiar odor in his wake. A smell like fish . . . mixed with gasoline.

It was him.

Sable edged around the door and ran out into the hall. There was no one outside in either direction, so she darted into the unmarked door on the other side of the hall. It turned out to be some kind of supply closet, complete with stacked rolling carts of clean linens.

What do I do now?

She couldn't stay here; she had to get away. She needed clothes.

A rack of white lab coats hung on one side of the closet, and she grabbed one, then nearly screamed as the gap revealed the motionless body of the young X-ray technician. The whites of his eyes were pink and his jaw sagged; there were dark bruises around his neck.

He'd been strangled.

Her stomach surged as she reached down and checked for a pulse, but found none. She threw a wild look at the door. Would he come back? Would he look for her in here?

Find J. D.

She went to the door and eased it open a fraction of an inch. The stink of fish and gasoline hit her nose, and she saw a man's back only a few inches away. The man was still wearing a yellow hard hat. He was standing right in front of the closet, waiting.

Watching for her.

Sable pulled the lab coats back to conceal the technician's body, then retrieved a pair of surgical scrub pants spotted with dried blood from a soiled linen bin. After yanking on the pants and tucking her patient gown inside, she pulled on the lab coat she'd taken down. A quick search of the shelves produced a plastic shower cap and a pair of elastic shoe coverings, which she used to cover her hair and feet.

With a silent prayer she grabbed one of the clean linen carts, and used it to push the door open. The man automatically stepped aside and glanced at her, but she kept her head down and quickly turned her back to him. "Pardon me."

She pushed the bin down the hall toward the red EXIT sign.

Just a few more feet.

"Hey—hey, wait."

When she glanced back over her shoulder, she saw him running after her. In desperation she swung the bin around and shoved it at him, then ran into the stairwell. She hurried down the steps to the next floor, where she darted inside the ward. She didn't dare stop to ask for help. He was coming after her; he could catch up at any second.

She had to get away.

The lab coat made her invisible to the nurses and doctors she passed as she followed the signs to the elevators. No one spoke to her or even glanced her way on the elevator, or tried to stop her when she left the hospital.

For a moment she stood outside and thought of J. D. waiting in the ER for her, then through the glass saw the man in the yellow hard hat step off the elevator. He was scanning the faces of the people in the lobby.

For the first time she got a good look at his face, and recognized him. Billy Tibbideau, one of Caine Gantry's men.

Caine had been fighting tooth and nail to keep commercial fishing out of the bayou. Marc had owned one of the largest commercial-fishing companies in the state.

Billy started walking toward the front entrance.

She had to find J. D. Sable hurried down to the ER entrance, then stopped when a sedan pulled up in front of her, blocking her path. The elderly driver got out and walked toward her, leaning heavily on the cane in his right hand. His left was wrapped in a bloody kitchen towel.

"What happened to you?"

"Durn stray dog bit me," he said, then scowled and nodded toward the sedan. "I left the keys in the ignition—you go on and park that for me. I'm about to keel over." Without another word he hobbled on into the hospital.

Sable glanced over her shoulder to see Billy step outside. *No more time.* She ran around the car and jerked open the driver's door.

"Cortland is returning early from Biloxi," Elizabet Gamble told her housekeeper, Mae Wallace, as she inspected the new floral arrangement in the dining room, and tucked a wayward fern leaf back behind a full-bloom rose. "Would you set an extra place for him at dinner tonight?"

"Yes, ma'am." Mae went to draw the blue satin curtains open. "Looks like it's going to rain."

"Better now than this weekend." Elizabet frowned at her slightly blurred reflection in the surface of the long mahogany table, which had been in her family since the French Revolution. There was nothing wrong with the short, neat arrangement of silver curls, but she lifted the glasses hanging on the chain around her neck to inspect herself anyway. "Either I've grown two more eyebrows, or this table needs polishing, Mae."

The housekeeper chuckled. "I'm sure it's the table, ma'am." The phone in the kitchen rang, and Mae excused herself. She returned a moment later. "It's Ms. Moriah Navarre for you."

"I'll take it in the library. Which reminds me, would you call the florist and make sure she has enough gardenias in stock for the party? I don't want to have to scramble for flowers at the last minute." Elizabet picked up her planner from the table. There was so much to do, and only a few days left. "Oh, and please let me know when the caterer delivers the serving tables—we'll need an extra one for the cold buffet."

The week of New Orleans's biggest holiday of the year was always hectic, but Elizabet Gamble had grown accustomed to handling the challenges. Aside from the annual Krewe of Louis Dinner, which her husband held at his restaurant for his business associates, the Noir et Blanc Gala was the most important social event on the family calendar. Since assuming the role of hostess from her mother twenty-five years ago, Elizabet had followed tradition and driven herself to put on the most elegant, perfect party of the season.

Tradition was a wonderful thing, but in the last few years keeping up with it had started to wear on her. *I'm getting too old to be running around like this every Mardi Gras.*

As she went into her husband's library, Elizabet wished for the thousandth time that she had a daughter of her own. Her daughter-in-law, Wendy, might have taken over the family duties, but she and Evan insisted on living on a ranch in the middle of godforsaken Montana, of all places. Still, Elizabet had two more sons to marry off, and as soon as Jean-Delano settled down with Moriah, she could pass the torch of tradition.

Now if I can just convince him to propose to the girl. She knew how stubborn her son could be, but it wouldn't hurt to drop a gentle hint. An engagement announcement at this year's gala would be the perfect highlight of the party. Once he was married, then she and Moriah could work on getting him out of the police department and into an occupation that wouldn't require him to carry a gun to work.

She picked up the phone on her husband's desk. "Moriah, my dear, how are you? What excellent timing—I was just thinking about you." The smell of strong liquor made her frown, and she opened one of the desk drawers, where her husband had left a bottle of cognac and a small snifter. She suppressed a sigh—Louie had promised her and his doctor that he'd stop drinking—and closed the drawer. "I've been meaning to have you and Jean-Delano over for dinner this week; would the two of you be free tonight? Cort will be home early, so we all could have a little pre-gala celebration."

"Elizabet, I'm sorry, I can't. Something terrible has happened." Moriah sounded uncharacteristically hoarse and unhappy. "Marc LeClare was killed this morning."

She slowly sat down in her husband's chair, unable to speak as Moriah related the appalling details of what had happened. Elizabet thought of Marc, who had been friends with her husband since childhood, and how devastated Louie was going to be when he heard the news. Tears stung her eyes as Moriah told her about Laure LeClare's near-catatonic state, and how vicious the media were being.

As the girl's voice trailed off, Elizabet rallied herself. "I'll call Louis; we'll bring some food from the restaurant over for Laure. Will you be staying with her, honey? I don't think she has any family in town."

"Yes, I think I'd better." Moriah sighed. "I've been trying to get hold of J. D., but they say he's at the hospital with the woman they found with Marc."

"A woman?" Elizabet frowned. "Who is she? Why is she at the hospital?"

"She was hurt or something; I'm not sure. They're having a press conference about her on television in a few minutes." An uneven voice spoke in the background, and Moriah added, "I have to go—Laure's calling me. You will come soon, won't you, Elizabet?"

"Yes. Try to get her to rest in the meantime, and don't speak to any reporters. I'll see you soon." Elizabet switched lines and dialed her husband's restaurant. "Philipe? Would you ask my husband to come to the phone, please." She listened for a moment as the maître d' explained that Louis was supervising a delivery. "Very well, then, please ask him to call me back as soon as possible. It's extremely important."

She removed the used snifter from Louie's desk before she went to the entertainment center and turned on the television. The chief of Homicide was already on, delivering a statement to the reporters. She disliked George Pellerin, who had come from New York City and had little respect for the way things were done in Creole society. She only invited him to her functions out of deference to her son. The sooner she convinced J. D. to leave the police force and take up a safer profession, the better. Until then she could put up with almost anyone.

"Isabel Marie Duchesne has been moved to a medical facility for treatment of a head injury," the captain was saying. "At this time I have no update on her condition."

"What was she doing at the warehouse, Captain?" one of the reporters called out. "Was she involved with Marc LeClare?"

Pellerin's face reddened. "Ms. Duchesne is a witness in an ongoing investigation. That's all I can tell you now."

The balloon-shaped glass fell from her hand unnoticed, shattering on the hardwood floor. *Isabel Marie Duchesne.* After all the prayers she had made, hoping never to hear that name again.

Elizabet looked up at the shadow box on the wall, which Louie had built to display what he considered their most precious heirloom—a small square cassette box in which his family's original matriarch had brought her trousseau with her from Paris. Elizabet's own family could trace its roots back to Jean Baptiste

Le Moyne, sieur de Bienville, King Louis XV's builder and founder of New Orleans. For this reason, she had always considered her husband's pride in his "casket girl" ancestress to be slightly embarrassing. The girl had really been no better than a prostitute, selling herself in marriage in exchange for a pitiful dowry and free passage to America. The same way Isabel Duchesne had tried to use Jean-Delano to better her situation.

I won't let her hurt my son again.

In a panic, Elizabet went back to the desk and dialed the restaurant again. Her fingers shook so much that she had to dial it twice. "Philipe? I don't care about the delivery. Tell my husband to come to the phone at once. Yes, it's an emergency."

Unable to sit down or relax, J. D. went to the windows of the ER lobby to watch the evening traffic roll by. If Sable had to be admitted, he'd have to post an armed officer outside her room. Hell, he'd stay and guard her himself—maybe when she regained consciousness, she'd be more in a mood to talk to him.

"Was that your wife you brought in?" a gentle voice asked.

J. D. turned to see a middle-aged woman standing next to him. She had on a faded housedress and looked tired, but her smile was sympathetic. What she'd asked him finally registered—she thought Sable was his wife.

Something twisted in his gut. "No, ma'am. She's . . . a friend."

"Well, don't you worry. This here's a good hospital." She nodded toward the treatment rooms. "My husband's in there now. He gobbles down two of my po'boys at lunchtime; then he says he's having chest pains."

Her tone was amused but he could see the worry in her eyes. "Maybe it's nothing serious."

"Indigestion, most like. He'll blame it on the peppers and onions, like always." She laughed at herself. "I keep telling that man he's got to stop eating so much and so fast, but does he listen to me?"

He smiled a little. "Hard for a man to do when his wife's a good cook."

"I suppose." She eyed him. "Your girl looked like she bumped her head real bad—you all get in an accident?"

"No, ma'am. She fell." He looked back through the window. "I tried to catch her, but I didn't get there in time." All he seemed to do was try to catch Sable while she slipped through his fingers.

A nurse called out a name, and the woman patted his arm. "That's me. Don't you fret, son. You just take care of her now, and she'll be fine." She walked over to the nurse, then laughed and accompanied her back to the treatment rooms.

J. D.'s attention strayed to a figure in a lab coat and scrubs talking to an old man outside. It was a woman, but her back was to him. A stray shaft of light broke through the gathering storm clouds, making her red hair blaze like dark fire.

That can't be—

He swore as he ran for the exit, but the driver of the sedan blocked his path.

"Watch where the hell you're going!"

"Sorry." J. D. paused long enough to steady the old man before trotting outside.

Sable was already behind the wheel of the sedan

and backing out. She'd not only faked him out; she was ditching him.

Over his dead body.

J. D. could call the station and explain how the only witness to Marc LeClare's death had just stolen a car, and wait for backup. Or he could catch her.

He didn't even have to think about it.

A minute later J. D. caught up with Sable on the highway, but kept back three car lengths so she wouldn't spot him. He knew where she was headed—the Atchafalaya, just as she had the night of the dance.

Only this time, she'd made a serious mistake.

Sable probably thought he was still some lovesick boy who couldn't see straight around her. She didn't realize he'd spent the last ten years dealing with death and destruction. Tracking down killers had changed him, had removed every ounce of pity from him, and had tempered him into what he was: an efficient, cold-blooded hunter.

She could run all she wanted, but there was no place on this earth where she could hide from him now.

Terri took the predicted chewing out from Pellerin alone and in silence, only speaking up when required to answer. Like the press conference, it had not gone well, mainly because no one could get in touch with J. D., and the hospital still hadn't called back with any prognosis on Sable.

"I don't care if her brains are leaking out of her ears," the captain said toward the end of his rant. "You get on over to Mercy, have them slap on whatever Band-Aids she needs, and bring her back here for questioning. She stays in protective custody until we get the autopsy on LeClare, and no one—including her—talks to the press unless they clear it through me.

I want a full progress report typed on my desk in two hours. Are you straight on this, Sergeant?"

Terri would have to get J. D. to do the reports, if she could pry his hands off their witness long enough for him to type them. He owed her for this. "Yes, sir."

Pellerin's phone rang for the fifth time since Terri had entered his office, and he gave it a disgusted look. "Go on, get outta here."

Terri escaped the station house and headed for her car, lighting a cigarette on the way. She'd been meaning to try to quit again since the beginning of the year, but nicotine withdrawal turned her into a total bitch, and she figured she was doing the world a favor by waiting until she went on vacation.

Only now she wouldn't get any downtime until they cleared the LeClare case—which wouldn't be soon, unless Isabel started remembering something. And then there was the very strong possibility that Terri might have to break in a new partner.

Good-bye, vacation. She took a deep drag and then released the acrid smoke from her lungs on a sigh. She really did need to quit, and soon. *I sure hope she's worth it, J. D.*

"Terri."

She swung around, expecting to see her partner. "Where the fu—" She cut herself off as soon as she met green eyes instead of blue. Every emotional wall inside her went into full lockdown. "That was quick." As a couple of uniforms stopped to chat outside the main station entrance a few feet away, she took another drag from her cigarette, making the tip flare. "You appropriate a plane for yourself, Marshal?"

Chief Fire Marshal Cortland Gamble looked the way he usually did—pressed, polished, and pissed-off. He was a few inches taller than J. D. and a little broader in the chest, and his hair was brown instead of black. Otherwise he could have been his brother's twin.

All except the expression on his face, and his mouth. The expression said he ate smart-ass female detectives for breakfast. The mouth said he'd start at the toes and work his way up.

Quit thinking about his mouth.

"Come here." He took her arm and hauled her around the side of the building, out of hearing range. "What's going on? Where the hell is my brother?"

"Easy on the jacket. It's dry-clean only." She eased herself from his grip. "J. D.'s over at the hospital, getting our witness patched up." She glanced at her watch. "I've been taking messages for him all day, though. Why don't I have him call you when he gets back?"

"Why aren't you with him?"

"Because we're not joined at the hip." She'd taken a lot of official crap for J. D. on this case already, and she wasn't going to take it from his big brother. "But if you've got a problem with how we handle our cases, Chief, you can speak to Captain Pellerin." Unable to resist, she took another drag and exhaled a little smoke in his face.

"I intend to." Cort plucked the cigarette from her hand, dropped it, and ground it out under his shoe. "This woman, Isabel Duchesne—what did she say?"

"She said she can't remember anything." She had an urge to light another one, but he'd probably rip up the entire pack, and then she'd have to punch him. "It's pretty obvious that she's trying to protect herself, or LeClare. My guess is, she was his mistress."

"*Fuck.*"

She arched a brow. "You kiss your mother with that mouth?"

He looked around for a minute, as if the patience he needed were hovering somewhere near. "I want an update on everything you've got."

"I want a Maserati, myself. Something in a nice cherry red, with lots of gold detailing. It's the insurance that holds me back." Feeling stupid, she pushed past him, heading for the parking lot and the quickest means of escape.

He caught up to her. "This isn't funny, Terri."

"Hey, my boss is all over my ass like a bad tattoo, your brother is about to trash his career, and I've got an injured witness to interview and a case to solve. Believe me, it's not been a bag of chuckles today." She pulled her keys from her trouser pocket and fumbled with them until she got the driver's-side door of her car unlocked.

"I need to know what's happening."

"You can talk to the desk sergeant. I'm a little too damn busy to hold your hand right now and tell you your little brother's going to be all right."

When she opened the door, he put out a hand and slammed it shut. "My brother is not getting involved in this shit with Isabel Duchesne."

She lifted her brows. "Here's a news flash for you: I tried to talk your brother into ditching this case. He wouldn't hear of it. J. D. *wants* to be up to his ears in this shit with Isabel Duchesne, and it looks like that's where he's staying. But if you think you can pull him out, have at it."

"I'll have the case transferred to my arson task force; it's our jurisdiction anyway."

"You do that." The cell phone in her car rang, and

she nudged him aside to open the door and answer it. "Vincent."

She listened as the dispatcher relayed the latest news from the hospital, and closed her eyes briefly, wishing she could slam her head into something. *Sorry, J. D., I did what I could.*

"Got it. Relay this to Captain Pellerin—tell him I think we ought to issue an APB for Duchesne. Right. Keep me posted." She ended the call.

"Is it J. D.?"

"Sort of. A technician was found strangled at Mercy. He was taking X rays of our witness, who was last seen driving away from Mercy in a stolen car." She met Cort's gaze. "Your brother went after her."

Cecilia Tibbideau heard the front door of the trailer slam, and glanced around the tiny, spotless kitchen before she set down the basket of laundry. "Billy?" She rubbed her palms against the front of her apron. "That you?"

"Goddamn bitch." His footsteps made hollow, heavy thuds on the floor as he strode into the kitchen. His thin face was flushed and shiny with sweat, and he was carrying a half a six-pack and a bottle wrapped in a brown bag. "Get me a glass, Cee."

She went to the cabinet and took down her husband's favorite drinking glass, a beer stein he'd stolen from a local bar. She made sure it was clean before she set it down on the table in front of him. "You hungry, honey?" Sometimes he didn't get so drunk if he had something to eat first. "I kept your plate in the oven—"

"Shut up." He opened the bottle and poured a measure of whiskey into the stein, then thumped the bottle down on the table.

Cecilia hadn't expected him home so late—he'd

said he had a job to do that would take all morning, but he wanted dinner hot and on the table at five. It was past seven now. There were fresh bruises on his face, and his bottom lip was split. *Caine Gantry had done that.*

He met her gaze. His eyes were bloodshot, and one looked like it was starting to swell. "What you looking at?"

"Nothing, Billy." She ducked her head. "I'm sorry."

"You're sorry. You're damn right, you're sorry." His gaze moved around the kitchen, then focused on the basket of wet clothes. His voice went low and soft. "You ain't got your chores done yet?"

Cecilia looked down at her folded hands. "It's the last load. The rain got to them before I could."

He made a snorting sound and took another drink. "You been sittin' round watching game shows all day again."

"No, honey. I cleaned the kitchen and did the wash and fixed you a nice dinner." He'd forgotten that he'd gotten mad watching the evening news and thrown the set across the room.

Billy wasn't a big man, but he could move fast when he wanted to. He was up and had her by the shoulders before she could blink. "Don't you lie to me."

"The TV set's broke." She cringed away from his hot breath. He'd never hit her yet, but there was something different about him today—something frightening in his eyes. "I can't watch it."

"But you want another one, don't ya?" He slammed her back against the refrigerator. "A bigger one? A better one?"

"I don't. Really I don't, Billy." She could hardly breathe, caught between his weight and the hard flat door. "I—I don't like TV."

"You got something better to do?" His eyes narrowed. "You been talking to that dyke next door again?"

She shook her head.

"Better not."

Billy hated Lilah, their next-door neighbor, but it wasn't because she was a lesbian. Cecilia suspected that her husband had tried to hit on Lilah more than once, and she'd flatly refused.

Maybe sex would calm him down. "How about I make you feel better, honey?" She licked her lips, the way he liked her to.

"Been wanting it, huh?" He stared at her breasts. "Can't get enough of me."

She hated sex with him, but it was better than tiptoeing around him for the rest of the night.

His eyes went to the window, and his expression changed. "I ain't got time." He let go of her and went back into the bedroom. He came out with his shotgun and a box of ammunition. "I'm going hunting. I'll be back later."

He hadn't gone hunting in years. "All right."

"Don't sulk now." He yanked up the hem of her skirt and ground his palm against her crotch. "I'll take care of you later."

After her husband left the trailer, Cecilia didn't move. Only when she heard his truck pull out onto the road did she pull down her skirt and let the tears go. She felt so dirty when he touched her like that—like she was some whore instead of his wife.

"Cecile?"

The sound of Lilah's voice made her wipe her face with her apron. "Just a minute." She didn't open the screen door. "Did you need something?"

"I heard Billy shouting." The busty blonde peered out from under her umbrella. "He hit you?"

"No, I told you, he never hits me."

Lilah walked up the steps and closed the umbrella as she opened the door and stepped inside. Under her coat she was wearing one of her work outfits—a spangled orange minidress that hugged her voluptuous curves—and the glitter made Cecilia blink. "I heard him clear across the yard this time. You got to get yourself away from that man, girl."

Get away from Billy Tibbideau? She almost laughed. She had no family to go to, and she'd dropped out of school at sixteen, so no one would hire her. Billy was all she had.

"I could help you get a job." Her neighbor tugged up the edge of the low-cut bodice. "Bartholomew's hiring."

Lilah danced five nights a week at Bart's Strip Club, but she had a gorgeous body and no qualms about showing it off. Cecilia didn't even like undressing with the lights on. "Thank you, but I couldn't do anything like that."

Her neighbor rolled her eyes. "You'd be waiting tables, honey, not stripping."

Lilah kept talking about the job, but Cecilia couldn't concentrate on what she was saying. She kept thinking of Billy carrying the shotgun out to his truck.

"Thanks again, but I'm fine," she interrupted her neighbor in midsentence, and opened the screen door. "Excuse me now, I've got some work to do."

After Lilah left, Cecilia went to the phone. She'd call Caine and tell him Billy had gone out to do some hunting. Caine would have to decide what, exactly, her husband intended to hunt.

Chapter Five

Sable didn't slow down until she was out of the city and on one of the lesser-traveled back roads into the bayou, and even then she couldn't stop shaking.

How did he find me so fast?

J. D. had told the ER staff they weren't to tell anyone she was there. Marc's murderer must have followed her from the fire to the police station, and from there to the hospital. Or one of the cops had told him where to find her.

He'd strangled that young technician so he could get to her. What else was he capable of doing?

Now that she'd stolen a car, she'd have to move quickly, and stay on the move. If the police caught up with her—if J. D. caught up with her—she wouldn't get another chance to run. And she had to see Caine first.

Caine Gantry had a lot to answer for.

The turnoff to Gantry Charters was marked by a neat, hand-lettered sign at the corner of a narrow dirt road, and as she turned she heard the faint sound of outboard motors and men shouting. Caine's boats were coming in from a long day out on the water, which meant his entire crew would be on the docks, unloading their catch and whatever passengers they'd brought along for the ride. It was Monday, so there probably wouldn't be too many tourists wanting to fish.

As she shut off the headlights and coasted to a stop a few hundred yards from the dock, she saw the silhouette of the big man standing at the end of the pier, dragging a bulging net dangling from a deck hoist over the side of a big charter boat. He centered the net and lowered it almost into a huge, square wooden barrow, then released it. The oysters hitting the wood clattered like dishes someone had dropped breaking.

He won't do anything to me in front of his crew, she promised herself as she got out of the car and headed for the dock. *After what Remy did for him, he wouldn't dare.*

"I took him around dat good spot over by Darel's place, 'n' dat's where I heard dat hummin' again," Tag McGee, one of the older men on the crew, was telling the others as they unloaded their catch. The lean, weather-battered Cajuns who worked for Gantry had lived on the water all their lives, and if they weren't fishing or hunting, they were talking about it. "It bein' a full moon 'n' all, I tell the Yankee mebbe it's the old black slaves what drowned in the bayou during the War a' Northern Aggression. Then he say, 'Can we go on back now? I think I done caught enough.' "

All the men chuckled at that. Caine said something low to the old man, who threw up a hand.

"I showed him it weren't nothing more than a shoal a' black drum fish, hummin' together under the water, boss." Tag shook his head in disgust. "He say, 'I don't want catch me no haunt fish.' "

"Still spooking the paying customers, Tag McGee?" Sable said in a soft voice, drawing every eye and bringing the work to a temporary standstill. "You ought to be ashamed of yourself."

Caine turned toward her, but with the sun setting behind him, his face remained in shadow.

"Evenin', Ms. Duchesne." Tag looked from her to his boss, cleared his throat, and then waved his arms at the men. "Y'all get your asses in gear 'n' move these barrows over to the wet house."

Suddenly everyone was busy again except Caine, who merely waited and watched as Sable walked steadily across the silvered planks to his boat. Only when she halted a few feet away did he speak. "You're supposed to be in the hospital with a bump on your head."

"It wasn't much of a bump." She eyed the short-handled shovel he picked up. "Did you hear about the fire?"

"It was all over the radio and TV." He thrust the shovel into the pile of oysters and picked up the end of the barrow. The big muscles in his upper arms knotted, but he pushed it past her as if it weighed no more than a baby carriage. "Everyone in the state knows. Go home, Isabel."

Sable followed him back to the wet house, where the men would clean the fish and the oysters before loading them into huge refrigerated bins. Caine took his barrow to the side of the shack, where one of the men was staking a sheet of chicken wire over a dug-out pit of glowing coals. After using an outside hose to spray down the catch in the barrow, Caine started shoveling the oysters onto the chicken wire. The water dripping from the shells made the coals hiss and steam rise from the pit. "Caine, we have to talk."

"No, we don't." He paused to wipe some sweat

from his brow and eyed the tree line. "Go to Remy's. He's worried about you."

"It's important."

"I got a crew to feed." He went back to shoveling the fresh oysters onto the chicken wire, then took some burlap sacks from a bucket of salt water and draped the mound of shells. "Turn 'em in ten minutes," he told the man tending the pit, then shoved the barrow to one side and went around Sable.

She stopped him with a single question. "Were you in the city this morning, Caine?"

Something crackled in the bushes.

Caine stared out at the swamp before he turned on her. "You go on home, Isabel," he said, his voice as flat as his black eyes. "You go on home right now."

"Oh, I'm not leaving." With the light in his face, she could see the change in his expression. "Not until you tell what you've done."

"What have I done?" He came to her and took her by the arms, his grip hard. "You come in here." He marched her to the wet house, and pointed to the big refrigeration cases. "You see those? I'll be paying on them, and the ones I had to install on my boats, for the next five years. They're making me buy a separate charter license for each of my boats now, too. Most of the small outfits round here have been shut down because they can't do the same." He released her. "I didn't do that, Isabel. LeClare did that to *us*."

She knew the old argument. Laws had been passed requiring oyster fishermen to refrigerate their catch almost immediately after harvesting the beds, to prevent contamination. There was also much stricter licensing now, as well. Marc had been one of the primary movers on the legislation. "It's to keep people from getting sick, Caine," she reminded him.

"LeClare and his kind have been harvesting beds where there's sewage spill-off," he snarled. "No one fines them for the oysters they fish out of the shit washed down from the city. No one blames them for making people sick."

"The state is closing down those beds and you know it." She sensed the men gathering around them in the dark, but refused to let them intimidate her. She was Remy Duchesne's daughter, and she'd known most of them from the time she could walk. "Billy was at the warehouse, wasn't he?"

"I fired Billy," he told her. His expression changed, became more withdrawn. "You'll have to ask him where he's been."

"Did he do it on your orders? Are you telling your men to set fire to Marc's properties?"

The anger faded from his face as he let his gaze wander down to her shoes and back up again. "Only fires I light are under the covers, *chère*," he drawled, reaching out to glide his callused fingertips along the curve of her cheek. "They take a long time to burn."

She knew what he was doing—he couldn't scare her off with his legendary temper, so he was falling back on the other thing he was famous for. Hilaire had told stories about Caine's appetite for women, how he sometimes brought two girls home with him so he wouldn't have to go out a second time, but Sable hadn't really believed that. She could only remember the shy, silent boy who had worked for her father.

The boy had grown up, she realized, swallowing hard as he gathered a handful of her hair and rubbed it between his fingertips. And maybe his rep was a little understated. "I'm not interested."

He smiled and bent down, holding her by the hair when she would have stepped away.

"Aren't you, Isabel?" He breathed the question against her brow as he slid his thumb across her lower lip in a slow, taunting caress. When she opened her mouth to reply, he rimmed the inside, testing the edge of her teeth. "Don't you feel just a little hot now?"

Some of the men chuckled.

She ignored the blatant sexuality and focused on his eyes. She knew he was putting on an act—wasn't he? She turned her head to one side to avoid his probing thumb. "Why are you in such a hurry to get rid of me?"

"You're not interested?" He dropped one hand on her shoulder, and the other over her heart. "Then why are you trembling, little girl?" He revolved his hard palm over the peak of her breast. "Your nipple is hard. You cold?"

"No." Shame, not desire, made her shiver. She didn't want Caine, but she couldn't stop her body from responding to the stimulation. "I'm disgusted."

"With me?" He cupped the back of her neck and tipped her chin up to brush a featherlight kiss over her lips. "Or yourself? Maybe those city boys didn't teach you right."

Dread settled in the pit of her stomach as she remembered something Marc had told her. "If Marc had become governor, he would have introduced new legislation to hire more Fish and Game wardens, to stop illegal harvesting and smuggling. That would have put you and your friends out of business. You knew that."

Caine lifted his head. "Now he won't. Run along, Isabel."

She wanted to shriek at him, to claw his face. "I never thought you'd follow in your father's footste Caine."

His smirk disappeared. "You don't know the first thing about me."

She remembered falling onto Marc's body, and the blood on her hands. "Did you kill him, Caine?"

"No, but I'm glad he's dead." Now he had his hands on the lapels of her stolen lab coat, but there was nothing seductive about it. "You got anything else you want to say to me before I toss your smart ass in the river?"

"You're pathetic." She looked at his crew, who were silently watching the exchange. The impassive faces outraged her. "Don't you know what they'll do? Marc LeClare was a powerful man. The police *will* come in here looking for Billy, and anyone who helps him *will* go to prison. Including your idiot boss here. Then who's going to provide for your wives and your children?"

An angry murmur ran through the crew.

Caine didn't like that. "You'd best worry about who's gonna take care of you now, *chère*."

A shadow separated from the trees, and dull metal glinted as a man pointed a gun at Caine's head. "That's enough," J. D. said. "Let her go."

The big Cajun slowly took his hands from the white lab coat. "Well, now, ain't this a night for reunions?"

Sable stared at J. D., torn between horror and relief. How had he known where she would go? Would he get her out of here?

"Come here, Sable." J. D. kept his aim level and motionless. "Now."

The crew moved forward, forming a tight wall behind Sable and Caine. She glanced over her shoulder and saw oyster knives appear in tight hands. "This isn't finished, Caine. I'm going to tell them."

"You do that, Isabel." The big man gave her a small

push in J. D.'s direction. "But take your cop boyfriend on outta here first, before he ends up like *your* daddy."

Moriah watched as Laure sobbed against Elizabet Gamble's shoulder. She wished she could do the same, but anger and guilt had somehow frozen her inside.

She'd tried to do what she could for Laure after she'd met her at the police station, but when Moriah had seen Isabel Duchesne, it had rendered her almost completely speechless.

Of course Laure had adored her husband, and was simply devastated. Moriah knew she should have been able to say something, summon some words of condolence, but instead she'd merely hovered and tried not to think about Isabel Duchesne, or how she could have known Marc LeClare.

She'd failed, naturally. She had never completely forgotten about Sable. The image of the shy girl in her cheap lace dress had haunted her for years.

Moriah had called her mother, but she was out shopping, so she had been obliged to drive Laure home. The only other person she could think to call was Elizabet Gamble, who happened to be one of Laure's oldest friends. She had come, and was now providing the sympathy and comfort Moriah couldn't.

She was glad that Elizabet and Louie had come, but Moriah had never felt more useless in her life.

A kind hand touched her shoulder. "Why don't we go on into the kitchen?" Louie Gamble murmured. "Give the ladies some time to talk."

Moriah nodded and followed Elizabet's husband out of the parlor and down the hall to the darkene kitchen. Laure had sent the horrified servants ho earlier, but the cook had left out gourmet cold me cheeses, and sliced breads on one of the cour

Take-out containers from Krewe of Louis stood in neat stacks beside the sandwich platters.

Funeral food, Moriah's mother called it. *People like to have something to nibble on when someone dies. Makes them feel better.*

Her stomach clenched tighter as she looked away from the expensive spread. "I don't think I can eat anything, Louie."

"You sit down." He guided her to a chair, then took off his jacket and rolled up his sleeves. Unlike his sons, Louie Gamble was a short, stocky man who paid no attention to his own receding silver hair and the extra pounds he carried. He went through the cabinets with the confidence of a man who had spent most of his adult life in a kitchen, and in a few minutes had a pot of hot tea and some shortbread on the table.

Moriah accepted the tea he poured for her and tried to summon a grateful smile. She felt cold, so cold that it wouldn't have surprised her to see frost form over the steaming cup between her palms. "Thank you."

When she didn't add anything to the brew, he reached across and put two spoons of sugar in her cup. "It'll help," he assured her, stirring it in. "You feel like talking about what happened down at the police station?"

Politely she took a sip of the too-sweet tea. "They wanted to get a statement or something, but Laure was too upset to talk to anyone. There were reporters all over the place. They went crazy when they saw that girl."

Seeing Sable had shocked her, but not as much as seeing J. D. with his arm around her. For a moment she felt as if they had all been transported back in time to that night of the dance, only J. D. was there and saw what Moriah and the others had done.

Does she remember me? What if she tells him?

"I expect they'll send someone to the house to talk with Laure tomorrow." Louie rubbed his forehead. "Can you stay with her, honey?"

"Of course." No matter how she felt, there was no question of her leaving the poor woman alone. "I'll take care of her, and I'm sure my mother can come over in the morning." Her hands started trembling again, and she set down the cup quickly.

He watched her hands. "I could ask Eliza to stay with you."

"No, we'll be fine." She met his kind gaze. "Louie, do you remember Sable Duchesne?"

"Of course I do." He thought for a minute. "You knew her, too, didn't you? Back at Tulane?"

What would he say if she told him that she and her friends had tortured the girl?

"I remember her dating J. D.," Moriah said, keeping her expression blank. "I think they broke up right before he graduated." *Thanks to what we did.* "I didn't know her very well."

"She was a sweet girl. Odd that Marc never mentioned her to me." Louie took a piece of shortbread and absently crumbled it over his napkin. "J. D. will look after her."

Moriah hadn't given J. D. a single thought since Laure had called her from the police station. When the desk sergeant had told Moriah he'd be the detective handling the case, she had still been too shocked about Marc's death to register it. The disbelief and misery inside her gave way to new humiliation and anger. J. D. had been questioning Sable Duchesne when Moriah went to meet him for lunch. Terri Vincent must have known about that, and yet she hadn't breathed a word to her.

J. D. had never looked twice at Moriah when he'd been dating Sable in college. He'd been crazy in love with the Cajun girl, and everyone had known it. Especially Moriah.

Her only thoughts had been of poor Laure, until she'd seen J. D. and Sable come out of the elevator. She'd seen the way J. D. had looked at her.

That was mainly why Moriah hadn't been thinking about him. J. D. had never looked at her like that.

Elizabet Gamble quietly entered the kitchen. "I talked Laure into lying down in her room. Hopefully she'll sleep for a few hours." She began putting away the food. "Moriah, will you be all right here by yourself with her tonight? I'll come back first thing in the morning."

Moriah nodded quickly as she got up from the table to help her. "Thank you so much for coming."

"I'm glad you called us, honey." Elizabet pressed a brief kiss to her forehead before turning to her husband. "Would you go and bring the car around, Louie? Moriah and I will put these things away."

Her husband paused long enough to give Moriah an affectionate hug before leaving the kitchen.

Elizabet's smile vanished as soon as her husband was out of hearing range. "Did you hear about the girl they found with Marc?"

"Isabel Duchesne." Moriah snapped the top back over a container of chopped chicken liver. "I saw her at the police station."

"Why would Marc have anything to do with that girl?"

Moriah had no love for Sable, but J. D.'s mother loathed her. What his friends had done ten years ago had actually been for Elizabet. Oh, she hadn't come right out and told them to do anything to the girl, but she'd made it plain she'd be very happy to see Sable and J. D. break up. Moriah and her friends had taken it from there.

"I don't know." She took a handful of crackers and stuffed them into a plastic bag, breaking most of them in the process. "They're saying she was involved with him."

"I'm sure they'll be saying all kinds of things, but I knew Marc." Elizabet thumped a roll of foil on the counter. "He was never unfaithful to his wife."

Moriah sighed. "Are you sure about that?"

"As sure as I am of you, honey." The older woman put an arm around her shoulders. "Now, it's up to us and the rest of Laure's friends to make sure that the truth is known. We can do that, can't we?"

"Yes." Just not the whole truth.

J. D. remained motionless as Sable left the dock and walked toward him. Gantry and his men made no moves to come after her, but he wasn't taking any chances, not with all the knives they were carrying. He didn't like the way the big Cajun was watching Sable, either—of all of them, Gantry would be the most trouble.

As soon as she came within reach, J. D. hauled her back against him. With one arm locked around her waist, he dragged her into the shadows, out of sight.

"J. D., I—"

"Shut up."

Though there were some angry mutters, the fishermen turned around and went back to work. Gantry remained on the dock, staring in their direction.

Sable touched J. D.'s arm, straining away from him. "I won't—"

"I said, shut up." He turned her around and maneuvered her through the scrub, then marched her down the dirt road, keeping one hand clamped on the back of her neck.

She didn't resist, though his pace and the uneven surface made her stumble once or twice. When he felt sure no one was coming after them, he pushed his gun back into his shoulder holster, although he left the strap off in case he'd have to get at it again. The old man's car was where she'd left it, the keys still in the ignition. He marched her past it to his own car.

Sable stopped by the driver's-side door. She was staring at the ground, her shoulders hunched. "I'm sorry."

"Did he hurt you?" he demanded, looking all over her. He hadn't seen any wounds in the lights from the dock, but it was almost pitch-black here and he wanted to be sure.

She shook her head.

"Good."

He shoved her back against the car, pushing one of his thighs between hers, pinning her there with his weight. Her hands got caught between their bodies, one against his chest, the other sandwiched by his hip and her stomach. It didn't matter—she wouldn't be needing her hands for the next few minutes. He pulled her head back by the hair, too fast for her to do more than gasp.

That was fine, too—he wanted her mouth open for him.

He thought kissing her would be better than strangling her, and it was. Much better. Her lips were just as lush and soft as he remembered, and offered no resistance.

Not that J. D. would have tolerated any, even for a second. After ten years of not knowing what had happened to her, and everything she'd put him through today, and then seeing Gantry all over her?

He'd earned this much.

Her mouth tasted cool and sweet and slammed into him like the recoil of a .45 rapid-firing at a range target.

J. D. felt her fingers curl into his jacket as he spread his hand over her scalp, angling her face against his. Frustration and rage and fear made him rough, and he tasted a trace of her blood on his tongue, but she took that without opposition as well. She was taking everything he gave her without a sound, and that silent submission made the snarling desire inside him swell to the edge of madness.

Then she moaned under his mouth, and nearly pushed him over the edge.

J. D. knew he could have her under him on the car seat in three seconds. He could bury his hard, aching cock in her and, mindlessly pump into her silky heat until she convulsed around him and screamed his name. Then he wanted to flip her over and start again from that side. She wouldn't fight him. She was practically melting all over him now.

He dragged a hand down and filled his palm with the satisfying weight of her breast. He'd erase Gantry's touch from her, an inch at a time.

Right here, right now. The way she arched and shuddered under him as he played with her made his lips curl against hers. *She wants it like I do.*

Then she made another sound—a new sound that had nothing to do with hunger and sex and everything to do with fear. It penetrated the roaring in his head and made him wrench his mouth from hers.

"Jean-Del." She looked up at him, her eyes wide, her lashes spiky and wet. Her hand moved to rest over his, and he became aware of the frantic beat of her heart. "Don't."

"I don't want to." Oh, but he did. He wanted to be inside her, all over her. He braced himself against her and the car, fighting for control.

The sound of Caine Gantry shouting something obscene in French drifted from the docks.

He was no better than that Cajun son of a bitch, losing control like this. Disgusted with himself, J. D. pulled Sable aside and yanked open the door. "Get in."

She slid in and over to the passenger side as he got behind the wheel and started the engine. He could feel her withdrawing from him, huddling with her arms wrapped around herself against the door. She was shaking so much he could feel that, too. Then she did something that made him want to jerk her back into his arms for round two.

She held out her wrists.

He rammed the gear shift into reverse. "I'm not going to cuff you."

Slowly she lowered her hands into her lap. "But I ran away. I stole a car." As if she was trying to persuade him she was not to be trusted.

"Did you think grand theft auto would get you out of this?" He sped backward until he found enough clearance, then made a U-turn and headed back toward the main road. He stayed quiet until his temper had eased back from boil to low simmer, and then he glanced at her. "I have to know about you and Marc."

"You won't believe me."

"Try me."

"All right." She stared blindly out at the night. "My mother died four months ago. She had bone cancer."

Of all the things he'd expected her to say, that wasn't one of them. When they'd been together in college, she had barely mentioned her parents, but he had always gotten the impression they were close. She'd never let him see how close, but she'd always been a little secretive. "I'm sorry."

"I'd been working for Family Services in Shreveport, but I quit my job to come home and take care of her." She shifted away from the door, sitting forward so that her hair hid her face. "Marc called a few weeks ago when he'd found out that Mama had passed on. We talked on the phone first, and then Remy convinced me to meet him. I was pretty nervous, with him running for governor and all, but he didn't care about that." Her voice warmed a little. "He was so nice and kind, and interested in me. We hit it off right away."

Images began filling his head—Marc, with Sable. Marc, with his hands on Sable. Touching her. Kissing her. On top of watching Gantry do the same. He gripped the steering wheel until cracking sounds came from the hard plastic cover. "So you were involved with him."

"Not really. Today was only the second time we'd met." She looked down at her hands. "I mean, we would have met."

"Must have been one hell of a one-night stand." J. D. wanted to put his fist through the windshield. "Or was it love at first sight?"

"It was, for him and my mother." She pushed her hair away from her face and looked at him. "Marc Le-Clare wasn't my lover, Jean-Del. He was my father."

Somehow Isabel had gotten away from Billy at the hospital, but he knew where she'd likely run to. The old man still lived in the same shack where her mother had sold bait—just down the road from Gantry's outfit.

And wasn't that the height of convenience.

Billy figured he'd square things with Caine first, then do the girl. His luck only improved when he crept through the brush to have a look at the pier and saw Isabel standing there, just as bold as brass, quarreling with his boss in front of the entire crew.

"There you are." He shifted position, moving forward and crouching down behind a tangled bush for better cover. "You looking for me, you little rabbit? Here I am."

He listened to her run her mouth, and when she mentioned his name his head started to pound. From what she said, Isabel had seen his face, and she knew he'd been the one to set the fire.

For that, the prying bitch was going to die slowly.

Caine, on the other hand, surprised him. He could have told her everything, but all he said was that he'd fired him. Maybe Billy had been wrong about him. Maybe his boss had finally remembered what was important out here—loyalty to your own kind, over and above everything else.

"'Bout time." Billy aimed for the girl, but Caine moved between him and Isabel. "Now just get your big ass on out the way."

For the first time since that morning he started to feel better. When this was over, he could probably patch things up between him and Caine. Have themselves a sit-down and hash out their differences. All Billy had been doing was what Caine had wanted him to do. He'd gotten a little sloppy this time, but that would change. He'd have plenty of money now. Hell, he might even invest some of his money in the business.

"Gantry and Tibbideau," he muttered, trying it on for size. "Huh. Tibbideau and Gantry sounds better."

Billy was feeling so good that he didn't see the cop until he had his weapon out and pointed at Caine. His euphoria abruptly disappeared, and he lifted his shotgun, trying to get a clear shot at the cop. The cagey son of a bitch stuck to the shadows, making it nearly impossible to see him. By the time Billy thought to switch his sights to Isabel, she'd already disappeared into the dark with the cop. He heard a car engine start a short time later.

Good thing there was only one road out.

"We'll do everything we can to recover your vehicle, sir," Terri Vincent told the fuming old man when she'd finished interviewing him. From his excellent description, it appeared that their missing witness had indeed stolen his car. "You get some rest now and take care of that hand."

"I'm gonna go home and shoot that durn dog that bit me, is what," he promised her. "You catch up with that gal that took my Chevy, you toss her in the hoosegow, you hear? And throw away the keys!"

He had no idea how much she was tempted to do just that. "Yes, sir."

Since Terri had already interviewed the doctor who had treated Sable Duchesne, and the semihysterical nurse who had discovered the body of the X-ray technician, she left Mercy Hospital and drove over to the county coroner's office on Tulane Avenue. Although the building was closed to the public for the evening, a security guard let her in through the official business entrance and showed her back to the morgue.

Terri hated the morgue. She had to breathe through her nose so she wouldn't smell the stink of death and the chemicals used to preserve it. She didn't mind the man who ran it, though. "Hey, Doc."

Grayson Huitt looked up from the long incision he was making down the center torso of a middle-aged woman. His handsome grin appeared behind the transparent shield protecting his face. "Detective Vincent." He always said it the way he would *Pamela Anderson*. "Long time, no bodies. What brings you to my side of town?"

"No deliveries tonight, Gray, just some questions." She nodded toward his dissection table. "Can you spare me a minute?"

Grayson flipped up his face visor, revealing his classic Californian-surfer good looks, framed by plenty of shaggy, sun-bleached blond hair. His grin widened. "You mean, you're finally going to ask me to have dinner and gratuitous sex with you?"

"Not on a work night, Doc. Catch me during the weekend." The smell of formalin made her cough. "And can we do it in your office, please?"

"You cops are such wimps." He turned his head and bellowed, "Lawrence?" A bearded, pudgy technician ducked his head around the door to look in at them. "Take over with Ms. Maynard for me, if you would."

Grayson stripped off his gown and gloves, lightly washed at a sink near the table, then showed Terri into his office. As soon as he closed the door, she sighed with relief. "Want some coffee?" He had on a Springsteen concert T-shirt and well-worn blue jeans, both of which hugged his nicely built frame in all the best places. "I just made some a little bit ago. Yama Mama Java, imported from someplace hot and exotic."

"I'm coffeed out, thanks." She pressed a hand to what was already churning in her stomach in emphasis.

He sat down behind his desk and shoved a stack of

reports and a container with what appeared to be an eyeball floating in it to one side. "So if I'm not having sex with you on my desk—the offer of which will remain open indefinitely, by the way—what else can I help you with tonight?"

She tried not to stare at the eyeball. "Gray, how soon can you do the autopsy on Marc LeClare?"

"I did that one soon as I came in. Orders from up the line. I was just going to call in the report. Sit, sit." As she dropped into the chair in front of his desk, he shuffled through a stack of charts in his out box before pulling one and opening it. "Marcus Aurelius LeClare, forty-seven years old, the wife identified him by a birthmark on his hip. Ticked me off—I planned to vote for the guy." He looked up. "What do you need to know?"

"Pretty much everything."

"Well, let's see. Body came in with a bunch of debris, traces of wood ash, drywall, and fragmented glass adherent to the body—that's likely from the scene. Global charring with complete burning of flesh from multiple sites, extensive tissue destruction of the head, upper torso, and extremities."

"So he burned to death."

"Ah, no. Further examination revealed cranial fractures to the occipital bone—wound area basically covered most of the posterior of the head. Massive subdural hematoma, comminuted fractures of the occipital bone, fragments lodged within the cerebral tissue, the works."

The medical jargon confused her. "Which translates to?"

"Somebody bashed Mr. LeClare repeatedly over the back of the head until his brain imploded and he expired. Take a look for yourself." He showed her an autopsy photo of the back of Marc LeClare's head, from which the scalp had been peeled back to expose the pulverized brain.

"Jesus."

"Mary *and* Joseph," he agreed. "Depth of penetration indicates the injuries resulted from multiple blows delivered at a ninety-degree angle from behind the victim. From the fractures of the front of the face, I'd say the killer hit him once while he was standing, then went to town when he hit the floor. I checked the lungs, but there was no sign of smoke inhalation." He replaced the photo. "Official cause of death is blunt-force traumatic injury, not burning."

Terri rubbed her tired eyes. "So someone bashed his head in, and then set fire to the place."

"Probably. Can't give you a time of death until tomorrow." He grimaced. "No question that it was a homicide, though."

She tried to think of what else he could tell her, but finally had to settle for, "Did you find anything strange?"

He considered that. "Now that you mention it, there was something." He flipped through the chart, stopped, and read for a minute. "Right—I pulled a half dozen wood splinters out of his brain, and sent them over to SDIC for analysis. Don't quote me, but they looked like pine."

"Could he have picked them up from the floor?"

Gray shook his head. "Too deep and wrong side of the head. He went down face-first."

"So they came from the murder weapon—which could have been anything from a baseball bat to a table leg." She brooded. "How big was it, do you think?"

"Judging by the wounds, about the size of a baseball bat, maybe a little narrower in width." Grayson closed the chart. "How long did the fire burn?"

"I don't know, maybe thirty, forty-five minutes. They were able to put it out, but the building was destroyed." She saw the change in his expression. "What?"

He tapped a finger against his mouth. "Whatever was used to bludgeon this guy to death was probably heavy and pretty thick. If the killer dropped it at the scene, it might have burned slower than the body. Could still be some evidence left behind."

Terri wanted to go home and go to bed and stay there for a few weeks, but she resigned herself to one more stop as she got to her feet. "Thanks, Gray. I owe you."

"Pray I never collect, or you may have to run away to Cancún with me and two suitcases filled with skimpy black bikinis." He came around the desk and tapped the end of her nose. "See you, Ter."

Chapter Six

"Marc LeClare was your *father.*" The disbelief in J. D.'s voice was sharp as a slap.

"I told you, you wouldn't believe it." Sable tucked her cold hands under her arms and stared at the dried stains on the scrubs pants she'd stolen.

Caine Gantry had frightened her, but not as much as J. D. had, showing up out of nowhere. She'd barely pulled herself together when he'd jammed her against his car and kissed her.

If you call that kissing. She touched a fingertip to her bottom lip, which still stung where the edge of his teeth had cut into it. The violence of it had rocked her down to her heels—the Jean-Delano she had loved had never laid a finger on her in anger—but it had drawn something from her as well. A strange and deeply feminine response, one that had kept her from struggling under his hands and his mouth. It had made her acquiesce, and yet it created an intense desire to do more than simply yield to his anger. She'd wanted to revel in it.

Maybe I would have been safer staying with Caine.

J. D. slowed down, then pulled the car off to the side of the road and killed the engine. He sat in silence, not saying or doing anything for several minutes.

When he finally spoke, his voice remained hard and cold. "I've known Marc most of my life, and he never mentioned you. Not once. Not even when we were dating, for Christ's sake."

"He didn't know about me. My mother never told him that she was pregnant with me. She never told me that he was my father, either." Fresh grief spread inside her as she realized she would never know her real father now—she would only have that first, awkward meeting to remember him by.

"Your mother was a Cajun girl." It wasn't a question.

She knew what he was implying—Marc LeClare belonged to one of the oldest and wealthiest Creole families in New Orleans—he and her mother wouldn't have been introduced by mutual friends. "Evidently they met when Marc got lost in the swamp. My mother found him and brought him home. Her father, my grandfather, took him back to the city."

He turned toward her. "And just like that, they fell in love."

"Marc did, or at least that's what he told me when we met. I think my mother took a little longer to convince, but she was pretty young, too." She shrugged. "He came back to see her the next day, and he kept coming back. He told me that summer was the happiest time of his life."

"Marc LeClare and a Cajun girl." He shook his head, still projecting utter skepticism.

"Why is it so hard to believe, J. D.? My mother was a beautiful, gentle woman." Bitterness made her add, "Besides, you went slumming yourself once, remember? It happens."

His eyes narrowed. "I was never ashamed of you, Sable. I was proud of you. I *bragged* about you."

Never in her hearing. She shifted her shoulders again. "It doesn't matter. They're both dead now and no one ever has to know."

He started to say something, stopped, then asked,"Why didn't your mother tell you about Marc?"

"I don't know."

"Why wouldn't she tell Marc about you?"

"I think she was afraid. Papa remembered some well-dressed people coming down to the bait shop to see my mother toward the end of that summer. He thinks they might have been Marc's parents. He didn't know what they said to her, but she broke it off with Marc right after that. By then she must have known that she was pregnant with me." She traced a circle around one of the bloodstains. "My grandparents sent her to stay with her relatives in Mobile, and that's where I was born. She didn't come back to the Atchafalaya until I was a few months old."

He processed that in silence for a moment, then asked, "Is Marc's name listed on your birth certificate?"

She nodded. "She hid it from everyone, but I think she wanted me to know. It's hard to say—Papa said she never told him. He found my birth certificate only after she died. She had it and some letters from Marc that she saved from the fire."

"Fire? What fire?"

"A few weeks after my mother returned to the Atchafalaya, someone set fire to the old bait shop. Remy—my papa—got me and my mother out, but both of my grandparents died in the fire. Remy was burned so bad they didn't think he'd live, either, but he survived. Bud Gantry was arrested, and Remy and my mother got married and moved back deep into the swamp, where his family lived."

"Bud Gantry?"

"Caine Gantry's father—he set fire to the house."
She glanced back toward the road that led to Gantry's
outfit. "Bud always claimed it was his own idea, but
folks around here were pretty sure someone had hired
him to do it—he had money the week before, and he
bragged about getting more on top of that. He died the
second day he was in prison, before anyone could find
out who paid him to do it."

Something cracked and whined, and metal pinged.
Sable barely had time to register the sounds when J. D.
grabbed her shoulder and shoved her forward.
"Down!"

There was a second sharp crack. Glass exploded
over her head from a hole in the windshield, pelting
her with sharp fragments.

Gunfire?

"Stay down."

J. D. rammed the car into gear and pulled back onto
the road, then lunged over and swore violently as the
driver's-side window shattered. Sable watched him
jam his foot down on the accclerator and clutched the
seat, bracing herself as the car fishtailed wildly.

"J. D.!"

He had his gun in his hand and fired twice at someone through the ruined window. The explosive sound
of the shots he fired and the smell of the gunpowder
made her bury her face in the seat with her hands over
her ears.

There were two loud, different explosions beneath
the car, and the front end of the car dropped without
warning.

"Hold on!" J. D. hit the brake as the car slid sideways. Sable was thrown from the seat and into the ceil-

ing liner as the car skidded off the road and jolted wildly through the brush.

There was a moment that felt like they were flying through the air, then a tremendous crash. Sable felt J. D.'s hands on her a fraction of a second before dark, cold water blasted through the hole in the windshield, flooding the interior.

"Grab on to me." He kept an arm around her as he turned and used his foot and arm to force the driver's-side door open. More water and a tangle of weeds rushed in as the car began to sink quickly. The smell of *floutant* was raw and strong. J. D. checked her face, then clutched her closer. "Grab my shoulders and hold your breath."

Sable held on as he dragged her out of the car and under the water. The water was dense and numbing, and it pressed against her ears. He kicked them free of the car, and then hauled her around to the front of him. She swam with him, using her legs to propel them away from the sinking wreck. Just as her vision grayed and she thought her lungs would burst from the lack of oxygen, he guided her up to the surface.

The first breath she took almost made her cough, but J. D. put a hand over her mouth and spoke close to her ear. "Be quiet. Someone's coming."

Fresh horror spread through her as she realized whoever had been shooting at them had come to see if they'd survived the crash. She nodded and swam beside J. D. to the far side of the sluggish river, where he pushed her up through a thick patch of cordgrass onto the bank, then hoisted himself from the water.

There was movement through the scrub on the other side of the river, and the sound of the last of the air bubbling up from the sunken car. J. D. covered her with his body, pressing her down in the thick tangle of weeds and cypress leaves. She held her breath and felt her heart skip a beat when she spotted a shadowy form appear on the very edge of the river.

After an eternity of silence, the figure turned around and retreated back to the road.

Sable closed her eyes and let all the air she'd been holding out in a rush. She was bruised and cold and wet but she was alive. *They* were alive.

"Sable." J. D. lifted himself up and to the side, then gently turned her over onto her back. "Baby, are you all right?"

She couldn't speak—her mouth wouldn't work—and then she realized she still had her jaw clenched. She lifted a hand to push herself up but it was shaking badly. "I think so."

"It's okay." J. D. helped her to sit up and cradled her with one arm, still watching the other side of the river. "Looks like he's gone. I'll get you out of here and to someplace safe."

What he was saying didn't make sense. "I thought you were going to take me to jail. For stealing that car."

"No. We're going to find out who killed Marc," he said, pushing the wet hair back from her eyes, "and who's trying kill you."

She thought of Caine Gantry, whom she had known all her life. She had never thought him capable of murder—and if he'd wanted her dead, why had he tried so hard to chase her off tonight? It didn't make sense.

If she told J. D. about seeing Billy Tibbideau at the hospital, he'd have Caine arrested and Gantry Charters shut down—just as she had warned Caine's crew. A lot of families would suffer; the same families she was trying to help. She couldn't allow that to happen.

Sable had never agreed with the way that Cajuns protected their own. It allowed too many men to operate outside the law and get away with it. Yet until she had indisputable proof that Caine Gantry was behind Marc's murder, she had no choice but to do the same.

After hearing from Terri Vincent that J. D. and the only witness in the LeClare case had vanished, Cort went directly to speak with Captain Pellerin. The chief of Homicide refused to turn the case over to Cort's arson task unit, and used the media frenzy and the victim's high profile as the main reasons for keeping it under his control.

"Since your brother is the lead detective on the case, you two should have no problem working together." Pellerin sounded indifferent, but he looked like he'd been put through a hand wringer backward. "Let us know what you and your team find, and keep the lines of communication open."

Cort didn't bother arguing, but left the station and went to the warehouse district and the crime scene. A fire truck remained parked at the curb beside the ruined building, where it would stay until an all clear was given by the chief scene investigator. Since the city had followed standard emergency procedure and cut power to the entire block, temporary auxiliary lighting hooked up to portable generators provided lighting. Yellow barrier tape ringed the entire building now, and a staging area had been set up to provide work space for the investigators.

The unmarked white van used by Cort's task force had been backed up to what had been the entrance of the building, and its rear doors remained open. As he parked and approached the van, he saw two of his techs carrying out evidence bags filled with broken glass. Both men were dressed in disposable outerwear and heavy-duty gloves, which served to protect them from any residual heat while keeping them from contaminating the crime scene.

"Marshal." One of the men, Gil McCarthy, placed his bag in an open tub in the back of the van and stripped his gloves off as he came over to him. "Warren said you'd be back tonight."

Cort stared at the broken, blackened walls. The air smelled of wet, burned wood, melted plastic, and exhaust from the portable generators. "Give me an update on this."

"We've already done the safety sweep—didn't sniff out any airborne toxins or secondary devices. Structure's pretty much totaled, but the building inspector has marked a couple of potential collapse areas inside. Whoever did this knew what he was doing." Gil nodded toward the van. "We found remnants from what we're pretty sure were six individual gasoline bombs."

"All clear glass bottles with cotton rags?"

Gil nodded. "Same type used for the other two."

Cort's team dealt every week with the most common of incendiary devices, which were often made from improvised materials. Flammable liquids like gasoline, along with gunpowder and kerosene, were readily available to the public, and the easiest tools with which to build a firebomb. "Where did you find the body?"

"On the second floor. We got pictures and video of everything before we let the coroner move him. Pretty cut-and-dried, though—he wasn't moved." Gil gestured toward the temporary mapping station set up next to the front entrance, where plans for the building and a detailed grid map of the scene had been placed. Inside the front entrance, numbered Day-Glo orange flags marked spots where evidence had been collected.

"We've restricted scene access to essential personnel

only, but it hasn't been easy." Gil glared at two news vans waiting just beyond the official security perimeter. "Had some asshole with a camera climb the barricade and try to get a shot of the body when we brought him out. Reporters have been dogging us all day."

"Do the walk-through with me."

As he and Gil entered the building, Cort concentrated on getting an overview of the scene from Gil's description of the blaze and how the building had burned. Evidence was not limited solely to components of the devices used to start the fire—ash and debris were collected for testing, and certain interior fixtures and freestanding objects would also be removed and analyzed.

"We've got a preliminary theory going. Looks like three bottles were ignited on the second floor from the inside; then another three were thrown into the building through the rear windows in the alley." Gil stepped around a puddle of dirty water. "Not a lot of concrete so she burned fast. NOPD canvassed but there weren't any witnesses other than the Duchesne woman. The surrounding buildings are unoccupied, and no delivery or service people were in the vicinity immediately prior to the fire."

Cort knelt to inspect a fallen beam, which was charred and had broken into several pieces. The heat inside the building had been intense, and the fire likely spectacular before it was brought under control. "We get a videotape of the crowd?" Arsonists often stayed to watch the buildings they torched burn, and it was standard procedure to film the spectators.

Gil nodded. "Got them from all angles. Photographer will cover the funeral, too."

"All right. I want the evidence-processing team on

this tonight. Make sure the access and recovery logs are completed and a full photo and ledger inventory is made back at the lab before testing. Call in whoever's up for overtime and tell them we're making this priority one. No one goes in or out; I want officers posted here until I release the scene."

"Somebody need a cop?"

Cort rose to his feet and turned to see Terri Vincent standing a few feet away. "What are you doing here?"

"I thought I'd stop in, see what progress you all have made." She switched her gaze to Gil. "You boys find anything that looks like a baseball bat or a table leg?"

"Not so far, ma'am." Someone called his name, and Gil excused himself.

Cort watched the lanky brunette as she carefully stepped over the beam and peered at a blackened set of aluminum shelving. He'd already had his fill of her smart ass remarks back at the station, but he suspected she hadn't come to check on the investigation or talk to him. "What are you looking for?"

"Murder weapon. It's official—someone caved in the victim's skull before they torched the place. Possibly left whatever they used behind." She went around behind the shelves, then emerged and gestured toward the stairs leading to the second floor. "Mind if I take a look?"

"I'll go with you."

He accompanied her up the staircase to the loft storage area, where smoldering spots had left the air thick and hazy. Water used to put out the fire still dripped from a fragment of roof that hadn't collapsed. "Any word from J. D.?"

"No."

He watched her as she walked around the white

tape used to outline where Marc LeClare's body had been found. She'd shed her jacket sometime since he'd cornered her at the station parking lot, and the unadorned white blouse she wore looked wrinkled and wilted. Her short dark hair resembled a rat's nest. Weariness made her sharp cheekbones stand out even more.

Cort had never liked Terri Vincent, or her natural talent for getting under his skin in less than sixty seconds. But she was a good cop and probably his brother's best friend.

"If this is blood"—she knelt down and bent over until her nose nearly touched a dark uneven stain still visible under the puddle of wet ash—"then he was killed up here."

"Forensics should be able to tell from the trace residue and the spatter pattern." He watched her hands, which were as long and elegant as her body, but she didn't touch anything.

She stood and scanned the immediate area around the tape, then tilted her head to look up. "Came up behind him, maybe, from over there." She pointed to the pile of crates which had been scorched but still remained in a semiorderly stack.

One of his men appeared at the top of the stairs. "Gil said you'd probably want to see this, Marshal." He held out a large evidence bag with the remains of a man's leather briefcase inside. "It was empty, but you can still make out the monogram. Initials are *MAL* ."

Cort took the bag and turned it over, examining the case. Everything had been removed except for two pens stuck in a side pocket. He handed it back to the tech. "Make sure that's processed inside and out for fingerprints."

"Yes, sir." The tech retreated.

Terri was pacing around the outline now. "Okay, so the killer whacks him; he goes down; he whacks him a few more times. Then Isabel walks in, he whacks her twice, and then he sets fire to the building and leaves her to burn with Marc."

"He went out to the back alley to toss the last three gas bombs through the windows." Cort went to stand at the base of the outline, and then crouched down. He looked to the left and the right before rising and walking over to a tangled pile of wood.

"Why did he leave the girl alive?" Terri followed him. "He'd already killed Marc. Why didn't he bash her head in, too?"

"Maybe he thought she was dead."

Terri went over to the window and glanced down at the alley before turning to look back at him. "He beat Marc's skull to a pulp, but then he only gives Isabel a couple of love taps? Doesn't sound right."

"He could have been pressed for time."

"We got something here." Gil came up the stairs and handed Cort another, smaller evidence bag. "Recovered part of a key from the front-door lock. Looks like it broke off."

Terri glanced down the stairs. "When your boys responded, was the front entrance locked?"

Gil nodded. "They had to break it down."

"So he locked her in. Coldhearted bastard." She blew out a breath. "That makes it murder and attempted murder."

Cort looked at a pile of wood, then went over to it. He removed a handkerchief from his pocket and used it to cover his hand as he pulled a long, heavy length of pine from the pile. The entire piece was burned, but not heavily, and one end had splinter marks and dark stains along the wood grain.

Terri and Gil came over and stared at the wood for a moment. "Shit."

Cort watched her face. "This your murder weapon?"

"Might be. Sable has defensive wounds—wood splinters in her palms." She gnawed at her bottom lip. "Gray Huitt found splinters in Marc's brain, too."

Gil took the club in his gloved hands and turned it over as he examined the odd-shaped end. "This looks like a tool of some kind, but not one I've ever seen."

"It's a culling pole." She met Cort's eyes. "Really handy when you go oystering out on the bayou."

The cold air made Sable shiver as she stood up with J. D. Her legs wobbled as she tried to find her footing, but he kept his arm around her and didn't let her fall.

"We can't go back to the road," he said, scanning the immediate area around them. "Someone might be waiting there."

"We can't stay out here, either." She pulled a hank of wet weed from the back of her collar and shook it off her hand. "Aside from the gators and the snakes and the bugs, the temperature's dropping fast, and it'll probably rain again before dawn."

J. D. took a cell phone from his jacket, and held it up to watch the water dripping from one corner of its leather case. He removed the case and pressed a button before holding the device up to his ear. "Phone's dead."

She took a look around to get her bearings and saw the old path that led from Gantry's dock back into the cypress. "I know a place nearby where we can go for the night."

"Where?"

"My cousin's grandparents live about a quarter

mile from here." She climbed up the bank, then turned when he didn't follow. "They'll help us, Jean-Del."

"The way Gantry was helping you?"

His reluctance was understandable, but she was tired and wet and cold, and not inclined to curl up in a patch of poison ivy or a nest of nutrias. "Caine isn't my family. The Martins are." She held out her hand. "Come on."

After a noticeable pause, he took her hand and followed her into the woods.

She stopped once along the way to tug the ruined shoe covers from her bare feet. Luckily the path was worn smooth from generations of Martin women walking from their home down to the piers to meet Martin men coming in with the boats.

He watched her. "You want to wear my shoes?"

She eyed his feet, which were almost twice as big as hers. "No, thanks. My feet are pretty tough." As she straightened, a sharp arrow of pain pierced her right shoulder, and she took in a quick breath. "I'm going to be one big bruise in the morning anyway."

"Take it easy." He slipped his arm around her waist as they started walking again. "How much farther?"

She peered through the darkness and spotted a flickering light. "It's right up there."

Seeing the familiar, moss-draped silhouette of the high, steep-pitched gable roof made Sable want to weep. Like most of the elderly Cajuns on the Atchafalaya, the Martins lived in a small house that had been built from native trees felled and split with the help of family and neighbors. Heavy blocks of cypress kept the house raised two feet from the ground, to avoid flooding, heat, and insect problems. Over time weather had seasoned the riven logs to appear as ancient as the scraggly trees surrounding the house.

A lamp near one of the front windows cast golden light out on the flat stone walk leading up to the white-washed porch. Smoke drifted from the top of the clay and stone chimney at the back of the house. Two hand-caned rocking chairs sat on the porch beside the narrow front double doors, and there was an orange marmalade cat curled up on the seat of one of them.

A short, stout elderly man opened the doors almost as soon as J. D. knocked, and looked out of the center gap with wide eyes. "*Qui est-il? Que voulez-vous?*"

"*C'est moi,* Isabel." She stepped into the light so he could see her face and smiled. "We've had a bit of an accident, *grand-père.* Can we stay with you for the night?"

"*Mais oui,* come in, child." The old man opened the door. "Why are you all wet? You fall in the river?"

"Something like that." She gave J. D. a rueful glance before adding, "This is Jean-Delano Gamble, my . . . friend."

Old Martin gave him a suspicious look. "You throw our Isabel in the river, boy?"

"No, sir," J. D. said with a straight face. "I fished her *out* of it."

The old man snorted out an appreciative laugh, then ushered them in.

The Martins' home was equally unprepossessing on the inside, with horizontal *barreaux* slats between the vertical posts and angular braces that held the home-made insulation of clay and Spanish moss *bousillage* in place. Lighting came from kerosene lamps of smoke-laced glass, with bits of colorful flannel and rock salt floating in their bases.

Most of the furnishings Old Martin had made himself, out of the cypresses growing around his home, but here and there were heirloom antiques made of cherrywood, which had survived *le Grand Dérangement*—his Acadian ancestors' trip from Nova Scotia to Louisiana after being expelled by the British in 1755. A primitive painting of the same determined ancestors occupied a place of honor between framed religious portraits of Jesus and the Virgin Mary.

Martin's wife, Colette, came into the front room, drying her hands on her apron. Unlike her husband she was tall and very thin, and wore her iron gray hair in a tidy wreath of braids. "Isabel! *Mon Dieu*, what are you doing here this time of night?"

Sable explained as Colette fussed over both of them and brought out towels and prepared mugs of hot tea. After Colette went to locate a change of clothes for them, J. D. related an abbreviated version of what had happened. Sable noticed he didn't mention Marc's murder, the stolen car, or the shooting, for which she was grateful. The old couple didn't need the worry, and she wasn't sure they'd be so sympathetic toward J. D. if they knew he was a cop.

"Here, *bébé*," Colette said as she handed Sable a stack of clothing. "You go on in the bathroom and take a shower. Then your man can have a turn." She turned a measuring eye on J. D. "My husband's not as big as you, *cher*, but I found an old pair of jeans my grandson left here that might fit."

Sable felt better after cleaning up and changing into the flannel nightgown and robe Colette had provided, but her arm and shoulder were sore and there was a place she couldn't reach on her back that felt raw. She came out to ask Colette to check it for her, and heard Old Martin say to J. D., "We don't have no phone, but you can walk down and use the one at my granddaughter's place in the morning."

"My cousin runs a country store near the main

road," Sable added, then winced as she tried to tighten the belt on her robe and new pain streaked down her arm.

J. D. got to his feet. "What's wrong?"

"I think I wrenched my shoulder. Feels like I scratched up my back, too." She rolled her shoulder carefully, grimacing. "I'll have Colette look at it."

"She's rinsing out your clothes." He got up and came to her. "Let me take a look."

She led him back to the tiny bathroom, where she shrugged off the robe and turned her back to him as she unbuttoned the nightgown. "It's just below my right shoulder blade."

He worked the fabric down until her upper back was exposed and muttered something too low for her to hear. "You've got a couple of nasty grazes." He opened the old-fashioned tin medicine chest next to the sink and searched through it, then removed a brown bottle and some cotton swabs. "This is going to sting."

"I've been through worse." She hissed in a breath as cold antiseptic touched the raw place, and fiery pain spread down her back. "Ow. I lied."

He rubbed, and put his hand on her shoulder when she flinched. "I know it hurts, but hold still. I need to clean them out." He took care of each spot quickly but gently, then turned her around. "Can you lift your arm?"

She raised her right arm, then groaned when the throbbing in her shoulder increased. "Yes, but I don't want to." As she lowered it, she grabbed the sagging front of the nightgown before it slipped over her breasts. Her fingers collided with his, and heat flooded into her face. "Sorry."

He stared down at the pale skin between them, his

dark eyes intent. "I'm not." He trailed his fingers slowly over the exposed top of one breast.

Her mouth went dry as her nipples pebbled under the soft flannel. "Yes. Well." She pulled the edges of the gown together and edged around him. "I'd better leave you to take your shower."

Before she reached the door, he caught her elbow. "Don't go anywhere without me," he said. "I'm done chasing through the swamp after you."

She nodded and slipped out.

The roadhouse was one of a handful on the outskirts of the bayou, catering to local fishermen, truckers, and anyone who was interested in a cold beer, hot crawfish, and a serious game of darts or pool. The only women who frequented the place did so in the company of their boyfriends or husbands, or they came looking specifically for more temporary companionship. The jokes were raunchy, the arguments loud, and every other voice spoke in French.

It may not have appealed to the visitors who drove past on their way to New Orleans for Mardi Gras, but if someone wanted to know what was happening on the bayou, it was information central.

Terri Vincent drew a lot of attention when she walked in, until she was recognized and the patrons went back to drinking, eating, and complaining about the tourists. Terri had grown up a few miles away, and while few of the locals approved of her job, she was accepted as only a native could be.

She paused and inspected the interior before she saw the man she wanted sitting at the shadowy end of the bar. His dark eyes zeroed in on her long before she sauntered over and slid onto the empty barstool beside him, but he made no sign of welcome. "Hey, handsome." She nudged him with her elbow. "Buy me a drink?"

Caine Gantry didn't look up from his beer. "Why? You broke?"

"I'm happy to see you, too. Okay, I'll buy you one." Terri caught the bartender's eye, pointed to Caine's bottle, then held up two fingers. "What are you doing down here?"

He turned a little and propped one foot on the bottom rung of her stool. "There a new law says I can't have a drink after work?"

"Nope. Just not like you to drink around other folks. You're more the homebody drinker." She took a pack of cigarettes from her jacket, turned it over in her hands, then removed one before tossing the pack on the bar. "I gotta quit smoking."

Caine took the cigarette from her, lit it, then took a drag before handing it back. "So quit."

"It's not that easy."

"Then don't." He lifted his beer to his lips. "Either way, quit bitching about it."

"Hey, Terri." The bartender, Deidre, brought two bottles of beer and a clean ashtray. Light from the neon beer signs over the bar made rainbow streaks in her tinted hair, and she picked up a tip left two stools down the bar and tucked it into the front of her low-cut blouse. "This is old home week tonight—haven't seen either of you here for ages."

"We've been busy, I guess." Terri glanced at the man beside her before lifting the bottle and taking a sip. "Thanks, Dee."

"You got dirt on your face there, honey. Yell if you need anything." Deidre went to get orders from a pair of bikers, leaving them alone.

"Damn." Terri squinted at herself in the mirror before grabbing a cocktail napkin and rubbing at the smudge. She needed a shower. The smell of smoke from the warehouse still clung to her clothes, too. "I hate arson cases."

Caine met her gaze in the mirror. "What do you want, Therese?"

She took a drag from her cigarette. "Some answers, *cher.* Starting with where you've been today."

"Out on the water."

"You didn't happen to stop by the warehouse district in the city, did you?" When he shook his head, she took another drink of her beer. "Someone was. Someone torched LeClare's warehouse, with LeClare and a woman in it, but I expect you've heard about that."

He nodded.

"You know the woman—Sable Duchesne." She caught the faint droop of his eyelids and the subtle way his hand tightened on the edge of the bar. "Now, why do you think she'd be in an empty warehouse with the future governor of Louisiana?"

He lifted his shoulders. "Maybe she liked his campaign speeches." He reached for his beer, and the light revealed the battered condition of his hand.

"Those are nasty." She ran a fingertip just below the swollen, lacerated knuckles before he moved his hand out of reach. "How's the other guy look?"

"Worse." He drained the bottle with two swallows and pulled out his wallet to pay for the drinks. "I'm going home."

She sighed. "Look, cos, I've had a really long, ugly day. You sound like you have, too. Don't make this more difficult than it already is."

"I was out on the water from sunrise until dark. Ask around." He nodded toward a cluster of men drinking and playing darts in the corner. "That it?"

She sighed as he stood. "I ought to get out the cuffs and haul your oversized ass downtown."

He loomed over her. "You can try."

"Maybe tomorrow, after I eat my Wheaties." She patted his arm. "One more thing. You or any of your men see my partner or Sable Duchesne around here?"

"No." Caine tucked his wallet into the back pocket of his jeans. "See you around, *chère.*"

Billy watched Caine leave, then followed his truck as far as the private road that led to his house. *I can't go to Caine, not yet. Not until I have my money.*

The cop and the girl were surely dead. That car had careened right into the river. Even if Billy hadn't shot them, they must have drowned.

He drove to the first pay phone he could find. "They're dead. No, I'm not going home—I'm going to celebrate. You just be on time tomorrow night."

Chapter Seven

Darkness settled around the Martins' home with creaky evensong provided by the swamp's expansive choir of frogs and crickets. Sable wished she could sit outside on the porch and watch for fireflies the way she had when she and Hilaire were little girls, trying to catch them in empty pickle jars. Being so close to J. D. and having to keep up a pretense of normalcy for the Martins was going from difficult to impossible, especially after the way he touched her in the bathroom.

They couldn't stay here, either. *What happens tomorrow, when we have to go back to the real world?* He'd acted like he wanted to protect her now, but he was still a cop, and she was still the only witness to Marc's murder. Would he really protect her, or had he said that only to gain her trust?

After Colette refused to let her do anything but drink sweet hot tea, Sable curled up in one of the ancient armchairs and listened to the baseball game Old Martin was following on his ancient Philco radio. She tried not to notice when J. D. came out of the bathroom, wearing the grandson's well-worn jeans and shrugging into one of Old Martin's faded plaid shirts, leaving it unbuttoned because it was three sizes too small for him. He glanced at her before disappearing into the kitchen, and didn't come back out.

She tried to concentrate on the game, but the sound of J. D.'s voice and pans rattling finally drew her from the armchair. He was probably only keeping the old lady company while she prepared the evening meal, Sable told herself, then stopped in the doorway to the tiny kitchen.

J. D. was standing in front of the Martins' old gas stove, and he was shaking a small green can over a bubbling pot while stirring it at the same time. "It looks thicker than my father's version," he said to Colette as he sampled a spoonful. "Tastes better, too."

"Folks in the city use kidney beans instead of proper Luziann' red beans." Colette was seated at the kitchen table and placing rounds of biscuit dough on a tin baking sheet. "End up too mushy. Real red beans like to simmer all day on the stove while you hang out the wash—that's why we have 'em on Mondays. You use the bone from Sunday dinner, and you don't have to tend it close."

J. D. placed a lid on the simmering pot and removed another, smaller saucepan from the heat. "Might be the ham hock, too. I've never seen one that size." As Sable joined him at the stove, he held up the spoon. "Try this."

She came over and sampled it. Red beans and rice was a classic Monday night dish that Cajuns ate almost religiously, and any other time she would have loved it. Yet now she could hardly taste the spicy stew. "It's wonderful. I didn't know you could cook."

His mouth hitched. "Mrs. Martin did the hard part; I'm just keeping it from scorching." As Colette came over to pop the biscuits into the oven, he guided Sable over to a chair. "We've got it covered. Sit."

As she watched J. D. help the old lady prepare the simple dinner, Sable tried to make sense of it. When they were dating in college, J. D. had taken her to the finest restaurants, often his father's place, and had been very nonchalant about ordering rich Creole dishes and expensive bottles of wine. The one time she'd had dinner with his family, the meal had been prepared by a cook, and served by the housekeeper and a maid. That was one of the reasons she had never taken him home to meet her parents. She could never see the rich, pampered boy she had known being comfortable peeling steamed crawfish over newspapers spread on her mother's battered dining room table.

Now he was stirring pots and joking about back woods recipes being better than his father's gourmet dishes. *Maybe I didn't know him as well as I thought I did.*

The surreal quality of the evening didn't end over dinner. Without batting an eyelash, J. D. set out the Martins' worn earthenware plates and utensils that were pitted and scarred from continuous usage, then helped Colette dish out the spicy andouille pork sausage along with the red beans and rice. After joining in a short prayer of thanksgiving with the old couple, he ate heartily and with visible pleasure.

His parents ate off fine china, Sable recalled, with enough polished silverware at one meal to outfit three Cajun families for life.

"So how'd you end up going with the police, son?" Old Martin asked. "Seems like an educated city fella like you'd be a lawyer or a doctor or some such."

"When we were kids, my brother and I were caught in a kitchen fire at my father's restaurant, but a beat cop and a firefighter kicked in the door and got us out."

"What a terrible thing to happen to you boys." Colette put an extra helping of rice on J. D.'s plate. "Y'all weren't hurt, were you?"

"No one was, thanks to those two men." J. D. passed the plate of sausage to Old Martin. "I never forgot what they did for us, and when the NOPD recruiter came by campus just before I graduated, I decided to check out the academy program. My brother went to the fire department."

Sable picked at her food and listened as he talked about the heroic police officer and fireman. It was obvious that he had admired the two men deeply, but again it didn't make sense. Elizabet Gamble might have given a hefty reward to the beat cop and the firefighter for saving her family, but she wouldn't have wanted her sons to follow in their footsteps—both Cort and J. D. had been enrolled in prelaw at Tulane.

"Did you ever go to law school?" Sable heard herself ask during a lull in the conversation.

"I tried." The smile faded from his face. "I dropped out after the first semester."

That puzzled her. "Why didn't you go back?"

"The idea of spending my life in courtrooms lost its appeal." He rose and began collecting the dishes, for which Colette scolded him soundly.

"You done enough, boy, and Isabel looks about ready to fall over," she said, shooing him away from the table. She caught Sable's eye. "I put clean sheets on the spare bed in the *garçonnière* upstairs, *chère*. Best I can do for you young folks tonight."

Sable had forgotten the Martins only had one small bed in the attic loft—reserved for visiting relatives—which meant she and J. D. would have to sleep together.

"That will be fine, *grand-mère*, thank you." She rose carefully, wincing at the pull on her bruised shoulder, and automatically leaned against J. D. as he put a hand on her waist to steady her. The heat of his palm made her stiffen a little.

"Thanks for the great meal, Mrs. Martin," J. D. said, guiding Sable toward the stairs. "Good night."

The Martins' spare bedroom was cool and dark. Moonlight from the attic window showed it was mostly empty, except for the old rope bed and a battered wooden clothes chest at the foot of it.

The bed was covered with a thick old quilt, but was only slightly bigger than a twin. She watched him strip off Old Martin's too-small shirt and said, "I can sleep on the floor."

He reached down and untied the belt of her robe. "You'll sleep in the bed, with me." He slipped his hands inside to rest them against either side of her waist. "We'll fit."

Only if she wrapped herself around him and slept on her side—assuming she could close her eyes under such conditions. "I don't think that's a good idea." Actually, standing here, a few inches from the muscular wall of his bare chest, she was convinced of it.

"You're safe. I won't jump on you."

"It's not that." More like her jumping on him.

"You said you weren't afraid of me." He gently eased her robe off her shoulders and dropped it on top of the clothes chest. "You change your mind?"

"Yes. No. Oh, I don't know." Exhaustion made her voice thready. "Jean-Del, this day has been one endless nightmare. I can't think straight anymore."

"You just need sleep." He led her over to the bed, and pulled back the quilt and sheets. "Get in."

With a sigh she climbed onto the thin mattress, then moved over to the edge as he stretched out next to her. She tried to preserve the scant space between their bodies, but his arm came around her waist and tugged her back against him before he pulled the covers over them both.

"Relax." His breath was warm against her hair, and the heat from his body penetrated the thin flannel of her nightgown. "Your shoulder okay?"

"Yes." She couldn't feel her shoulder. She could feel other things, though, and shifted her hips forward an inch, so that the curve of her bottom wasn't pressing into the crotch of his jeans. She could smell the soap he'd used in the shower, and felt the steady thud of his heart just below her nape.

Say something. "Are you comfortable?"

"I'm all right." He ran his hand over her hair, smoothing down some wayward strands. "I'm used to more room, though."

Didn't he have a girlfriend? "I have a double at home. As big, I mean, as tall as you are, I guess you'd need a king-size." Oh, God, she was starting to babble. She squeezed her eyes closed and faked a yawn. "I'll think I'll go sleep now."

He put an arm over her, letting it rest at her waist. "Good night."

It was not going to be a good night—she knew that three minutes into trying to force herself into unconsciousness. Where before she'd felt dull-witted and tired, now every inch of her skin seemed to bunch with nerves. It didn't help to be so close to him, not when he was generating so much heat that they could be lying naked without a sheet and she wouldn't feel the chilly night air.

Sweat prickled her brow as she recalled the last time she'd been this close to him. Since he'd lived at home with his parents, and she'd had a roommate, they'd never shared a bed at college. It hadn't stopped them—they'd made do with a blanket spread over the grass in a shadowy corner of the park, and once they hadn't made it out of the front seat of his car.

In those days, she'd been so awkward and inexperienced, and Jean-Delano had had to teach her everything. He'd never made her feel clumsy, though. He'd taken her from good-night kisses to more sensual delights gradually, making the time they spent alone into a journey of the senses. He'd lured her out of her embarrassment about intimacy, convincing her to explore him and showing her what he liked. At the same time he taught her things she had never known about her own body.

Touch me like this, he had murmured to her once when they were parked by the lake. He'd slid his hand into her panties and guided her fingers into the open zipper of his jeans. As she curled her hand around his hard, satiny length, and stroked him with the same slow rhythm that he was using to caress her, he'd groaned. *Like that, yeah.*

He'd never once forced her to do anything she didn't want, but he'd never had to. On the night they'd had sex for the first time, she had been more than ready to tear her clothes off and beg him to make love to her.

It's just a subconscious reaction, she told herself as she surreptitiously squeezed her thighs together against the growing, empty ache between them. *I've been running on fear and adrenaline, and my body wants some comfort.*

"Are you hot?"

She nearly jerked upright, and then turned toward him, ready to leap out of the bed if necessary. "What?"

"I'm hot." J. D. propped himself up on one elbow and wiped a trickle of sweat from her temple. As he did, her hip connected with the solid ridge under the front of his jeans. "So are you."

"I'm . . ." *Sweating, aching, wanting. Wanting to slip my hands in your jeans and stroke you, the way you taught me to do it.* "I guess we don't need the quilt."

He sat up and pushed the patchwork coverlet down toward the end of the bed. As he did, she watched the silvery light from the window play over the muscles of his back. The faint sheen of his sweat made her want to reach out and run her fingers over his skin.

No, I want to put my mouth on him and taste it.

Of all the men she'd ever been intimate with, only J. D. had ever made her feel so uninhibited and excited—and not because he had been her first lover. She'd tried to forget him and fall in love again, but she'd never experienced with any other man the emotional connection she and J. D. had shared. Every relationship she'd had since college had been brief and disappointing. Oh, she had enjoyed the sex, but she'd never found the sense of completion that she and Jean-Del had given each other—that indefinable feeling that they were whole only when they were together.

He wrecked me for good, she thought, suddenly filled with resentment, *but he probably didn't think twice about me after I left.* A pang of guilt shot through her as she recalled what he'd said about law school at dinner. He would have enrolled that fall, just after their breakup. *Or maybe he did.*

"Better?" He lowered himself down beside her.

"Yes." She shifted over onto her side again, but the question wouldn't leave her in peace. "Jean-Del?"

He moved in, cradling her with his frame. "Hmmm?"

"Did you quit law school because of me?"

He was silent for so long that she almost told him to

forget that she'd asked. Finally he sighed and said, "We'll talk about it another time. Go to sleep, Sable."

Absently she rubbed her hand over the back of her neck where his breath tickled it, then winced as her hair caught on the broken skin of her palms.

He tensed behind her. "What now?" He sounded impatient this time.

"My hand is a little sore, too." She flexed it, inspecting her palm with tired eyes in the scant light from the window. *The window* . . . She yawned. "I got them when I was trying to get out of a window. Upstairs."

He went still. "Got what?"

"This morning you asked me where I got the splinters in my hands. I tried to get out of a window at the front of the warehouse upstairs." She'd been so frantic to get away from the fire, she hadn't clearly remembered the moment. Now she was so tired she could barely keep her eyes open. "The windows were boarded up; I couldn't pull them off."

"Couldn't you find the door?"

"Downstairs?" She yawned. "I tried, but it wouldn't open."

Her last thought before she fell asleep was of the door of the warehouse—the same door she had used to enter it. It had been open when she came in.

Whoever had killed Marc and started the fire must have locked her in.

While Sable slept, J. D. stared at the chinking between the wooden planks of the ceiling. Several hours passed before he gave up on sleep and got out of the tiny bed. He watched as she rolled toward the now-empty space in the bed, unconsciously reaching for him before snuggling into his pillow.

He didn't have to stand there and look at her, but he

did. There was just enough light for him to see the serenity of her face as she slept on. Enough to penetrate the thin stuff of her nightgown and outline the way her breasts swelled and curved on either side of the buttons, the jut of the blunt angles of her hipbones, and the suggestion of a dark triangle at the top of her thighs.

He was tired, and bruised, and still as painfully erect as he'd gotten the moment he'd lain down beside her.

Get away from her before you do something more stupid than losing her at the hospital.

A quick check downstairs revealed that Old Martin and his wife were also in bed asleep. Silently J. D. went to retrieve his cell phone where he had left it to dry out in the kitchen, then slipped out to the porch. He needed time to think, to talk to his partner, to find out what was happening back in the city. He also needed to put some space between his imagination and Sable's body.

Once outside, he switched on the phone and was gratified to see it was working again. He checked his watch—2:34 A.M.—then dialed Terri Vincent's home phone number.

It rang six times before a disgruntled female voice slurred, " 'Lo?"

"Terri, it's me."

"I just got to sleep—me had better be God." There was a rustling sound, and a groan. "J. D.?"

He smiled in spite of his brooding mood. "How many partners do you have?"

"More than I can handle." She yawned noisily. "After he was done gnawing on my posterior, Captain Pellerin said to tell you that if you're not sick or dead, that you're on administrative suspension, effective yesterday. So tell me you're puking up a lung."

He could imagine what their boss had said to her, punctuated in words of four letters and little compassion. "I got shot at tonight—does that count?"

"Only if he hit a vital organ." There was a click and an inhalation as Terri lit a cigarette. "Who's shooting at you and how can I reward him?"

He gave her the details of what had occurred since he'd brought Sable to Mercy Hospital earlier that day. "We're okay now," he added at the end, "but I need to move her to a secure location."

Terri exhaled. "So bring her in and we'll put her into protective custody, like we were supposed to this morning. Our safe house is extremely secure, and it's protected by some very large, mean men with many guns."

"No." What he planned to do would likely cost him his career, but he couldn't think about that now. He couldn't trust Sable's safety to anyone else, not until they nailed whoever was trying to kill her. "I'm not bringing her in, Ter."

There was dead silence for a minute, and then Terri snarled, "You're aware that you're out of your tiny fucking mind, I hope."

"Probably."

"She stole a car—"

He rubbed his eyes. "She borrowed it."

"*Stole*, J. D. And now you're building a little swamp love nest with her?" Terri's voice became strangled, and she coughed for a minute. "Jesus Christ, Pellerin isn't just going to take your badge—he's going to enamel your molars with it."

"I can take the heat."

"Let me turn up the thermostat, then. Marc LeClare

was murdered; someone beat his skull in before setting the fire. An X-ray technician who was working on Sable at Mercy was found strangled. Have you noticed how men are dropping like flies around this girl?"

"It's not her fault."

She drew in some smoke and blew it out. "Has she told you anything yet? Or is her memory still on vacation?"

"We haven't had time to talk."

"Sable Duchesne comes from the bayou, and bayou people stick together. She could be trying to protect someone."

"No, not her." He reined in his temper. "She came after Caine Gantry by herself tonight. When I got there, he was about to beat the crap out of her. In front of his crew."

"Bullshit." But suddenly Terri sounded uncertain. "J. D., I found the murder weapon tonight. It was a culling pole."

"Then you should be checking out Gantry."

"I will, but in the meantime, Sable is our only witness. She's the only one who knows who it belongs to." When J. D. didn't say anything, she sighed. "What am I going to tell the captain? Or your brother, for that matter?"

He hadn't considered what his family must be thinking, either. "Cort's back in town?"

"Oh, yeah, just like Jesus—Cort's back, and he's really pissed." She sighed. "Don't do this, J. D. Tell me where you are, and I'll come out and help you bring her in. We'll keep her in protective custody while we run the investigation. Be reasonable."

"Someone told the killer that she was at Mercy. The only people who knew where she was were cops. I can't risk it. Sorry."

"Is there something you're not telling me here?"

He trusted his partner. "Off the record."

"Hell, yes."

"Marc LeClare was Sable's biological father."

There was another lengthy silence as Terri absorbed that. "Holy shit. Are you serious? You are. Holy *shit*."

"They didn't know about each other until a few weeks ago." He told her what he knew of Sable's fledgling community program to get health and educational services to the Cajun people living on the bayou, and how Marc had intended to support his newly found daughter's work. "They were meeting at the warehouse to see if it would serve as headquarters for her project. Knowing Marc, I'd bet he intended to publicly acknowledge her as his daughter, too."

"Okay, I agree—that puts a different spin on things," Terri said. "But I can't keep something like this to myself. I have to talk to the wife about it."

He considered that. "All right. Ask her, but try to keep it quiet if you can."

"What about you?"

"I'll do what I can from this end," he told her, "but I'm depending on you to work the case from the city. Question Gantry and his crew. If anyone can find out who was after Marc, you can."

"Sure, I can fit that in between catching bullets in my teeth and leaping over tall buildings in a single bound." She snorted. "I'm already regretting saying this, but all right. I'll see what I can track down."

"You'll handle it. Tell me about the murder weapon."

She described the wooden culling pole. "Oh, and after we dropped it off at forensics to be tested, your brother mentioned something about the bayou."

"Like what?"

"Like tearing it apart with his bare hands until he finds you, and you know how your brother is. So if you don't want to get caught between him, Gantry, and the would-have-been-governor's daughter, I suggest you two get the hell out of Dodge."

Cort would be a problem. "Can you stall him?"

"Not without using a syringe, but I'll try." She yawned again. "You know, I really need my vacation. I think when this is all over, I'll spend a week down at the cottage."

J. D. watched an egret fly across the moon. Terri's parents had left her a vacation home on the north shore of Lake Pontchartrain, and she'd lent it to him and Cort a couple of times when they'd gone fishing. The cottage sat back away from the edge of the lake, secluded in the middle of the twenty acres of trees on the property. His partner liked to go there at a moment's notice, so she always kept it stocked and left a key in a planter on the porch. She also kept her Harley there, locked up in a shed—also with a spare key hidden in the fender.

"Nothing like a couple days where it's quiet and nobody around to bother me, you know?" Something rustled and Terri sighed. "Now I've got to get up in three hours and go lie to our boss and your brother. You be careful and call me tomorrow."

Caine watched the first hint of blue sky appear behind the gray green top of the tree line. Soon the sun would rise to burn off the low-lying shroud of mist blanketing the water and skirting the knobby cypress roots, and would reveal the brown and green and silver of the bayou's colors. It was usually his favorite time of the day, when he could sit on the empty dock and watch the world wake up.

He was tired. Despite the long hours of work from the day before, and three beers at Dee's, he hadn't been able to sleep.

I won't be able to until I find Billy and finish this.

He thought of Sable, and how she had looked at him last night. He shouldn't have touched her like that, shouldn't have kissed her. He'd only been trying to get rid of her. But the feel of her under his hands had made him forget about Cecilia's phone call, and Billy, and every other rational thought in his head. He'd thought about humiliating her, for what she'd done to him.

Instead? He'd nearly begged her to forgive him.

Sable had never known that he had watched her most of his life, from the day her mother had brought her back to the bayou as a baby to the night she'd run away from Tulane. He had appointed himself her guardian, keeping an eye on her when she was little, always hovering just out of sight so he wouldn't scare her. Sable had grown from a sweet child of light and laughter into a hauntingly beautiful young woman before his eyes, and his feelings had changed accordingly.

He would have set himself on fire before telling her how he felt, though. Especially after last night, when he'd done everything he could to chase her off.

His fist knotted against his thigh. He was done with her, had been done with her ever since the night she had shown up at the boathouse, running from her rich Creole boyfriend. She'd made it clear she had nothing but contempt for who and what they were. It had killed the love that he'd carried inside him for so long. He'd gone out the very next night and buried himself in willing women, and hadn't emerged since. He didn't need her approval, didn't want it. The hell with Sable Duchesne and what she thought of him.

Billy was at the warehouse, wasn't he?

Terri Vincent's coming to talk to him was only the final sour note on the entire night. Since she'd left the bayou to become a cop he hadn't given her much thought, but she was smart, she knew him, and unless he took care of this business with Billy, she'd be back.

"Hey, boss." The pier planks creaked as his new foreman, John, wandered out to the boat. "You're in early. Hear about the accident down the road?"

"What accident?"

"They found that cop's car in the river about three miles from here." John nodded in the direction of the road. "Somebody took some shots at him and Isabel."

Caine's throat closed up. Billy hadn't been hunting him after all. "Anyone hurt?"

"Don't rightly know. Seems they might have gotten out of the car before it sank, but there's been no sign of them since."

Isabel, alone in the swamp with that city boy cop. With Billy hunting them.

Caine put aside the trap he was repairing and checked the sky. It would soon be light enough to get the boats out on the water, and he intended to have all of his crews out today. He picked up the newspaper he'd gotten on the way home from Dee's and handed it to John. "Make sure everyone who didn't see her last night gets a look at her." He tapped the article that showed Sable's photo.

John frowned. "You think she's gonna come back here?"

"No." Caine stepped into the boat. "We're going to go and find her." *Before Billy does.*

*   *   *

Elizabet had just finished breakfast when Mae announced that Laure LeClare had arrived, and she quickly rose from her place at the table. "Thank you, Mae," she said before she hurried to the front of the house.

"Laure!" It wrenched her heart to see her dearest friend looking so wan and lost, but she kept her expression welcoming and came forward to kiss her on both cheeks. "You should have called; I would have come over to you."

"Forgive me for intruding at such an ungodly hour." Laure's voice sounded slightly hoarse and uneven.

"Don't be silly. I'm glad you're here. Come in." Elizabet guided her friend into the parlor, and glanced back at the hovering housekeeper. "Please bring tea for us, Mae, and some pastries."

"Don't fuss, Eliza." Marc's widow sat down carefully on one of the fleur-de-lis tapestry love seats, then straightened her shoulders and worked up a ghost of her usual charming smile. "I promise, I'm much better today. I'm sorry to bother you so early. I just . . . needed to get out of the house."

"You did exactly the right thing." Elizabet sat down beside her friend and took one of her cold hands in hers. "I thought Moriah said her mother would be stopping in this morning."

"I slipped out before she arrived. Moriah's still sleeping; the poor child stayed up half the night pacing the floor and watching over me." Her voice shook as she added, "Marc thought a great deal of her, you know."

"She is the sweetest girl." Elizabet pressed her hand to the other woman's hollow cheek. "I am so sorry, Laure. I would do anything to spare you this pain."

"I truly am feeling a little steadier today." She made a vague gesture. "Aimee will help with the arrangements, and the governor promised to send someone to coordinate the media. It's simply getting through the next week now, is all." She bowed her head. "I've been so . . . muddled, Eliza. I couldn't put two thoughts together that made any sense."

"You shouldn't be trying to push yourself to do things. We'll see you through this, I promise." Elizabet nodded to her housekeeper as she came in bearing the tea tray, and Mae placed it on the low table in front of them before withdrawing from the room. "The police will find who did this, and in time it will seem like only a bad dream."

"Or they won't find him, and it will turn into a nightmare that never ends," Laure murmured, her eyes shimmering with unshed tears before she rapidly blinked them away. "My poor Marc. How could this have happened to him? Was it me? Did I push him into taking on this campaign?"

"Nonsense. Marc loved you and you were a great asset to him. As for the campaign, you know how he thrived on it. He would have been a fine governor." Elizabet prepared a cup of tea and dropped two sugar cubes in it. "Have you spoken to Jacob?" she asked as she handed it to Laure. Jacob Pernard, Marc's attorney, was one of the most influential attorneys in the state as well as the city, and could do the most to help Laure through the difficult days ahead.

"I think I remember him calling." She looked down at the delicate cup in her thin hands as if unable to fathom what to do with it. "He said something about the district attorney wanting to speak with me, although I can't imagine why."

"They'll have questions about Marc and what he

was doing yesterday." Elizabet added cream to her own tea and kept her expression and voice deliberately bland. "You heard about the young woman who survived the fire, didn't you?"

Laure nodded. "Isabel Duchesne—her picture has been all over the television."

"Did you or Marc know her?"

"I think Marc did, a little. He mentioned that he was making a contribution to a charity she was involved in." Laure lifted her shoulders. "I had the feeling he was worried about her, but he didn't say much." She sipped from her cup.

So the little tramp tried to sink her claws into poor Marc, as well. Elizabet squelched a surge of outrage. "Did he tell you why he was meeting her yesterday?"

She nodded. "He was going to let her use that old warehouse as a welfare center of some kind. I couldn't understand why he'd want to, considering how much trouble the Cajuns have created for the business, but you know Marc. He was so forgiving toward everyone."

For a moment Elizabet debated what to tell her friend. It was one thing to shield Laure from the ugliness of Marc's tragic death, but quite another to watch Isabel Duchesne ruin Marc's good name. Elizabet remembered how J. D. had been after the girl had run away—he'd walked around like a ghost for months.

Laure wasn't nearly as strong as her son had been.

"I knew Isabel Duchesne ten years ago. She dated Jean-Delano while they were at Tulane. They broke up after she was involved in a terrible incident. She attacked some of his friends." Elizabet nodded at her friend's shocked look. "Yes, I felt the same when I saw her photo on television. I couldn't believe she'd come back to New Orleans, not after what she did."

Laure's jaw sagged. "Was she the girl who made him decide not to go to law school?"

"She did, but that wasn't the worst of it. She broke his heart. After she left, for a time Louie and I thought J. D. might try to harm himself." Remembering those long, terrible weeks made Elizabet rise and go to open the curtains. "He was never the same after her. He never trusted another girl again."

"How did he get involved with her?"

"Oh, you know how some of these poor girls get into college on scholarships. I think they only do it so they can trap some boy into marriage." She curled her fingers into the velvet edge of the curtain. "I warned J. D. about her, but he thought he was in love and of course he wouldn't listen to me. For six months, I lived in terror that he would get her pregnant." She pulled aside the ivory tapestry drapes, and closed her eyes as the sun touched her face.

"She didn't try to trap him into marriage, did she?"

"Not at first." Elizabet turned around to face her friend. "She's not a stupid girl, you know. She worked her way into his life gradually, taking up more and more of his time, luring him away from his studies. Then she began poisoning him against his friends— the same boys he had known since grade school." Elizabet straightened one of the curtain hems before returning to sit beside Laure. "I knew when she nearly convinced him to quit the football team that she was serious trouble. You know how much J. D. loved playing."

Laure set aside her cup and leaned forward. "Did you speak with her?"

"No. I felt like I held my breath for about six months, though. When I heard she'd thrown mud at some of J. D.'s friends on the way to a dance, I wasn't

even surprised." She refilled her tea, then added a
drop to Laure's barely touched cup. "Although to this
day, I don't know what set her off."

"You remember the way we were at school?" Laure
sounded vaguely sad. "All those poor girls we
snubbed? I never was real comfortable with that."

"You've always been too softhearted for your own
good," Elizabet chided. "I know for a fact that J. D.'s
friends were kind to her, for his sake. They were all
such nice kids." She smiled a little, remembering. "Pity
she couldn't be the same."

"Maybe they were jealous of her," a male voice said.

Elizabet's head snapped up, and she saw her husband standing just inside the doorway. "Louie, you
startled me. What in heaven's name are you talking
about?"

"Isabel, and the way she was. She wasn't a schemer.
She was sweet, and smart, and a hard worker." Elizabet's husband folded his arms. "I couldn't say the
same about J. D.'s other friends."

Laure set down her cup and stood. "Perhaps I
should go."

"I will be happy to take you home, chère." Louie
gestured toward the front of the house. "Would you
give me a moment alone with my wife first?"

"Of course." Laure kissed Elizabet's cheek,
squeezed her hand, then departed.

"What are you doing, Elizabet?"

"I'm caring for my friend." She wasn't intimidated
by her husband's visible displeasure. "I'm also letting
her know who she's dealing with. Have you forgotten
what that girl did to our son?"

"I remember it a little differently. So should you."

She set aside her cup. "Sometimes the memory be-
comes unreliable over time."

"So now I'm an old man."

"No, you're not. That would make me an old woman." She went to hug him, but he drew back. It didn't worry her. Louie never stayed angry for more than an hour or two before he reverted back to his charming, irreverent self. "You shouldn't worry about Isabel Duchesne. I expect she'll land on her feet. Her kind have a knack for doing that."

"I have adored you since the moment I first laid eyes on you," he said, his voice snapping out the words. "But I have never been as disappointed in you as I am now."

That hurt, but she kept her expression smooth. "You'll get over it, Louis, like you always do."

Elizabet didn't flinch when he slammed the door on his way out. She already had a lengthy mental tally of Isabel Duchesne's sins against her family, and this was simply one more item to add to the list.

Chapter Eight

"Get up, boy."

J. D. opened his eyes to find himself alone in the Martins' spare bed, the business end of a double-barreled shotgun wavering an inch from his nose. He remained still and gazed along the barrel until he met the angry gaze staring down at him from a heavily scarred face.

The man was short and lean, with patchy white hair and more burn scars than J. D. had ever seen on a living human being. He looked like hell had chowed him up and spit out the gristle.

"Who are you?" J. D. looked around, but Sable was nowhere in sight. His gun was tucked under the side of the mattress, but he didn't want to move until he could distract the old man.

His attacker sneered, emphasizing his grotesque disfigurement. "I am the devil—what do you think, boy?" he asked, his voice a croaking rasp. "Am I not pretty?"

"Pretty, uh, no." Christ, he was going to be shot in the face by a lunatic, and where was Sable? "But you look hard to kill."

"I am." The old man jerked the shotgun up a notch. "Get up, now."

Sable came around him, carrying a stack of neatly folded clothes. She was wearing a calico shirt and a pair of baggy jeans, and had braided her hair back away from her face. Instead of being afraid, she gave the scarred man an exasperated look, as if what he was doing was only a minor annoyance. "What are you doing?"

J. D. used the distraction to slide his hand over the side of the mattress and extract his weapon.

"What I should have done ten years ago," Remy told her. When he turned back, his eyes widened.

J. D. kept the gun trained on the old man. "I'm a little hard to kill, too, old man. Sable, go on out of here."

"*Déposez le fusil de chasse*—put down the shotgun, Papa." She came to stand next to J. D. and gave him the same annoyed frown. "And I would appreciate it if you wouldn't shoot my father."

J. D.'s mouth curled. "Soon as he puts down the shotgun."

She turned to the man. "Papa?"

"This is how he protects you? I could blow his head off while he slept." Remy made a sound of disgust, but slowly lowered the weapon. "City boys." He rubbed his chest.

J. D. lowered his gun and sat up, scrubbing a tired hand over his scalp. "You can shoot me after I've had a cup of coffee."

"These are clean. Colette washed them." Sable left the stack of his clothes on the end of the bed, then went to her father and tugged on his arm. "Come on, Papa, let J. D. dress. We can talk downstairs after you take your pills."

"I hate pills," the old man grumbled, but went along with her.

J. D. dressed and left a few twenties under the lamp

by the old bed, where Colette would find them later,
then went downstairs to find Old Martin and Remy arguing in French. The battered table was almost groan-
ing under the weight of a huge country breakfast.
Remy's shotgun stood leaning against the wall by the
table. Sable was standing beside Colette at the stove,
holding a plate the old woman was stacking with pan-
cakes. They were conversing in French, too rapidly for
him to follow, but it was something about someone
named Billy.

"*Chère*," Colette nudged her when she saw him,
then gave him a big smile. "Look who didn't get his
head shot off."

He glanced back at Remy. "Yeah, lucky me."

"I got your reward for surviving Isabel's papa." She
handed Sable her spatula and filled a mug from a battered speckle ware pot, which she brought to him.
"Here. This will open your eyes the rest of the way."

"Thanks." He took a swallow and closed his eyes as
the savory/bitter chicory washed the cobwebs from
his mind. "Dear God. Divorce Martin and marry me."

She giggled like a young girl. "You are lucky I am
Catholic, *cher*, or I might just run away with you. Sit
down—I have hotcakes, *grillades*, and grits."

He took the empty chair across from Remy, who directed his next remarks to Sable. Sable brought more
food over to the table, then sat down and launched
into a rapid exchange with Remy, also too fast and di-
alectal for him to follow. Old Martin snorted a f
times, gesturing and interjecting a few words,
threw up his hands.

When there was a pause, J. D. touched Sabl
"He still upset about me?"

"You, and other people." She rested h
against her hand for a moment. "Papa th

leave the parish and go stay with family. He doesn't believe anyone was shooting at me. He thinks they were after you because you're a cop."

But that wasn't all Remy and Sable had said; he'd definitely heard *"comme un fils à moi," "son meilleur ami,"* and *"ta mère"*—*like a son to me, his best friend,* and *your mother.* "What about Marc's murder?"

"He thinks it has to do with Marc's political campaign." She turned toward Remy when he muttered something. *"Vous savez que Caine a eu quelque chose faire avec ceci, Papa."*

That J. D. could translate—*You know that Caine had something to do with this.* "Is Gantry involved in the attacks on Marc's businesses?"

Sable hesitated before shrugging. "I'm not sure. No one has said he is, but Caine and the other Cajun fishermen in this area have been hurt by some legislation Marc supported. They're now required to purchase special equipment and individual boat licenses to stay in business, and many of them couldn't afford it. A lot of people are angry, as you saw last night."

"That's why you went to see Caine alone?" He put down his mug and curled a fist around it. "Didn't it occur to you that he may have killed Marc, and told his men to toss you to the nearest gator?"

Remy said something low and vile under his breath.

"No. Caine and those men have known me since I as a baby," she snapped. "They may be a little rough stubborn, but they're not killers, and they would hurt me."

they'd burn down someone's business to make wouldn't they?" He watched the doubt appear s, then noticed Remy was listening to him v. "Whoever torched that warehouse mur- rst, then tried to do the same to you."

She pushed the tines of her fork through the grits on her plate. "Or maybe whoever started the fire thinks I saw them kill Marc."

"*Grand-mère?*" Hilaire rushed into the kitchen and skidded to a stop when she saw Sable and J. D. She wore an old-fashioned white pinafore over a red puff-sleeved dress with a very short skirt, and a straw hat on top of her curls. J. D. thought she looked exactly as if she'd stepped out of a 1940s pinup. "Oh, thank goodness—I thought you might still be here."

Sable got up and went to hug the girl. "I was going to stop by the store to see you before we left." She glanced back at J. D. "You remember my cousin, Hilaire Martin. Hil, this is—"

"I remember who he is." And her memories obviously weren't fond ones, from the way she flicked her long nails at him before taking Sable's hands in hers. "You have to get out of the bayou, right now. Caine is looking for you."

J. D. went to check the windows, then came back. "No sign of anyone. What does he want?"

"Dee at the roadhouse said a policewoman came over last night and questioned him. Then he sent out all his boats at dawn this morning, but not to fish. Jessie called me and said to look for you and the cop. They'll be here soon."

"Why would Caine do that?" Sable's brows drew together. "He couldn't wait to get rid of me last night."

"Jessie said everybody is angry, but Caine is th worst." Hilaire shot another dark glance at J. D. "I his fault—he doesn't belong here. He's making ev body nervous."

And Caine most of all. J. D. could think of a f sons why.

"I will go to Caine," Remy said, risin

table. "He expects me to be looking for my Isabel; I can lead him away from here."

"Here." Sable came over and tucked a brown plastic pill bottle in the pocket of his shirt. "You take these when you're supposed to, or you won't be leading anyone anywhere."

"We need transportation," J. D. told her. "Does anyone around here have a car we can use?"

Sable shook her head. "People walk or use pirogues. The police might be watching the roads, too."

"I brought my boat," Hilaire said. "I can take you both out of the bayou and no one will see you."

"Can you get us over to the lake from here?" he asked before he swallowed the last of his coffee.

"Yes, but what's at the lake?"

"A safe place." He rose and shook hands with Old Martin. "Thank you for putting us up for the night." To Remy, he said, "I'll look after her."

"You'd better, *cher*." Remy shouldered his shotgun. "Or next time, I won't wake you up first."

"Here, Isabel." Colette brought a large, covered basket to the table. "I packed some things for you. Hilaire, you be careful on the water." She twisted her hands in her apron as she turned to Sable. "And you, *chère*, you don't do anything foolish. Stay with Jean-Delano—let him take care of you."

Sable kissed her thin cheeks. "I will."

ecilia didn't see Billy's truck until she walked out
       clothesline. He wasn't in the trailer, so she put
            he basket and walked around to their narrow

              curled up on the front seat, a mostly empty
              skey cradled in his arms.

He's sleeping with his true love, she thought. *Instead of me.*

"Pssst." Lilah waved at her from the door of her trailer. "Come here."

Cecilia checked Billy again, but from the deep way he was snoring, it appeared he'd be out for a couple hours. Carefully she walked across the yard and up to Lilah's trailer. "What is it?"

"Come inside." For once Lilah looked nervous. "Hurry."

Cecilia climbed up the stairs. Lilah had a nice double-wide, and she'd decorated the inside in her favorite colors of orange, red, and purple. Billy said it looked like a whorehouse on wheels, but Cecilia always thought the bright colors were cheerful.

"I saw Billy in the truck when I got home from work this morning." Her neighbor led her back to her bedroom. "I looked inside and saw this on the floor, so I took it." She pointed at the quilt on her bed.

Cecilia stared at her husband's shotgun and the box of ammunition. "Oh, Lilah. He'll be so mad."

"No, he won't—and he won't go shooting anyone, either."

"You can't keep it. What if he comes over here? What if he finds out you took it?"

"I don't think he will, but . . . ." Lilah opened the shotgun and removed the cartridges, which she put in the box. She bent over and stuffed the box under her mattress. "There. Now he can't shoot me if he does."

"I can't let you do this." Cecilia reached for the gun. "You don't know how angry he gets."

Lilah tossed the weapon back on the bed and took her hands. "Honey, I've been listening to that man get angry at you for two years. I'm not afraid of him. He's just a drunk and a bully." She touched Cecilia's cheek. "I can't sit back and watch him hurt you anymore."

"He doesn't hit me."

"I know what he makes you do." She glanced at her bedroom window, which was only a few feet from Cecilia's trailer. "I have to listen to it every night."

"Oh, Lord." Utterly mortified, she rushed to the door, but Lilah stopped her.

"CeeCee, wait." Her neighbor glanced over her shoulder at Billy's truck. "Now you've got me watching him all the time like you do. You have to leave that man, honey, or one of these days he's going to kill you."

"You don't understand." Cecilia shook her head. "I don't have anyone else."

"That isn't true." Lilah put her hands on either side of Cecilia's face. "You've got me."

"You sure you know the owner?" Hilaire asked as she and J. D. finished tying the moor lines of her boat to the lone pier jutting out from the empty-looking lakefront property. When he nodded, she sighed. "All right, then, but if anyone comes out here with a Doberman, I'm jumping back in the boat and you all are on your own."

Sable had been tense, ever since they had left the Tchefuncte River and cruised toward the northern shore area of Lake Pontchartrain. Hilaire had hidden both of them under a tarp, which had been a good thing, considering two of Caine's men had stopped her to ask if she'd seen them.

Lying still and silent under the tarp with J. D. right next to her had been worse than sharing a bed with him last night. At least then he hadn't held a gun in his hand.

After avaricious companies had nearly deforested the area while building the city of New Orleans, the former timber boomtown had been transformed into an exclusive resort area by one of the wealthiest members of Creole society. Wishing to escape the heat of the city, the rich man had bought up thousands of acres and had even built a plantation at the very edge of the lake, to which he invited his equally wealthy friends.

Now the property had been divided up and parceled out to several families, but all of them were rich, if not richer than the original settler. They were definitely back on J. D.'s territory.

"It's back a ways." He pointed to a white-painted boardwalk winding from the bank up into the thick groves of old oak trees. "It's safe. No one will bother us here."

"I hope so." Sable climbed onto the side of the boat to step up onto the pier, then reached up as J. D. helped her out.

"Can you stick around for a few hours?" J. D. asked Hilaire.

"I guess." She handed Colette's basket up to Sable. "I left Lacy in charge of the store, and she probably won't bankrupt me until after dinnertime. Why?"

"I need to borrow your boat."

Hilaire's pretty eyes went wary. "I don't know about that, Jean-Del. I'm more partial to this boat than I am to my mama's cherrywood hope chest."

"I won't let anything happen to it. We'll need some supplies." He pointed to one of the pretty marinas a few miles down the shoreline, where there were a number of shops. "I don't want to leave Sable by herself, and it's better if no one sees her."

"What about you?" her cousin demanded. "Caine's men are looking for you, too."

He took the straw hat from her head and put it on his own. "Better?"

Hilaire rolled her eyes. "Makes a bigger target."

"It's all right, Hil," Sable said. "He knows what he's doing."

"Don't make me regret this, Jean-Del." She sighed and handed him the keys. "And don't lose my hat."

He helped her up onto the pier and gave her one of his heart-stopping smiles. "You won't, honey."

As they left the pier and followed the boardwalk back into the woods, Sable noticed signs that someone had been caring regularly for the property. The ground cover beneath the trees had been allowed to grow wild, but the shrubs and flowers lining either side of the boardwalk had been neatly trimmed back. "Does your friend have a groundskeeper?"

"No, she takes care of it herself." He led them down a short flight of stairs and across a mowed expanse of short green grass to a charming little red-roofed cottage.

As Sable watched J. D. remove a key from a planter on the front porch, she felt her cousin nudge her. "What?"

"*She* takes care of it herself," Hilaire repeated in a whisper, and rolled her eyes. "Plus she leaves out a key for him. Now don't that beat all."

"So he has a female friend." Sable was trying hard not to dwell on it. "His partner is a woman, too. It could be her."

"A cop, with a place like this?"

"Okay, then a family friend." Jean-Del came from money; he would know people with money.

"Oh, yeah." Hilaire snorted. "I bet the man is just *surrounded* by female friends of the family."

J. D. let them into the cottage, which was beautifully

furnished with airy white wicker furniture and a distinct, crisp nautical theme. The combination was unusual—both masculine and feminine—but Sable liked it. He tried one of the light switches, and an overhead ceiling fan spun lazily into life.

"There's a kitchen and pantry, in through there," he said, indicating a door at the left. "Bathroom and bedrooms on the other side."

Sable handed the basket to her cousin. "Put this in the kitchen, would you, Hil?" When her cousin departed, she nodded toward the lake. "You are coming back."

"Yeah, I am." He came to her, and took one of her hands in his. "I don't like letting you out of my sight, either."

"It's not that." She looked down at the beautifully patterned rug under her feet. "Hilaire would kill you if you ran off with her boat."

"Then I'll hurry." He ran the back of his hand down her cheek, then nudged her chin up to give her a quick, hard kiss. "You stay inside and out of trouble."

She nodded and tried to ignore the feeling of impending doom as she watched him leave.

Cort made some phone calls and ran some case files on his computer at home, then dressed and went down to get a cup of coffee before he went in to work. His mother intercepted him in the kitchen and gently maneuvered him into staying to have a light brunch with her.

"I didn't get to finish my breakfast earlier, and I never have a chance to see you anymore," Elizabet chided. "Surely you can spare me thirty minutes before you go into work?"

Her smile wasn't reaching her eyes, Cort thought. Which meant trouble. "You look upset."

"It's hunger pangs." She steered him out to the dining room.

His mother didn't eat much, but she did talk quite a bit, all about her plans for the Noir et Blanc Gala and how important it was for Cort to bring a suitable escort.

"After all," Elizabet said, "Evan will be here with his wife, and J. D. will be escorting Moriah. We wouldn't want you to appear . . ." She made a small, graceful gesture.

"Hard up for a woman?" he offered.

She frowned. "Are you?"

"No."

"Good." She went back to picking at Mae's excellent omelette. "Because if you were, you know, I could arrange for one of Moriah's friends to accompany you."

"Don't worry, Mother." He kept the irony out of his voice when he added, "I'm sure I can find my own date."

"Please don't leave it until the last minute, Cortland." She didn't look up as his father walked in. "I would like to send a formal invitation out as a courtesy to whomever you invite."

"We should cancel it," Louie said.

Cort glanced at his father, and then his mother. From their expressions, it appeared he wasn't here to eat brunch so much as to act as a buffer.

"Why do you think that, Louie?"

"Marc's dead." He made an abrupt gesture. "I don't feel like that's something to celebrate."

Rather than reacting with horror at the suggestion, Elizabet refolded her napkin. "I know how you feel, my dear, but think. Marc would have wanted us to go on as if everything were normal."

"If I had been murdered," Louie flared, "my friend would not have thrown a party a week later."

"Very well." Cort's mother's expression went chilly. "If you can't see the importance of carrying on the family tradition, I'll cancel everything this morning. It should only take a few phone calls, although I will have to send out some telegrams—"

"No, no. Have your party. Do whatever you want." Louie stalked out of the dining room.

Cort was a little surprised—everything usually rolled off his easygoing father's shoulders. "He's not taking Marc's death well, is he?" Maybe that was the reason they were arguing.

"Marc was his best friend since they were boys." Elizabet stirred a spoon in her untouched coffee. "He simply has to come to terms with the loss, which he will."

"It isn't really about Marc, is it?"

His mother glanced at him, then sighed. "No."

"Do I want to be in the middle of this?"

Elizabet's lips formed a reluctant curve. "Probably not."

"Then I'm going to work." He rose and went over, and kissed the top of his mother's head. "Get him a box of cigars. That's always worked for me."

"Cortland!" Elizabet swatted at him.

On the drive to headquarters, he ran through a mental list of women to ask to his mother's annual fashion fest. Since Moriah had made J. D. her target for immediate engagement, Cort hadn't bothered to date among the social set much. His mother would know a suitable girl from a good family for him, but if he asked her to handle it, she'd want him engaged to the girl within six months. It would just be easier to ask someone from work.

I'm sure you'll understand that I'm a little too damn busy to hold your hand right now.

Why he thought of Terri Vincent at the moment was a complete mystery to him. His brother's partner probably didn't own a dress, much less know how to conduct herself at a formal social function. She was more at home drinking beer and eating peanuts with her cop friends in the Quarter. J. D. had always insisted their mother invite Terri every year, and yet she had never shown up once. Cort doubted she'd even bothered to RSVP Elizabet about the invitation.

The disapproval he felt faded into annoyance. *Christ, I'm getting as uptight as my mother.*

At headquarters he checked in with his task force commander, but no one had any new data or leads to report. It would take another twenty-four to forty-eight hours to process the evidence collected from the scene. Once he made a few calls, Cort could do a little canvassing of his own, out on the Atchafalaya.

Or would have, if Terri Vincent hadn't shown up in his office ten minutes after he'd arrived. She didn't announce herself or even knock—his door simply swung open and she sauntered in. "Hey there, Marshal." She wore another of her endless blasé suits, her jacket already rumpled. "How's tricks?"

"I'm busy." Although he didn't have to make a call, he picked up the phone. "You have something for me, Sergeant?"

"Yeah." She grinned. "Five-five-five, six-three-eight-seven."

He cradled the receiver on his shoulder. "What?"

"Five-five-five, six-three-eight-seven. It's a recorded weather report, updated every hour, and it loops continuously. I use it all the time when I want to get rid of someone." She planted herself in the chair in front of his desk and leaned back, propping one boot on the edge. "Or would you rather have the one for the high and low tides on the Gulf?"

He put down the phone. "What do you want, Terri?"

"My captain wants us to work together, remember?" She ran the toe of her boot along the edge of his desk. "That would require both of us to be in the same place at the same time, doing the same thing."

He got up and grabbed the NOFD windbreaker he wore when on official business. "I'm driving out to the bayou."

"Oops, too late. I already questioned Gantry last night. I was hoping you'd go with me to interview the widow." She got up and stretched, propping her hands against the small of her back. "She hasn't given us a statement yet, and you being so good with women and all . . ." She waggled her narrow dark brows at him.

He came around the desk. "Let's get something straight. You're my brother's partner, not mine."

She cocked her head. She was so tall she didn't have to break her neck looking up at him, like most women did. "You do have the most remarkable powers of observation. And?"

"I'm running this arson investigation, not you."

"Well, Marshal, the way I see it, we can go chase around the swamp, talk to people who will not talk back to us, and probably find out nothing," she said, her voice overly sweet. "Or we can go interview the woman who was married to the victim, knew every move he made, slept with him for the last twenty years, and who is a personal friend of your family." She pretended to think. "Whatever shall we do?"

It was throttle her or head out the door. With a faint pang of regret, he picked moving toward the exit. "Let's go talk to the widow."

"Cozy place J. D.'s friend has got here," Hilaire said as she emerged from inspecting the bedrooms. "No TV but all kinds of CDs and books. Two big cozy beds, neither of them twins. She's even got herself a cute little whirly-pool tub in the bathroom, built for two."

Unable to relax, Sable had paced in front of the lake view window, watching for signs of J. D.'s return. She didn't want to think about whoever owned the cottage, much less argue with her cousin about it. She turned and headed for the kitchen. "How about I make us something to drink?"

"*Grand-mère* packed a thermos of her coffee in the basket." Hilaire followed her in and gazed around at the white cabinets and small, neat appliances. "Should still be hot."

Sable found some clear glass mugs in the cabinet and poured two cups. She could feel her cousin watching her. "What's on your mind, Hil?"

"Like I said, this is a nice place." Hilaire leaned over the counter to look through the window over the sink. "Would you look at that? She's even got herself a brick charcoal pit right there in the yard—and an electric spit. Damn, could I make us some barbecue on that."

"Hil?" Sable held out the mug. "Get serious."

Hilaire took it and sighed. "You don't belong here, cousin. Not here, not with him."

Which was exactly how Sable felt, not that she'd admit it. "He's trying to help me—to protect me."

"For one thing, he's a cop, not a bodyguard. He nearly got you killed last night, or did you forget about all that shooting?"

"He saved my life." Sable nearly knocked over the thermos before she set it carefully at the back of the counter. "I don't want to talk about this." She left the kitchen and went to take up her post by the window.

Hilaire pursued her. "Isabel, I love you like you were my own sister, but you know I'm right. Look at what happened to you the last time you got mixed up with Jean-Del—what they did to you. You really think anything is different now?"

Sable whirled around. "We're not involved like that. He's only trying to help me."

"Oh, *chère*." Her cousin came over and hugged her before drawing back and looking up into her eyes. "You never did get over him, did you?"

She shrugged. "I'll be fine, Hil. If anything happens between me and J. D., it won't be like it was when I was at Tulane."

"Because Marc LeClare was your real daddy?" Her cousin shook her head. "His people aren't going to accept you any more than they did ten years ago. You go and tell the world about Marc and your mama, it'll only make things worse—can't you see that?"

Sable turned back toward the lake. "All I care about is finding whoever killed my father."

"And all I want for Mardi Gras is Harry Connick Jr. wearing nothing but a feathered mask and a double strand of blue beads." Hilaire sat down on the wicker rocking chair and rested her head against the high back. "I almost hope he does steal my boat. I don't want to leave you here alone with him."

"You need to get back to the store before Lacy sells it to a wandering gypsy." Sable opened the window a little, so she could hear the sounds from the lake. "Don't worry about me. I think I can restrain myself."

"Hmph. I've seen the way he looks at you, girl, and I bet you he buys a whole case of condoms while he's out making groceries."

The memory of a night when J. D. had taken her into the drugstore to do exactly that made Sable swallow. He'd nearly had to drag her inside, and she'd been so embarrassed, especially by the look the clerk gave her.

Why do I have to do this? she'd protested. *This is a man's thing to do.*

I might forget, and I'm counting on you to remember if I do, he'd told her, laughing. *And we're both Catholic, so if you get pregnant, both sides will be hauling out the shotguns for the wedding.*

She'd stared at the rack of condoms, feeling slightly resentful. *You would never marry someone like me.*

He'd stopped laughing and had taken her into his arms, right there in front of the clerk and all the customers. *No, I wouldn't marry someone like you. I don't want anybody like you. I want you.*

"What's in there?" Hilaire got up and opened the tall cabinet across from her chair, revealing an expensive stereo system. "I was wondering why she had all those CDs laying on her dresser." She poked at the receiver's buttons. "You want to listen to some music or the radio?"

"The radio." Maybe there would be some news about her father's funeral. Sable pressed her brow against the windowpane and closed her eyes as she remembered the one and only evening she had spent with Marc. Now he was lost to her again, forever this time, and she couldn't even go and pay her last respects.

There was some crackling of static as Hilaire tuned

the receiver; then an announcer's abrupt, loud voice came through the speakers.

"—witness escaped on foot from Mercy Hospital shortly before the disappearance of Homicide detective J. D. Gamble. At press time, Chief of Homicide Captain George Pellerin said the witness, Isabel Marie Duchesne, had not been found and is now considered a suspect. Sources within the NOPD indicated that an APB was issued and surrounding county authorities were alerted to the suspect's flight. State and local police, with the help of a helicopter, spent nearly five hours combing the immediate area around Mercy for the suspect before calling off the search for the night." The announcer gave a short description of Sable, then added, "If you see this woman, do not attempt to approach her, but contact your local police station immediately. In other news—"

Hilaire switched off the radio. She was white-faced and shaking. "*Mon Dieu*, Isabel, this is what they are saying about you? That you're a *suspect* now?"

Sable couldn't think. "They issued an APB for me." An incredulous laugh erupted from her. "For me."

"The police, they don't kid about things like this." Hilaire closed the cabinet. "Sounds like they got every cop in Louisiana out there looking for you."

Sable went to the sofa and sat down, burying her face in her hands. "I can't believe this—they think I did something to J. D.?"

"You're easy to blame." Her cousin came over and sat beside her, and slung an arm around her shoulders. "Like when they blamed you for starting that mud fight back at Tulane—and look how that turned out. They went and took away everything you earned and kicked you out of that school."

"I haven't done anything wrong." She stared at her cousin. "That has to mean something."

"It didn't last time, *chère.*"

"Jean-Del—"

Hilaire rested a finger against Sable's lips. "You listen now, because this is bad. When they catch up to you, and they will, they're going to force him to make a choice."

Sable cringed. "No. It won't be like that."

"But it is, *chère.* It always is. J. D. won't like it, but that's life. He's Creole; you're Cajun. Those folks in the city are part of his family, and his job, and everything he knows and loves. You're just an old girlfriend, honey." She tilted her head to the side. "They're not so different from us. We do the same for our own."

"He'll stand by me," Sable insisted. "He won't let them arrest me."

"For now. But when it comes time to choose, who do you think he's going to pick?" Her cousin looked sad. "Sable, think. It's not love on the line. It's not a scholarship. It's your life."

Chapter Nine

The Garden District may have been the loveliest jewel in the Crescent City's crown, but Terri Vincent had never felt at ease even when she'd been in uniform, patrolling its short, narrow, potholed streets. Everything from the electric-powered green streetcars running along St. Charles Avenue to the manicured jewel box gardens and the fancy little bookshops had always seemed a bit too pretentious for her liking. She was more at home in the Quarter, where life was free and easy, and the hours were counted by the bells of St. Louis Cathedral, which had the right to be ostentatious.

Too many fancy mansions, she thought as she pulled around to the back entrance of Marc and Laure Le-Clare's elegant home. *People don't live in these places— they curate them, like museums.*

Marc LeClare's widow must have hired a private security firm to watch over the property, because there was a small army of uniformed guards keeping the reporters and paparazzi from setting up camp. When one of them tapped Terri's window, she rolled it down to show her badge.

"Detective Vincent and Fire Marshal Gamble," she

told him. "We have an appointment to speak with Mrs. LeClare."

"Right." The guard checked his clipboard and checked off an item, then waved a hand to the guard operating the electronic gate. "Let them through."

A short drive over a sweeping interlocked-stone drive led up to the three-story, galleried structure painted a soft cream with elaborate burgundy modillion cornice trim.

"Wow." Terri put the car in park and sat looking up for a minute. "I don't remember seeing this place before."

"Marc recently had it renovated to restore the Chinese, Italianate, Eastlake, and Queen Anne revival elements from the original blueprints." Cort scanned the property, checking out the Mercedes and the BMW parked on the other side of the drive. "The original house was by Thomas Sully."

"So it's really old." Thinking of the termite problems alone made her shudder.

"And rare." He gave the mansion a brooding look. "Most of Sully's houses have been demolished."

"Who's Sully?" Not that she really cared, but Cort was apparently trying to relate something important to her, in his usual college-professor-lecturing way.

"He was the first architect to open a professional, large-scale firm in the city. In twenty-five years he built over thirty homes and churches, and changed the face of the Garden District."

Was he stalling her from going inside, or did he really want her to get all jazzed about an old house? "Wow. Some guy."

"He brought the city into the mainstream of American design. Marc thought the renovation was important; he considered it giving a piece of history back to the district." Now he looked at her. "He and his wife were both active in several charities devoted to architectural preservation."

"Fascinating stuff." She liked the great rounded porch that wrapped around the first floor, but thought the multipaned stained-glass windows were a bit much. It was a house, not a church—and for all their money, the LeClares were just people. "How do you know all this?"

He glared at her. "I grew up here. Everyone knows this *stuff.*"

"Uh-huh. This wouldn't happen to be your way of telling me to keep my common little mouth shut and let you talk to the lady, would it? You being a family friend and an authority on her genteel shack o' Sully here?"

"God, you are an obnoxious woman." He got out of the car and slammed the door.

"That's what I thought." She took her keys out of the ignition and thrust them into her pocket. "I can tell already that this is going to be a laugh a minute."

A maid complete with an apron answered the front door and ushered them into a sitting room. On the way, Terri noted the ornate ceiling medallions, heart-of-pine floors, and huge curving staircase. Paintings of important-looking but not very attractive people marched up the walls in irregular columns all the way to the fourteen-foot-high covered ceilings. There were so many valuable antiques around that one room probably cost more to furnish than what she had socked away in her pension fund for the last six years.

The message was beautiful, elegant, but still rather pointed: *We have money. You don't. Nah-nah-nah-nah-nah.*

The sitting room—or the morning room, as the

maid had called it—was decorated in a thousand shades of pale yellow, white, and ivory. Terri assumed it was supposed to give the impression of sunshine and happiness, but it made her feel like she'd walked into a bowl of movie theater popcorn. She had an urge to look for a tin shaker of salt and a wad of paper napkins.

Straighten up, Vincent—the woman just lost her husband.

Marc LeClare's widow appeared in the doorway a few minutes later. She was wearing a dark charcoal gray dress with soft lace cuffs and a marcasite and diamond brooch shaped like a Mardi Gras mask.

"Detective Vincent." She came forward slowly, as if unsure of her ability to reach her destination. "Thank you for coming." She turned to Cort. "Cortland, how kind of you to call."

"I wanted to make sure you were all right, Laure." He took her into a gentle embrace.

Terri waited until Cort finished hugging the woman, then offered her hand. Laure's fingers felt like thin, frozen sticks. "I'm so sorry for your loss, Mrs. LeClare."

"Thank you." She gestured to a daffodil yellow settee. "Won't you please sit down? Can I offer you something to drink? Tea, coffee, or perhaps something cold?"

"No, ma'am, but thank you." Terri took out her notebook and pen. "We won't take up any more of your time than we have to, but we do have some questions."

Cort sat down beside Laure and took her hand in his. "If you're not up to this, we can come back another time."

Terri gritted her teeth. "Of course we can."

"No, I'd rather . . . get it over with." Laure grimaced slightly. "Please, how can I help you?"

"Did you see your husband yesterday morning, before he left the house?" Terri asked.

"Yes, we had breakfast together as we always did, and went over the campaign schedule for the week." Laure frowned. "He mentioned he was stopping by one of the properties we have downtown before he went to his campaign headquarters. Then the police called, and . . ." She made another of her delicate gestures.

Terri made a note to check into Marc's scheduled appearances, but before she could move to the next question, Cort asked, "Laure, did Marc say he was meeting Ms. Duchesne?"

"He mentioned her to me, and that he was making a contribution to a community project she was involved in. I believe he meant to lend her the property for some office and storage space." Laure looked over her shoulder as the door opened and Moriah Navarre came in.

"Cortland?" The petite blond woman looked from him to Terri, and scowled. "What are you doing here?"

The Deb, naturally. Now my morning is complete. "It's official business, Ms. Navarre, if you wouldn't mind—"

"I do mind. Mrs. LeClare is a friend of my family, and she is in no condition to answer any questions." Her eyes shifted to the man sitting next to Laure. "I thought you were out of town."

Here we go with the helpless Southern-flower act, Terri thought, barely restraining herself from rolling her eyes. *She'll whimper something like, "Oh, Cort, you big strong hunk of testosterone you, I'm so relieved you're here. I can hardly stand upright without manly support. . . ."*

"I came back early." Surprisingly, Cort didn't look

very interested in Moriah. "We need to talk to Mrs. Le-
Clare now, Moriah, so give us a few minutes."

His dismissal seemed to annoy her more than
Terri's presence did. "Laure?"

Marc's widow nodded quickly. "I'll be just fine, my
dear. Would you check on how things are progressing
with lunch?"

"Sure. Call me if you need anything." With one last
steamed look at Terri, Moriah departed.

"Moriah is a little overprotective," Laure said.

Moriah is a little over-Guccied. "No problem, ma'am."
Terri felt sorry for the widow, but she had to shake her
out of her fog of devastation. "Mrs. LeClare, were you
aware of the relationship between your husband and
Ms. Duchesne?"

Laure's forehead wrinkled. "Relationship? I'm
sorry, I don't . . " She looked at Cort.

Cort reacted as if Terri had slapped the older
woman. "What relationship would that be, Detective
Vincent?" Terri ignored him. "Mrs. LeClare, did your
husband tell you that Isabel Duchesne is his natural
daughter?"

"Daughter?" Laure paled, then lifted a trembling
hand to her throat. "No. My God. He never said a
word to me. All these years . . ." She covered her face
and began to weep.

Her shock seemed pretty real. "According to my information, your husband only recently discovered that
Sable was his daughter," Terri told her quickly. "But if
he had known about her, would there be any reason he
would conceal this from you? Any payments he might
have made to the mother for her support, for exam-
ple?"

Cort made a low, harsh sound. "That's enough,
Terri."

The widow recovered quickly. "No, Cortland, I want to know about this," she said, wiping at her eyes with her fingertips. "Detective, Marc couldn't have known he had a daughter. He would have told me."

"And why is that, Mrs. LeClare?"

Incredibly, the older woman blushed. "We were never able to have children," she said, her voice low. "Marc and I tried everything—even fertility treatments—but nothing worked. I could get pregnant but I couldn't carry a child to term."

That must have sucked. "I'm sorry."

"The damage from all the miscarriages forced me to have a complete hysterectomy seven years ago." She sat up straighter, visibly gathering herself. "I know this is more information than you need, but let me assure you, my husband and I would have been overjoyed to welcome a daughter into our lives."

"Sable Duchesne's mother was a Cajun," Terri said softly. "Would you have welcomed her, knowing that?"

Rather than showing offense, Laure smiled a little. "I know what you're thinking, Detective, but I'm no snob. She could have been purple with pink polka dots and we still would have loved her." She sighed. "I don't understand. If she is Marc's daughter, why weren't we told? Did her mother keep her from us? Can I speak to the girl?"

"We don't have all the facts yet, Laure. Ms. Duchesne is presently in protective custody." Cort gave Terri a hard look. "It's possible someone was blackmailing Marc. Revealing her existence could have seriously damaged his election campaign."

Laure shook her head. "Marc wouldn't have cared about that. If she or her mother needed money, he would have given it to them. We would have done anything to help them."

Terri's brows rose. "He wouldn't have cared about his election being wrecked?"

"You didn't know my husband, Detective, and that's a pity. If you had, you would know what a wonderfully generous man he was."

Terri asked a few more questions, but Laure was unable to give them many details about that day other than her brief conversation with Marc at breakfast.

As she walked them out to the drive, Laure touched Cort's arm. "This poor girl—Isabel—is there any way I can help her? Does she need a place to stay?"

Now that's something you don't see every day, Terri thought. *The widow of an unfaithful husband offering to put up his illegitimate daughter.* "No, ma'am, but thank you for the offer."

Cort kissed her brow. "I'll keep in touch and let you know. You take care, now."

Terri expected Cort to chew her ear off as soon as they got to her car, but he said nothing. "Where to, Marshal?"

"You can drop me back at the station."

She wasn't going to let him shut her out just because she'd sprung a little surprise on him. Not without a fight. "I had to see how she'd react. You know the scenario: She's trying to get him elected as governor; he tells her he's been hiding an illegitimate kid; maybe she goes a little crazy."

"Laure LeClare is not crazy, or jealous, or a killer. She's a decent woman who has had her entire world destroyed, and you just shoved her face in the rubble." He turned fierce green eyes on her. "Who told you Sable Duchesne is Marc's daughter?"

"Your brother, the fugitive from work."

His cell phone rang, and he swore under his breath as he flipped it open to answer it. "Gamble." He listened for a moment. "I'll take care of it. Thanks." To Terri, he said, "You said you questioned Caine Gantry. Where do I find him?"

"Why?"

"The lab report confirmed two types of blood on the culling pole we found at the scene. The blood matches Marc LeClare's and Sable Duchesne's."

"Your cousin didn't want to leave." From the window, J. D. watched Hilaire's boat speed back across the lake toward the river.

"She's worried about me." Sable took one of the last grocery bags he'd brought down from the pier from him. "And she doesn't like you."

"Yeah, I picked up on that." He followed her into the kitchen. "Is it because we dropped in on her grandparents last night?"

"No." She opened the first bag and looked inside. "She just doesn't like you in general."

"Right." He noted the tension in her shoulders and the flat line of her mouth, and wondered what had happened while he had been gone. "The newspapers are having a field day. Election's shot all to hell, politicians scrambling to replace Marc." He'd decided not to tell her about the APB; it would only worry her more. "Mardi Gras is going well, though."

She began unloading the bags and sorting through the groceries he'd bought. "Uh-huh."

He decided to prod her a little. "They're running photos of you and him on the front page. I never noticed the resemblance before I saw them side by side. You have the same eyes."

"That's all we shared." She shoved a head of lettuce into the refrigerator.

"Maybe not." J. D. had never thought of Marc as the type of man who kept secrets, but Sable's existence proved that he had. Now what J. D. needed to find out was what she was hiding from him.

"He was running for governor and a millionaire; I'm a social worker who makes twenty-five thousand a year if I'm lucky." She slammed the fridge shut. "We came from completely different worlds."

"Not really." When she gave him a slightly incredulous look, he decided to change the subject. "What did you do while I was gone?"

"I watched the lake and prayed you wouldn't steal my cousin's boat. Hilaire snooped around the place. She thinks your friend has a nice bathtub." She folded one empty bag and went on to the next. "We listened to the radio, too. Evidently I'm now a suspect in your disappearance." She tossed a bag of rice in the cabinet. "Just in case you were wondering."

So she knew—no wonder Hilaire had looked at him like he was scum and Sable acted like she wanted to tear his head off. "I heard. I'll take care of it."

"I can't believe this." She slammed a can of coffee on the counter. "*I* didn't ask you to come after me. *You* decided to disappear all on your own. Why don't you report in or whatever it is you cops do when you're out chasing people?"

"I can't." He moved in and put a hand on her shoulder. "It doesn't mean anything. Settle down."

"Why should I?" She stopped unpacking and shrugged off his hand. "Your life isn't being torn to shreds, Jean-Del. Mine is."

She didn't say *again*, but the word hovered between them anyway. He had the feeling that she was relating the present situation to what had happened on the night of the dance ten years ago, but why? What did their breakup have to do with an APB?

Another item to add to the list of things they were going to settle before this was through. "You're not going to be arrested. I'll tell them the truth."

That made her laugh—and it was a sad, bitter sound. "When has the truth ever mattered?" She didn't wait for an answer but simply brushed past him. "I'm going to take a shower."

She was still running away—from trouble, from him. Always from him. Anger surged in him, but he shoved it down.

"My partner found a culling pole at the warehouse. Same kind used out on the bayou." He leaned back and watched her halt in the doorway. "They're testing it now, but it looks like it's the murder weapon."

She turned slowly around. "So?"

He let his gaze drift down to her hands, which were clenched into tight fists. "Your father—Remy—he's an oysterman, isn't he? I bet he knows all the other oystermen on the bayou, too."

Her face went blank. "Papa is not getting involved in this."

He already is, and you know something you're not telling me. "Where did he get those scars on his face?"

"As I told you last night, Papa was burned in the fire that nearly killed my mother and me when I was a baby. He was the one who rescued us." She folded her arms. "What's your point?"

"He must have loved you and your mother a lot."

"Yes, he did. But Remy had nothing to do with Marc's murder. If anyone did, it was—" She stopped and drew in a deep breath. "It could have been any-one."

"You mean it could have been Gantry." When she didn't answer, he switched directions. "Remy risked his life to save you and your mother. Then he married her and took you both away from here." He followed the taut line of her jaw to the tick of the pulse at the base of her throat. "You said Gantry's father was arrested right after the fire. That would have been while Remy was recovering in the hospital, right?" She nodded. "Then why did he take you and your mother away? Bud Gantry was in prison."

"Someone paid him to burn our house. My mother was afraid they'd try again." Her voice was tight. "She did it to protect me."

"Or maybe Remy was worried about Marc."

Her eyes narrowed. "I know what you're trying to say. My father may be nothing but a poor Cajun fisherman, but he's never hurt anyone in his life."

"He stuck a shotgun in my face this morning."

She strode right up to him. "That was just for show and you know it!"

"It must have been tough on him, knowing someone else got your mother pregnant, but your mother never telling him who. Then finding out after she died that your father could buy and sell him a hundred times over."

"He was happy for me."

"Happy that Marc could give you everything that he couldn't. Maybe it started to eat at him. First his wife, then his daughter—"

J. D. didn't try to avoid her hand as she swung and slapped him, hard. "Don't you talk about my papa like that again," she whispered through white lips. "Ever."

"You want the truth, baby? Sometimes the truth fucking hurts." He caught her wrist when she tried to hit him again and used it to pull her into his arms. "I'm not letting you sacrifice yourself to protect a killer. Not even if it's Remy. Do you understand me?"

"I don't *know* who killed Marc," she said through gritted teeth, twisting against his grip. "But it wasn't Remy. He ran into the fire to save me and my mother. He wouldn't leave me to burn then and he wouldn't have done it now."

He locked an arm around her. "Then tell me what you've been holding back on me. Tell me about Billy."

"This is a waste of time—it's barely noon," Terri grumbled. "I'm telling you, Gantry won't be there."

Cort should have left Terri Vincent back in the city, but she knew where Gantry's operation was, and he didn't feel like wandering around the swamp for hours trying to find it himself. "We'll check anyway."

"Of course we will." She sighed and turned onto a narrow lane leading into the swamp.

"Tell me what you know about Gantry."

"He's the meanest son of a bitch in the state." At his sideways glance, she sighed. "Okay, he's first runner-up. Should you ever be unable to carry out your duties . . ."

He silently counted to ten. "Give me facts."

"Gantry has a large outfit, runs about thirty boats, most with two- to three-man crews." As they approached the docks, she slid on her sunglasses. "He does mostly fishing and swamp tours. He keeps to himself and he doesn't like cops." She leaned forward. "Oh, hell."

"Hell what?" All he could see was a decrepit old Chevy parked on the side of the lane. "Let's run a check on that plate."

She didn't want to tell him, but finally dragged the

words out. "I don't have to. That's the car that was reported stolen from Mercy ER last night."

Which meant his brother or Isabel Duchesne had been here. Could still be here. Cort counted five boats and fifteen men at the dock as she parked. He got out. One of the men—the biggest one—was already walking toward them.

"That Gantry?"

"That's him." Terri put herself in front of Cort, holding up one hand. "Hang on, Caine. This is official business."

Gantry looked over her head at Cort. "You look like a Gamble."

"I am."

"Got a warrant?" When Terri shook her head, Gantry showed some teeth. "Then get the hell off my property."

Cort smiled back. "Sure. Soon as you tell us where my brother and Isabel Duchesne are."

"Fuck if I know." The big man looked down at Terri, and some of the hatred left his face as he put a hand on her shoulder. "You and I gonna go round about this again, Therese? I thought we danced enough last night."

Before he thought about what he was doing, Cort moved and shoved Gantry away from Terri. "You'll want to keep your hands off her and where I can see them, Cajun."

"Or what?" Black eyes measured him. "You might be big enough, Gamble, but I doubt you have the belly for it."

Cort centered his weight. "Try me."

"Whoa. Guys. I'm starting to choke on all the male hormones in the air." Terri put herself between them and placed a hand on Cort's chest. "Marshal, we're not here to brawl, just ask some questions. And you"—she turned to Caine and jabbed his sternum with her finger—"you're going to settle down and answer them."

"Gamble isn't here. Neither is Isabel." He jerked a thumb back toward his boats. "Ask my crew. We've been out looking for them all morning."

Cort folded his arms. "Why bother?"

"We're decent folks," Gantry said, his tone as bland as Cort's.

"Decent folks who take care of their own."

"Your cop brother and his slut don't belong to us." His upper lip curled. "You can take them on back to the city, as soon as we find them."

"Before or after you crack their skulls?"

Gantry's smile widened. "You got something to say, Gamble, go ahead and say it."

"Caine." Terri's voice held some kind of warning. "We need to know if you're missing any gear."

Black eyes moved to her face. "Like what?"

"Like a murder weapon." Cort started walking toward the wet house, but the big man got in his way. "I can come back with a warrant, and a Fish and Game inspector. The warrant will permit a search, but the warden will shut you down. The same way Marc would have."

"Bring it on. I run a legal operation here, and my lawyer loves to take assholes like you to court." Gantry turned to Terri. "What's this about a murder weapon?"

"Someone used a culling pole to kill Marc LeClare."

Gantry went still, then regarded Terri the way he would a poisonous snake. "You really do want to wrap things up in a hurry, don't you, *chère*?"

To Cort's surprise, the brunette flushed. "It's not what you think, Caine."

"I don't think—I know. It runs in the family." He eyed Cort. "So, you sweet-talk her into planting it, or was it her idea?"

Cort knew Terri's father had been a cop, but had been caught planting evidence at a scene and forced to retire. The disgrace was not common knowledge, however, and before he broke the Cajun's jaw he'd find out how Gantry knew about it. "Terri?"

"Caine's father is my mother's brother." She rubbed a hand over the back of her neck. "Much as I hate to admit it, we're first cousins."

Cold rage solidified inside Cort. "That's why you've been trying to dump the case."

She nodded. "As soon as I heard it was Marc Le-Clare. If Caine here didn't set that fire and kill him, then another member of my extended family probably did."

Gantry grabbed her arm and gave her a rough shake. "You don't go pointing fingers at kin, girl."

"Gantry." An ugly heat rose inside him. "I told you to keep your hands off her."

The big man released Terri's arm and chucked her under the chin. "Why didn't you tell him you were a coon-ass, *chère*? Might have gotten in his pants faster." He directed a sneer at Cort. "Won't make any difference if you turn the lights out, you know. Hell, a Cajun girl can teach you what you're really supposed to do with your dick."

It was as if the civilized switch in Cort's head suddenly clicked off for the first time in his life. He lunged, and Gantry met him halfway. They went down grappling.

"Cort!" Terri skirted around them. "Damn it, Caine, stop it!"

Gantry's heavy fist plowed into his jaw just as Cort

knocked the air out of his lungs with a punch to the diaphragm. He shoved the Cajun away, jackknifing to his feet at the same time Gantry did. The two men circled for a moment, waiting for an opening. The sound of a gun being fired three times made them both freeze.

"Now that I have your attention," Terri said, holding her weapon on them, "I'd like a little cooperation. Caine Gantry, you're under arrest for assault and whatever else I can think up on the way into the station. Marshal Gamble." She tossed a pair of handcuffs to Cort. "Do the honors, if you would." She turned to the advancing wall of Caine's men and shifted her aim. "John, you're in charge. How many of your boys do you want to take to the emergency room today?"

"Coldhearted bitch," Caine muttered as Cort cuffed him.

"Runs in the family," Terri agreed cheerfully. "John, you've been to my daddy's house—you've seen my marksmanship trophies in the hutch in the dining room. Let's not add to them."

"I'll call the lawyer, Caine." The foreman held out an arm, and the crew halted in their tracks. "Let them go."

Cort marched Gantry to the car and shoved him in the back before getting behind the wheel. Terri slid in the other side, keeping her eye on the surly faces of the fishermen.

"You're making a big mistake, *chère*," Gantry said. "He came at me—it was self-defense."

"It's whatever I say it was." She eyed him in the rearview. "You'll want to shut up now, cos."

Gantry subsided into silence, and Terri busied herself trying to call someone on her cell. Cort didn't trust himself to speak on the drive back to the city. He escorted the big man into police headquarters and handed him off to the desk sergeant before heading for the elevator. Terri called after him but he didn't hesitate.

He came back down to Processing a half hour later, and found her typing up the arrest report with Gantry still cuffed in a chair beside the desk. "Terri."

"Yo." She pulled the report out of the typewriter and hunted in the drawer until she pulled out a case file folder. "Just finishing up. You want to take his statement with me? It's bound to be a fiction of incredible proportions."

"Terri." Cort waited until she looked directly at him. "Detective Garcia will take over from here."

"What are you talking about?" She looked from him to the unhappy Garcia and back to him. "This is my collar."

"I've had you removed from the case." He nodded to Garcia, who took Gantry by the arm and pulled him to his feet. "You're assigned to desk duty upstairs until further notice."

He turned his back on her stunned face and walked away. The only sound that followed him was Caine Gantry's low, soft laughter.

Chapter Ten

Sable was glad she didn't have a culling pole at that moment; she'd have brained J. D. with it for sure. "I'm not holding anything back."

"Aren't you? What were you talking to Colette about this morning? Why did Remy argue with you about Caine and his best friend and your mother?"

She couldn't tell him what Marc had said that had troubled her on the night before the murder; he'd think it was ridiculous and she was crazy. Remy had thought so. "We were talking about something else."

"What?" When she didn't answer, his hold on her changed. "Then tell me, why does it have to be like this between us?" He pulled her head against his shoulder, stroking her hair until she relaxed against him. "I can't let you shut me out again, Sable. The last time about killed me."

"I didn't do so great, either." Her throat hurt, and her eyes stung, but she blinked back the tears.

"Then talk to me, baby. Please."

His anger she could handle, but his gentleness was going to drive her insane. She had to put a stop to this, make him understand. "Jean-Del, what we had in the past is over. We're different people now, older and I hope a little wiser. I care about you, and I'm grateful to you for helping me, but I won't get involved with you again."

He tilted her face up to his. "Too late for that."

Sable willed herself to remain still as his mouth touched hers. If she responded, he'd know she was lying, and that he could have as much of her as he desired. Being skinned alive would have been less painful, but the alternative would only lead to heartbreak and ruin. Like him, she couldn't handle that again.

I don't want this. I don't want him.

It would have been easier if he'd been angry and rough, the way he had after hauling her away from Caine Gantry. But J. D. drew her into a quiet place full of darkness and heat where the world went away and there was only the two of them. He deepened the kiss at the same time he put his hands to work on her skin, stroking and gentling her, and the double assault made her head swim.

He lifted his head and buried his face in her hair. "Do you remember the first time I kissed you?"

How could she forget? They'd been caught in the rain outside her dorm and huddled together under the scant protection of a narrow overhang, trying to say good night without getting soaked.

That night he'd smiled down at her—*It's only a little water*—and he'd pulled her out into the rain, whirling her off her feet. She had wriggled and shrieked with laughter, covering her head. They'd both gotten soaked to the skin within seconds, but then he'd stopped suddenly. Sable had slid down the front of him, expecting to feel the ground beneath her feet again, but she'd never reached it. Instead he'd held her suspended between his hands and looked all over her face in wonder before staring at her rain-wet lips. *God, you just glow. Like you're lit up from the inside.*

In that moment, she'd lost herself in his blue eyes. *You make me feel like I am, Jean-Del.*

J. D. looked at her the same way now. "I never saw anyone so beautiful, the way you were that night." He bent his head, and murmured the last words against her mouth. "And the next night, and the next, and every other night I held you in my arms."

If there were a hell for lovers, it had to feel like this—she wanted him and feared him and could not escape him. The old pain blended with new as she felt herself reaching for him, threading her fingers through his dense black hair, moving against the press of his hard body on hers. "Kiss me again."

He did. The desire he'd drawn from her intensified, became as scalding as his hands and mouth were urgent, scorched through her body until she thought her skin would melt under the relentless heat. She moaned when he took his mouth away, almost mindless with need.

"You want me?" His voice teased her left ear as he stroked his hands from her shoulders to her hips.

He needed reassurance? "Yes." She turned her face, wanting his mouth again, but he was doing something to her throat—something with his tongue and his teeth that was going to make her scream. She must have made some sound, because she felt his smile against her skin.

"You trust me?"

That hurt a little. She'd given him so much already—didn't he see that? But if he needed the words, needed to hear them from her lips, she would give him those, too. "Yes. Please, Jean-Del—"

"It's okay, baby. I know it hurts. I hurt, too." He was

walking backward now, drawing her out of the kitchen. "I'm going to make it better for both of us."

Her legs were starting to give out, and she clutched at him. "Now?"

"Right now." He halted at the threshold of one of the bedrooms to kiss her again. "Sable."

"Mmmm? . . ." She chased his mouth again. If he teased her much longer, she'd rip all their clothes off herself and knock him to the floor.

He started on the other side of her throat. "You are going to tell me about Billy, aren't you?"

That softly murmured question was as effective as a bucket of duckweed-slimy swamp water. Sable went immobile, locked in disbelief that he would use her own response to him like this.

We protect our own, Hilaire had said, *and so do they.*

She didn't hit him again, mainly because she was afraid she wouldn't stop if she started. No, now she had to be clever, more clever than Jean-Del was.

But he was already looking into her eyes, and there was resignation in his. "I shouldn't have pushed. I'm sorry."

Actually she thought he'd done quite well. He'd almost gotten her crazy enough to tell him whatever he wanted, just to have him. If she told him what Marc had said, what she was thinking now that only made sense to her, he would have to make a terrible choice.

And he won't choose me.

Carefully she extricated herself from his embrace. "I really do have to take a shower." A long shower. A long, *cold* shower. She made her expression soften. "It'll be okay, Jean-Del."

"I need to make some calls anyway, see about this APB." He sighed and rested his brow against hers. "Don't take too long."

Not long. Only the rest of her life. "All right." She kissed one of his dark eyebrows before she slipped out of his arms. "Make us something cool to drink, will you? I think we're going to need it."

Sable could almost hear her heart breaking as he chuckled and wandered back to the kitchen. She went into the bathroom and locked the door, then studied the dimensions of the window. It was a simple, single-paned crank type, and large enough for her to fit through comfortably. She popped the screen out and hoisted herself over the edge, looking in both directions before dropping to the ground. She'd have to avoid the front of the house and the lake, but she could hear the sound of traffic in the distance. She followed it until she emerged from the scrub pine on the edge of a busy road leading from the lakeside to New Orleans.

Before she'd even thought about where to go from there, a red convertible filled with a pair of laughing college students pulled off the road a few yards away from her. "Hey, sweetie!" One of the girls waved to her. "You need a ride?"

She couldn't go back to the bayou, not with Gantry and his men looking for her. Jean-Del wouldn't look for her in the city. She smiled and started walking toward the car. "That would be great, thanks."

J. D. emptied the ice he had crushed into the pitcher of lemonade, and tried not to think about Sable naked in the shower. With a little more patience he'd get her to tell him about Caine and Billy, and then he could spend the rest of the night in bed with her.

Night, hell. We'll be lucky to come up for air, food, and water in a week.

Sable's insistence that Remy was innocent didn't bother J. D.—she was only being loyal to the man who had raised her—but there were too many coincidences. If he could find evidence that the fire at the warehouse and the one that nearly killed Remy were somehow connected . . .

Cort would know. His task force had been collecting evidence and data on arson cases for years, entering them into the database so that repeat offenders could be identified and stopped more quickly. But Terri had already indicated that he was pissed off, so J. D. didn't want to call him directly.

On impulse he dialed the private number to Krewe of Louis.

His easygoing father answered the restaurant phone with a snarled, "What you want?"

"Some of your gumbo would hit the spot right now," J. D. said. "How about you?"

"I'm out of my mind with worry about you and near ready to divorce your damn mother. There ain't enough cognac in New Orleans to make me happy." Louis exhaled heavily. "You want to come on home now, boy?"

"I can't just yet. Dad, I need you to do something for me." He explained the situation to Louis and how he needed Cort to get whatever records he could on the old arson case. "Tell him to compare the evidence from that one to the warehouse fire. I need to know if there were any similarities at all."

"Your brother's out hunting for you all, but I'll see what I can do." The old man sounded tired. "J. D., you watch yourself and look out for that girl, you hear me?"

"I will, Dad. Talk to you soon." J. D. switched off the phone and frowned. He knew from experience that the shower in Terri's bathroom was strong and noisy, but he still hadn't heard any water running. Then he recalled how big the window was in there and ran from the kitchen.

She wouldn't.

He didn't bother to knock, but used his shoulder to force the locked door in. The bathroom was empty and the window wide open. He swore as he climbed through the window and dropped down, looking in all directions. The sound of running feet through the pine needles made him take off toward the side of the house, where Terri kept her motorcycle in a utility shed.

J. D. used the spare key Terri kept in a magnet clip under the fender to start the Harley, then rode it through the woods and got to the road in time to see Sable take off in a red convertible with a couple of kids. He automatically memorized the license plate as he took a moment to pull on Terri's black helmet and snap the dark visor down to conceal his face before he pulled out and followed the convertible toward the city.

As Laure related what Terri Vincent had told her, Elizabet forgot her mother's ironclad rule about ladies always governing what they said with the utmost decorum. "I see. Ms. Duchesne has truly outdone herself this time."

Moriah picked up the tea tray. "I'll put this away, Laure." The girl hurried from the room.

"I don't know. I know Marc was involved with someone before he and I . . ." The other woman seemed ready to collapse at any moment. "Eliza, I don't know what to think or do. If she really is Marc's daughter—I know he would want me to help her—"

"But don't you see, Laure? That's why she made up this whole elaborate story, to gain your sympathy."

Elizabet gestured at the portrait of Marc above the mantel. "I've known Marc since you two were newly-weds, and not once was he unfaithful to you. For her story to be true, Marc would have had to get her mother pregnant a month before your wedding. Do you really think he would have had an affair while you were engaged?"

Laure paled. "We weren't engaged all that long, but no, I don't think so."

Gratified that she had settled that matter, Elizabet smiled. "I've called all my friends and talked to them about what we can do. The most important thing is to present a united front. Jacob has already scheduled a press conference today to denounce this girl's claims. I think you should give an interview to the *Daily News* and do the same."

"I don't think that's a good idea." Moriah, who had been hovering in the doorway, walked slowly over and sat next to Laure. "I knew Isabel in school, Laure. She wasn't as bad as everyone said she was. She was a genuinely nice girl."

Elizabet gave her a hard look. "She has fooled a lot of people into believing that, Moriah."

"I think I need some time to myself." Laure got to her feet. "I appreciate you all looking after me, but you should go home to your own families now."

Moriah ducked her head. "There's something else you should know, Laure. Isabel Duchesne has very dark brown eyes. They're the color of black coffee." She let out an unsteady breath. "Just like Marc's were."

Sable was relieved by the time her ride dropped her off in the French Quarter. Besides insisting that she share in the bounty of their lukewarm beer, the two students had pulled off the road several times to buy souvenirs and once to stop for lunch, where they spent nearly an hour gobbling up Cajun fries soaked in ketchup and arguing about who was hotter, Elijah Wood or Justin Timberlake.

"Justin's got a great voice, but Elijah's eyes rock."

"Britney never dated Elijah."

"That's 'cause Elijah thinks Britney is a slut."

"Well, so does Justin."

What should have taken an hour turned out to take three with the stops and the traffic. By the time they reached the city, the girls tried to talk her into going with them to their hotel, where a local radio station was holding various contests.

"You got a beautiful pair," the young coed said, patting Sable's breast as casually as she would a cute puppy. "Plus they pay three hundred dollars if you flash your tits for the guys videotaping everything. It's easy." She got up on her knees as another car filled with students passed them, and jerked up her T-shirt to jiggle her bare breasts at the ogling boys. "See?"

Sable could only laugh. "Thanks, but I've got somewhere to be."

"Your loss, honey." The girl had handed her a badge. "Listen, if you still want to earn a few bucks, take this and go to parade staging on Canal Street. You can take my place; I'm supposed to work one of the floats tonight." She burped and giggled. "Only I'm so drunk I'd just fall off."

Now that Sable was back in the city, she actually didn't have anywhere to go. Dancing, costumed tourists sloshing their plastic go-cups of beer choked the streets in unbelievable numbers, but she still felt uneasy, and looked over her shoulder several times. She negotiated her way out of the rows of bars and into the somewhat less crowded shopping district, but found the main streets had already been barricaded for one of the nightly Mardi Gras parades.

She took out the pass the girl had given her and almost laughed. *Sure, I could work a float. Watch the murder witness on national television, tossing goodies to the unsuspecting tourists.* She clipped it to her lapel. *It might come in handy if someone stops me, though.*

She followed the barricades for about an hour, looking for a pay phone she could use, but there were lines at every one she saw and she didn't want to wait. As it was she felt like everyone was staring at her, and when she saw two patrolmen working their way through the crowded street toward her, she abruptly turned around. A trio of glassy-eyed coeds bedecked in strings of flashy beads nearly collided with her before someone grabbed her arm and tugged her to the curb.

Her heart nearly jumped out of her chest as she stopped in her tracks and looked up into a stern, perspiring face.

"Hey." It was a man wearing a black jacket with KREWE OF ORPHEUS and PARADE OFFICIAL emblazoned on the breast in white letters. He took the pass from her nerveless fingers and scowled at it and her. "You're in the wrong place, and you're an hour late. Why is your hair red?"

"Sorry." She tried to think of an excuse. "Traffic was insane. I got tired of being blond."

"Good choice, you're prettier as a redhead. Come on, I'm headed that way myself—I'll give you a ride." He took her arm and steered her toward a waiting car. "You haven't been drinking, have you?"

"Uh, no, sir."

"Good. Half the performers we've got are already too soused to stand upright." He opened the door for her.

The official took her to the parade-staging area,
where gigantic papier-mâché floats sat lined up and
waiting for the night's festivities. Hundreds of performers in outrageous glittering costumes wove in and
out, helping each other with enormous headdresses,
adjusting feathers and shouting out to technicians
putting the final touches on the various props and
wires on the enormous floats.

"Get over to costuming," the official told her, giving
Sable a push in the direction of a huge striped tent just
beyond the car.

Everyone was sporting some type of mask, so Sable
walked into the tent. Until she could find a way to get
in touch with Hilaire or Remy, she needed the camou-
flage. The moment she stepped through the flaps, two
women seized her from either side. "You're a size six,
right?" one of them asked while stretching a measuring tape across her chest.

"Seven." She winced as someone tugged the ponytail holder out of her hair. "Hey."

"She's the right height," the second woman said to
the first, then asked Sable, "You ever wear a hoop skirt
before?"

An hour later Sable stepped down from a dress-
maker's stand, completely transformed. The two
women had wrestled her into what appeared to be an
exact replica of Scarlett O'Hara's green gown from the
movie *Gone with the Wind*. The emerald velvet high-
collared bodice and outer skirt shimmered against the
lighter lime underskirt. Her red hair was hidden under
a bubbly wig of chestnut curls and a hat festooned
with black feathers and golden tassels.

"These are too loose." One of the women adjusted
the golden cords around her waist, which duplicated

the drapery pulls Scarlett had worn. "There. I think even Rhett Butler himself would be impressed."

The other woman humphed. "Remember, whatever you do, don't sit down in this thing. The hoop will pop right up in your face, and everybody in New Orleans will be looking at your panties."

Someone shouted for Scarlett from the front of the tent.

"Go with Gary." The woman pointed to a man hovering at the front of the tent. "He'll help you onto the float."

The technician gave her the once-over before handing her a huge armful of colorful plastic necklaces. "Have you ever done this before?"

Sable shook her head and gingerly arranged the beaded strings over one of her forearms.

"Okay, three things to remember—you wave, you smile, and you throw your beads. Four things—you try not to move around too much." He led her to a huge float where other performers were already being positioned around a miniature model of an old plantation house.

"What's the theme?"

"Great Southern movies—you're *Gone with the Wind*. Did you go to the bathroom? It'll be an hour before the parade starts, and you won't get off until nine or ten tonight."

She nodded and followed him up the roll-away scaffold stairs to the side of the float, where two waist-high metal braces rose from a small flat circle. There was a black satin oval backdrop behind it, and two spotlights at the front.

Not so high that I can't jump down to the ground as soon as we get out of here. She'd have to pull the hoop out, but as soon as she deflated her skirt she'd be able to blend right in with the crowd.

Gary helped her climb on, then got behind her and fiddled with something. "Tell me if this is too tight." He wrapped a transparent plastic band around her waist. "If you get into trouble, just call down to one of the street performers. They can help you and they'll chase off anyone who tries to grab you."

She swallowed. "They do that?"

"All the time, sugar, all the time. You can always give them a good kick in the crotch, too—that always sends the message." Gary finished making the adjustments behind her and patted her shoulder before stepping off onto the scaffold. "Just relax and have fun."

She reached behind her to feel for the strap release. "Um, how do I get out of this thing?"

"You can't." He grinned back at her. "I'll take you out of it when the float gets back."

Terri talked her boss into letting her have five minutes with her cousin, although she didn't know why she was bothering. Caine had done more harm to her career in one day than her father's lousy reputation had done in eight years.

Don't forget about Cort blowing the whistle on you, a snide little voice inside her head reminded her.

Yes, she owed Cort, too, but first she'd deal with family.

Caine was lounging in the interview room, idly sipping from a Styrofoam cup of water. The first thing Terri did after closing the door and locking it was slap the cup from his cuffed hands. "Don't you look so cozy. You having a good time, cos?"

"The best." He rested his hands on the table and regarded her with a slight smile. "Detective Ga gonna get your boyfriend to drop the assault charges so I don't sue the city. But I thought you were riding a desk from here on out, *chère*."

"You country dumb-ass. Garcia told you that to give the DA more time to get warrants to search your house and business."

He shrugged.

"Captain's given me five minutes to talk some sense into you." She dragged back a chair and sat down. "Time to stop playing, Caine. I know you wouldn't kill Marc LeClare, but you know who did that fire. I know you do."

He laughed and shook his head slowly.

Terri waited until he was finished. "I called Billy Tibbideau's wife. She wouldn't talk to me, so I called the manager of the trailer park and got the number of her best friend, who happens to live right next door. Lilah had a lot to say to me."

The humor faded from Caine's face. "Billy didn't do anything."

"Lilah saw Billy leave home before dawn on the morning of the fire. Before he left, she saw him loading some clear glass bottles and a can of gasoline in the back of his truck. She said she saw him come back later that day and get a shotgun. She also said you fired him." Terri leaned forward. "You didn't mention that, or why your punching hand is all bruised and cut up." She waited a beat before she added, "Feel free to jump in here anytime now."

"You always had a nice imagination, Therese. You should write books."

"I deal in reality, cos. Here's yours: The DA will ̶d you on the present charges for twenty-four hours, ̶e Garcia and the arson task force try to place you ̶ scene. They've got motive. They'll check with your men, your friends, and your enemies. They'll impound your truck and have forensics go over it with a fine-toothed comb. They'll show your photo around the warehouse district, talk to people who were there that morning. I'm guessing they'll find enough evidence and witnesses to indict. If you were anywhere near that warehouse when it burned, they will charge you as an accessory to the murder."

"Let them."

"Billy went to the warehouse district, didn't he? And you went after him. Did you try to stop him? Is that how you bashed up your hand?" When he didn't move an eyelash, she sighed. Now she knew how J. D. must have felt, trying to get answers out of Sable Duchesne. "Caine, I'm not going to let you go to jail because Billy Tibbideau killed that man and burned down that warehouse before you could stop him. But if you helped him, even in the tiniest way, I'll lock you up personally and toss the key in Lake Pontchartrain."

"Poor cousin. I was wrong about you." All the anger vanished from his eyes, and for a moment he looked a little sad. "Go back to work, Therese. There is nothing you can do for me now."

Garcia came in, looking as happy as Terri felt. "You've had your five, Ter." He went around the table. "Stand up, Mr. Gantry."

She got to her feet. "Herb, please. I just need a couple more minutes with him."

"Can't do it." He took out his keys and removed handcuffs. "Mr. Gantry has some good friends s[ome]where." To Caine he said, "You're free to go."

Terri blinked. "Wait a minute. Does the D[A know] about this?"

"The DA's springing him. All charges[...]

dropped." Garcia pocketed his keys on his way out. "Have a nice day."

Billy waited in his trailer, and drank the rest of his whiskey while he waited.

She left me.

He'd woken up in his truck to find his shotgun and shells gone. He'd walked into his trailer to find Cecilia gone, along with all her clothes. He'd gone to Lilah's and kicked in the door, but their neighbor had packed and left, too.

She left me. His damn thieving wife had run off. *For a dyke stripper.*

Cecilia had made a tragic mistake this time. Billy would find her eventually. Caine would understand— he might even help him look. Caine believed in the sanctity of marriage.

Had she been with Lilah all this time? Sneaking over there behind his back? He wouldn't put it past her. They said once a woman violated God's law by diddling with another woman, it ruined her forever.

She left me.

Billy never wanted to touch her again. He'd only do what had to be done, what any self-respecting man would do. As soon as he had his money—which would be any minute—he'd hunt those two bitches down and send them to burn in hell.

The phone rang, and he nearly tore it off the wall swering it. "Cecilia? You'd better get your ass on e right now—"

wasn't his wife. "Mr. Tibbideau, Sable Duchesne live."

we of Orpheus parade flowed out from the in slow but majestic procession. Sable could hear the sounds of a beautiful man's voice singing a famous Sinatra tune as the screams and the whistles erupted from the packed streets. Her own float was toward the end of the line, so she tried again to release herself from the brace strap.

She couldn't feel a snap or a tie or anything to tug on. "What did he do, sew me to it?"

Finally the *Gone with the Wind* float bumped over some potholes and onto the street, and Sable looked down to see the escort of street performers take position around the floating plantation home. They were dressed like Confederate and Union soldiers, and marched in double lines while spinning the rifles they carried.

"Hey, Scarlett!" a man in the crowd shouted. "Down here!" He wore a mask shaped like a weeping clown. "Throw me something!"

She plucked one of the bead strings from her forearm and tossed it to the delighted man. As soon as he caught it, a dozen other voices called to her and a flurry of hands stretched over the barricades.

"Throw me one!"

"Here, honey, right here!"

"I give a damn, beautiful!"

For a few minutes she concentrated on smiling and throwing her beads to the crowd; then something jogged her arm and she dropped some of the necklaces. The cinch strap caught her as she tried to bend over to get them at the same time that two hands clamped on her hips.

"Don't move."

Chapter Eleven

As soon as she heard his voice, Sable did the exact opposite of what he said—or she tried to. The strap held her bound to the brace rods. "Jean-Del. How did you know it was me?"

"I followed you from the cabin." He bent closer, putting his mouth next to her right ear. "And I told you I was done chasing you, Isabel."

Renewed anger flooded through her. "I don't need your help. Your kind of help gets APBs put out on me."

"You need new lines, baby. No, what did Rhett say to her in the movie? 'You need kissing, and often.'" He used his teeth on the curve of her ear, biting down to almost the point of pain before kissing the stinging spot. "'And by someone who knows how.'"

In front of her, people in masks and costumes shrieked and waved, still calling for her to throw them something.

"Go on." J. D.'s low voice turned harsh. "At least give *them* what they want."

She felt him press closer, and her hand trembled as she tossed out several of the gaudy strings. She glanced over her shoulder, shocked to see that he had donned a mask as well—black edged with gold, a pirate's mask. That and his black T-shirt and trousers made him almost invisible against the black satin backdrop behind them. "What are you doing here?"

"'How fickle is woman.'" His breath touched the back of her neck. "Why did you run this time? Decide you couldn't go through with it? Finished using me?"

"I never used you." She twisted against the strap, straining away from him. "I can take care of myself. I don't need anything from you."

"Wrong." His hands pressed against the velvet folds of her skirt, sliding down to her outer thighs. "You're just like her, you know. 'You're like the thief who isn't the least bit sorry he stole, but is terribly, terribly sorry he's going to jail.'"

"I'm not Scarlett O'Hara and I am not going to jail. I didn't do anything wrong." If she got him angry enough, maybe he'd leave her alone. "But you are. Why don't you run on home, now, before your mama finds out you're trifling with swamp trash again?"

"Trifling?" He laughed, low and nasty. "Baby, I don't trifle."

She thought of how he'd touched her back at the cottage, using and tormenting her to get what he wanted. "If you want to get laid, you can go pick up someone in the street," she said, making her voice cold as she threw out another string.

"Why cat around when what I want is right here?" He reached down and grabbed the back of her skirt hoop, lifting it until the cool night air washed against the back of her thighs. "You want it as much as I do. Is that why you ran away? Because you're afraid of this?"

"No." She bucked against his arm, and then went still as he splayed a hand over her hip and pressed her bottom against the front of his jeans—which were open. All the blood in her body rushed in two directions—to her face, and down between her thighs. "Don't do it, Jean-Del."

"If you hold still and throw your beads," he murmured against her ear as he pushed his hand under the elastic of her panties, "no one will see."

"You can't—" She looked around wildly, but the street performers were watching the spectators, and the other performers on the float were too busy laughing and tossing out beads to pay any attention to her. Then she felt his hand yank at her panties, ripping the side seam. "Please. I'm sorry. I'll do whatever you want."

" 'You're such a child,' " he said, still quoting Clark Gable. " 'You think that by saying, 'I'm sorry,' all the past can be corrected.' "

"I'll come back with you."

"You'll come right here and right now." He dropped her torn underwear, and it landed on her right foot. "And I'm going to make you scream for me when you do."

She couldn't free herself—she couldn't even turn around. Hundreds of people were staring straight at them. This was beyond decadent, beyond insane, and yet she had never felt more terrified—or excited—in her life.

"That's it." He worked his fingers against her, parting her folds and pressing them up into her softness. "You're wet, baby. Wet as I am hard." He brought her right hand back behind her, and forced her palm against the open zipper of his jeans. His erection nudged her fingers, and she reflexively curled them around the swollen length of him.

A pair of teenage boys gawked up at her. The girl between them yelled, "Throw me something, lady!"

She flung all of the strings in her free hand to the girl, making the teens squeal with delight.

"Generous." J. D. pushed through the circle of her fingers, nudging her legs apart with his knee. "What are you going to do for the rest of the parade? Besides ride me?"

Sable couldn't believe he would go through with it, even when he tugged her skirt back to better conceal what he was doing to her under it. Then she felt the weight of him between her thighs, the full satiny dome of his penis following the curve of her bottom, hunting until he seated himself against the elliptical part of her that was already slick and pulsing and aching to take him.

"J. D." Lights and colors and sound swirled around her in a dizzy collage. "I can't do this."

"You will." He didn't try to enter her. Instead, he stroked that silent mouth, gliding over it to nudge the hard knot of her clit before drawing back to nest against her once more. When she tried to move to accept him, he used his hands to hold her hips in place.

He wasn't making love to her. He was punishing her, torturing her—and the whole world was watching him do it. "Please, J. D."

"Please . . . what? Stop? Go on?" She could feel the throb of his heart beating in the rigid column, so hard it made goose bumps rise on the delicate skin of her inner thighs. "Be more specific, baby. You never want to talk to me—well, now you have to. Tell me you want this."

Would he stop if she said yes? *Maybe.* Would she scream if he did? *Yes.* "I can't."

"So shy." He licked the tiny beads of sweat from the back of her neck as he put his hand back under the skirt and cupped her from the front, still stroking her from behind. His fingertips spread her, exposing more of her for quick, glancing prods. "No one will hear you but me."

If he didn't do more soon, everyone in New Orleans would hear her shriek. "I want you. I want you to do it. Just do it."

"I can make you come." He used a featherlight touch to tease her, caressing her clit with a few strokes before easing them away. "Like this."

She shook her head. People were screaming at her and she didn't know what to do. Her face was burning up, and she was breathing so fast it sounded like she was sobbing. "All of it. Please."

He shifted, angling himself against her now. "More. More of me?"

"Yes." She jerked her hips, but he still controlled her with his hands. "What else do you want? Do you want me to beg?"

"I want you to tell me what you want." He pushed against her, insistent. "Tell me everything."

Tears of frustration spilled down her cheeks. "I don't know what you want me to say."

"You know." He moved his mouth to the side of her throat. Against it, he murmured, "Say, 'Give me your cock, J. D.'"

"I want you, Jean-Del."

"You're not listening." He breached her a scant inch, just opening her enough to make her forget to breathe. "Say, 'I need you to make me come, J. D.'"

Desperate, she dragged in air. "I need you, Jean-Del."

"Last chance." He pushed in another inch. "Say, 'I want you to fuck me, J. D.'"

"No." She turned her head until her neck nearly kinked, so she could see into the slits of his mask.

What they were doing was erotic and dangerous, but it wasn't only lust. Gently she brushed her lips over his. "I want you to love me, Jean-Delano. I want to feel you inside me, loving me, I—" A cry jolted out of her as he thrust into her, hard and fast.

Her vision blurred as one of the street performers came over to the float. He was saying something, asking her something. Was she all right? Did she need something?

"Beads," J. D. said against her ear.

"Beads," she blurted out, showing the performer her empty hands. "I don't have any more . . . beads."

"Here." The soldier tossed up another packet of necklaces and golden krewe coins. "Smile, honey— you're the prettiest girl in the parade."

She couldn't breathe until the man returned to his position in the line, and then her body clamped down involuntarily.

"No." J. D. used his hands to move her hips as he worked his way in, past the convoluted, constricted tissues. "Don't you fight me now."

The burning, stretching ache grew almost too much to bear, but he didn't stop, even when her cry became a strangled whimper. It seemed to go on for an eternity, and then she felt his thighs against hers and the coarse brush of his body hair against her tense flesh.

A low groan rumbled from him as he held her impaled on him, not moving except for his chest heaving against her back. "God Almighty . . ."

Show tunes were blaring, the crowds shouting, the performers dancing, but the slow restoration of the heat and need inside her made her blind and deaf to everything but Jean-Delano—and he was shaking now, his fingers dragging up and digging into her waist as he fought for another kind of control. She couldn't see him, couldn't draw his mouth to hers, couldn't comfort him.

There was only one thing she could do—move.

Slowly Sable lifted herself, stretched up on the balls of her feet until there was a small space between their bodies; then she lowered herself again. He didn't try to stop her, and the motion eased a little of the tightness. She tried it again, biting her lip. Relaxing allowed him to press deeper inside her but the discomfort ebbed and a different kind of throb began.

"Do you know what you're doing?" His voice grated on the words.

"No." She made a tiny circle with her hips, adjusting their fit. "Do you like it?" He muttered something low and filthy in French, and a strange laugh emerged from her throat as she tore open the bag with shaking fingers and threw out more beads to the reaching hands beneath them. "I thought so."

J. D.'s breath went ragged as he moved with her, sliding back by gentle degrees as she lifted, and moving up into her as she came down again. She felt herself go liquid around him, easing the way for his return. At the same time, the pulsing ache intensified, spreading from the gliding friction created by the moving union of their bodies, up into her belly and her breasts. She felt smothered by the green velvet dress now, beads of sweat gathering in the hollow of her breasts and under the confines of her wig.

He tightened his grip at her waist, still moving slowly. "Does it still hurt?"

Breathless, she shook her head.

"Good." He reached up and took off the hat and the wig, dropping them to the side before combing his fingers through her damp hair. "Be better if you were under me."

"I can't wait that long," she whispered, bearing down on him until he was lodged impossibly deep inside her. She looked down at the avid faces, wondering how she looked to them. Then he put his arm around her waist and she didn't care anymore. "I need you now."

"I'm here." And he was, his big frame cradling her as he pushed into her body, filling her faster, stroking the ache that was now eating her up alive. "I'll make it better, baby."

He did more than that—he made the Quarter and the tourists and the city dwindle down to a distant hum as he loved her. Every memory that she had carried inside her from their youthful affair paled as well. The boy she had loved had teased and cherished her, but the man he had become gave her more, and demanded the same.

He's going to take all I am this time, she thought, just as her body hurtled up through the darkness to smash through icy-hot waves of wracking pleasure. *I'm going to give it to him.*

"Say my name," he muttered, his mouth hot on her throat and his hips jerking against her faster.

"Jean-Del." The plastic bag ripped apart in her hands, spilling beads and gold coins down the front of her skirt.

His grip tightened to the point of pain. "You're never going to leave me again. Swear to me."

"No . . ." She writhed against him, trying to hold on while he buried himself in her, then convulsing as a second volley of fiery delight rushed in, eager to burn and consume her. The golden coins left in her hands bruised her fingers as she closed them tight. "I swear, I won't."

"Isabel." He clutched her as he drove into her one

last time, and then shuddered as he pumped his seed into her. "You're mine," he rasped against her cheek. *"Mine."*

Sable stretched out her arms, scattering the last of the krewe coins to the eager hands below. She was again, as she had always been, his.

Caine walked out of the police station to see Billy and John waiting by the curb for him in front of his truck. His former foreman was grinning like a gator circling a sinking pirogue. Caine could smell the liquor on him before he got within three feet of the men, but that didn't surprise him. Jack Daniel's had been Billy's mouthwash of choice since they were boys, and no amount of threats from Caine had ever persuaded him to give it up.

"Boss." John tossed his keys to him but wouldn't meet his gaze.

Billy, on the other hand, had only a little difficulty doing that, and only because he was drunk. The black eye and bruises Caine had given him were more colorful than ever, but he held out a bottle of beer in an unsteady hand.

"Where y'at, Gantry?" He looked up at the lettering over the entrance. "Oh, right, you been in jail this time. Guess what? My wife left me for a lesbo." He laughed as if that was the funniest joke he'd ever heard.

Caine ignored him and checked over his shoulder before glaring at John. "What the hell is he doing here?"

"He showed up at the pier, looking for you." John shrugged. "I figured, kill him or bring him along."

"What, you think them cops gonna come out here and arrest me? After they done had to let *you* go?" Billy laughed and weaved a little as he shuffled toward the steps. "Lemme take care this. I tell them how it was. I know all about it."

Caine was familiar with his former foreman's stages of drunkenness, which ranged from rampant outrage to sodden self-hatred. Evidently he'd drunk enough to feel guilty about what he'd done. "Not now, Billy."

"No, I swear, I'll do it right this time." He waved his arm back at them. "You can have all the money. Cee, too, if you want her. She'd no damn good in bed, but maybe the two of them'll go at it and let you watch."

Caine caught Billy around the waist before he could mount the first step. "We're going to see Cecilia tomorrow, when you're sober." He took the beer out of his hand and spun him back toward the truck. "We got to talk about other things first."

The drunken man scowled. "I tried to talk to you and you wailed the tar out of me for it." He peered up at Caine. "You know I was only fixing things like you said you wanted them."

Terri or Garcia could come out of the station at any moment, and Caine couldn't risk them hauling Billy in for more questions. He handed the beer to John and scanned the immediate area for cops. "We got other things to fix now."

"Well, shit, if you don't want it, give it to me," Billy said, swiping at the bottle. "I sure as hell—"

"Take a nap, *cher.*" Caine drove his fist into Billy's jaw with a quick, snapping punch. The foreman crumpled like a dry-rotted net.

John helped Caine drag Billy over to the truck and hoist his limp body into the back of the open bed. "They really drop the charges?"

"I made a deal." Caine went around to the cab and got inside. "Anyone find the cop or Isabel?"

"Lacy said Hilaire Martin got them out to the lake

on her boat." John nodded in the direction of Lake Pontchartrain. "Looks like they were at your cousin's cottage on the north shore for a bit, but when Darel and Caleb got there, they were gone."

Caine tried to imagine where Sable could have gone. With the cop helping her, she could be anywhere. "She'll call Hilaire. Tell Lacy we need to know when she does, but from where." He checked the rearview, turned around, and swore.

Billy was gone.

He'd just had her, and all J. D. wanted to do was stay inside Sable and take her a second time. Thinking of that and all the things he wanted to do to her made him hard again. But the parade was nearly at the end of the Quarter, where he knew a small army of reporters waited to film the celebrities on the lead floats. Slowly he slipped from her body and adjusted himself, zipping up his jeans.

"Jean-Del." She reached back for him.

He caught her hand and pushed the hoop skirt back down. "We have to get off this thing."

"I can't—they strapped me in."

He found and released the strap from the support brace, and then had to grab her as she sagged. He'd been too damn rough with her. "How bad did I hurt you?"

"I'm okay, just a little dizzy." She regained her balance but kept a steadying grip on his arm. "Where will we go?"

He looked ahead, and saw an opportunity in a parked delivery truck narrowing the road. They were too far from his apartment, and it was probably staked out anyway. "I'll find us a place for the night."

"Every hotel in town is booked solid," she said, biting at her lip.

He wanted to bite her lip, too, but settled for a quick kiss. "I know a place. I'm going to get down up there." He pointed to the truck. "Wait until I'm on the ground before you jump."

She measured the distance to the ground, and then regarded him. "Don't drop me."

"Never." He touched her cheek, saw the answering flare in her eyes. "Stop looking at me like that."

She smiled a little. "Then stop touching me."

J. D. watched the street performers anticipate the impasse and march ahead to make room. As the procession reached the narrow lane and the float slowed, he dropped down behind the truck. Sable waited until he held his arms out before she did the same, and he caught her in a bundle of velvet.

"Come on." He set her on her feet and led her around the truck, concealing them from the eyes of the spectators and the street performers. "We have to get that costume off you—it's too conspicuous."

"You ripped off my panties," she reminded him. "All I have left on underneath is a bra." Then she looked over his shoulder and gasped.

The driver of the truck, who was balancing twelve crates of fruit on a hand truck, had stopped to listen in.

J. D. grinned at the man. "Couldn't help myself."

The driver eyed Sable from her tousled red hair to the rumpled hem of her skirt and sighed with delight. "*Laissez les bons temps rouler.*" He put down the hand truck and shrugged out of his jacket, holding it out to J. D. "Here—this keep her warm until you can."

"*Merci, mon ami.*" He quickly wrapped the overlarge jacket around Sable before he pulled her through the crowded confines of an open bar to the exit on the other side of the block. From there it was three blocks to the hotel he wanted.

Sable looked around at the darkened streets and stayed close to him. "Are you sure about this?"

"I know somebody." He spotted the neon sign for the Lagniappe Inn, which flashed a red NO VACANCY. "Over here."

"You take me to the nicest places." Her laugh was as soft and husky as her voice.

"Trust me, baby." He stopped for a moment and cradled her face between his hands. "In a few minutes you won't even remember what state you're in."

"You can top making love in the middle of a Mardi Gras parade?" She looked down as he took out his cuffs and jangled them; then she drew in a quick breath. "Okay, I guess you can."

The clerk barely glanced up when J. D. approached the shabby front desk. "We ain't got no rooms, mister."

"Ronnie around?"

The clerk turned his head toward the open door behind him. "Ronnie! Man out here to see you."

Ronald Porter, a short black man with a woebegone expression, wandered out. "J. D." His gaze flickered over Sable. "Hey, I didn't know she was a working girl."

"She's not." He nodded toward the mostly empty key rack on the wall behind the clerk. "I need a room for tonight."

Ronnie's face went from sad to agonized. "Man, you gotta be kidding me. I got a busload of coeds due in any minute."

"Have a couple of them double up." When he still hesitated, J. D. added, "I do a floor-by-floor and find out you got more than coeds doubling up in here, you go back for a six-month vacation behind bars."

"No need for that." Ronnie grabbed a key from the rack and slapped it on the desk. "But you gotta be out by nine a.m., or take in a coupla roommates."

"Thanks." J. D. nodded toward the back room. "Let me see your lost and found."

Ronnie brought out a cardboard box full of clothes and turned to Sable. "You lose something, honey?"

She smiled politely. "You could say that." She glanced at J. D. "But I'm hoping to get it back where it was real soon."

J. D. nearly dropped the box. "You will." He rummaged through the pile until he collected what Sable would need for a change, then handed the perspiring man a fifty. "Order us in some dinner from Tailor's Dance. Call me when they deliver—I'll come and get it." He guided Sable back to the door leading to the first-floor rooms.

"What y'all want?" Ronnie called after him.

Sable reached up, putting her lips next to his ear. "You don't want me to tell him." Then she sucked lightly on his earlobe.

His head spun, his blood roared, and his zipper was about to castrate him. "Whatever stays hot for a while," he called back to Ronnie.

They made it inside the room, and he had enough sanity to throw the dead bolt and turn on the television. Then he dropped the borrowed clothes on top of the rickety dresser and took her in his arms, filling his hands with emerald velvet. "How much you think this outfit is worth?"

"I don't know." She pressed herself against him. "But I'm a good seamstress."

"Thank God." J. D. tore until he got to her skin. "I have to see you this time—all of you."

He backed her toward the bed, working her bra

straps down the sides of her arms, watching as the satiny cups peeled away from her breasts. They were slightly fuller now, but just as smooth and firm as when he'd first put his hands on them ten years ago. He brushed his fingers over her pretty, dusky pink nipples and hissed in a breath when they tightened and darkened for him.

"Jean-Del." She tugged at the bottom of his T-shirt, trying to drag it up. "I want to see you, too."

"Later." He pushed her back on the bed and tore off his shirt before dropping down on top of her. If he didn't get back inside her in the next minute, it wouldn't be for lack of effort.

"So shy," she mocked softly, curling a leg around the back of his and rolling until he was on his back and she lay spread-eagled on top of him. With a beguiling smile she propped her hands against his chest and slid back until the heat between her thighs rested against the rigid bulge under his zipper. She shimmied against him. "I want to see you now."

He pushed a hand into his front pocket. "Where are my cuffs?"

"You mean these?" She dangled them over his face, then snatched them out of reach when he grabbed at them. "Be good or I'll use them on you."

"I'll be good." He pushed his hips up, grinding himself against her. "Good and hard and deep for you."

"Oh, yes." Her eyelids drooped as she undulated against him for a moment. The cuffs fell somewhere beside them on the bed. She leaned down, brushing the hard tips of her breasts against his heaving chest, then slid back again. "Later."

Later, hell. "Baby, it's *now* or never."

"Now there are other things I have to do." She

reached down between them, popping open the button at his waist. "Things that need my immediate attention." She tugged at the zipper, easing it open over his erection, and then slowly pulled his jeans and shorts down to the middle of his thighs. His cock sprang up, full and still damp from taking her on the float, and as her warm breath touched it he curled his hands into the bedspread. "Wouldn't you agree?"

"Touch me."

"Touch you . . . like this?" She watched his face as she ran her fingertips in a feathery caress from the fluted opening at the top down to the base of his shaft. "Or like . . . this?" She bent her head, and did the same with her tongue before lifting up to look at him again.

"Christ." He tangled a hand in her hair, urging her lips toward the swollen, straining head. "Put your mouth on me."

Her breath caressed him again for an agonizing moment before her lips parted and she drew him into the incredibly soft, wet heat of her mouth. It took every ounce of his self-control not to thrust himself deeper as she gently sucked on him.

"Sable." The way she used her tongue made him groan and wrap her hair around his fist. They'd never tried this back in college, and from her tentative touch he suspected she hadn't much experience with it since. "Have you done this before?"

"No." She met his gaze, concerned now. "Am I awful?"

He wanted to laugh, but settled for a tender smile. "No, baby. You're doing fine."

She drew back and reached for his other hand, then brought it to her face. She stared up across his knotted abdomen at him as she rubbed her cheek against his palm. "Show me how."

His eyes narrowed to slits as her mouth took him again, and he guided her head up and down. "Don't try to take too much. Tell me when to stop." Pushing into her lips this way, inch by slow inch, was sheer torture—but he wouldn't hurt her this time.

She wasn't stopping, though. She kept taking more and more of him, sucking at him and rubbing her tongue along the sides of him as he glided over her tongue and deep into the slick, tight pleasure of her mouth. He heard and felt the sounds she made—a low, yearning, eager hum that spilled from her throat and caressed him as much as her lips.

"Isabel." He didn't want it to end, but he felt his balls drawing up and tightening and knew he was only a minute from exploding. He tried to urge her away. "Baby, stop, I'm gonna come."

She wouldn't let go of him—if anything she drew him deeper. Seeing her mouth sliding over him, feeling the wet heat and the rhythmic tug, and hearing the sounds she made pushed him over the edge. J. D. held her head as the first surge shot out of him, and still she sucked and swallowed, taking everything he gave her.

When he had shuddered out the last, she closed her eyes and rested her cheek against his hip, letting him slide from her lips to the gentle cradle of her fingers. For a long time he lay like that with her, waiting for his heart to stop trying to jump through the wall of his chest.

"Jean-Del?"

He rubbed his hand against her hair. "Hmmmm?"

"Why didn't you teach me to do this before?" she murmured, stroking him.

"I don't know. I think we would have gotten to it eventually." He drew her up into his arms, turning so that they lay on their sides, and brushed a tangle of hair back from her misty eyes. "Oh, baby, don't cry on me now."

"Can't help it." She blinked. "All these years, and I never stopped missing you. God, we've lost so much time."

He caught the first tear as it beaded on her lashes, then transferred it to her bottom lip, spreading it across the slightly swollen curve before he kissed it away. "But we found each other, and I'm never letting you go again."

She kissed him back; then she went still and raised her head. "Look."

The late news broadcast was on the television, and a photo of Caine Gantry was featured beside the an chorwoman. J. D. reached for the remote on the side table and raised the volume.

"—charges against the commercial fisherman have been dropped. Officials refuse to comment, but a source inside the NOPD claimed lack of evidence as the reason Gantry was released."

Chapter Twelve

As Cort pulled up the old Crowley parish arson case files, one of the task force investigators looked around the edge of his door. "Marshal, I got some guy on the phone, says he wants to talk only to you."

"Take a message."

"He said he has some real good *lagniappe* for you."

Cort's head snapped up. "I'll take it. Close the door." As soon as he did, he picked up the phone and punched the blinking hold button. "Porter?"

"Nah, this is George. I work for Ronnie." The voice was oily-smooth. "So I hear you lost a brother. Any money in finding him?"

"Depends. How do you know it's my brother?"

"He's diddling the pretty redhead who got her picture in the paper."

Cort heard someone arguing on the other side of his office door. One of the voices was Terri's. "Where?"

"What's in it for me?"

"Fifty."

"Maybe you got something extra for the redhead?"

Christ, the asshole wanted to bargain with him. "A hundred and I won't kill you."

"Hey, now, easy." George uttered a nervous laugh. "Your brother and the girl are holed up here for the night. Ronnie'll be here until five a.m.—then he goes to get beignets. Best come then for them."

Cort's door swung open, and Terri strode inside. "Right. I'll be there."

"Don't forget my money." George hung up the phone.

The tall brunette kicked the door shut behind her. "You and I need to talk."

He sat back in his chair. "No, we don't, but don't let that stop you, Detective."

She stepped in front of his desk, shoving a chair out of her way. "I'm not a detective these days; I'm a freaking secretary, thanks to you."

"Take it up with Pellerin."

She stared at him the way she would a pile of dog shit she'd just stepped in. "I don't get you. I really don't. I thought you cared more about your brother than the goddamn rule book."

"I'll deal with J. D."

She slung a hand toward the window behind him. "J. D. is out there, somewhere, and I'm pretty sure he's in trouble. You can't do this one by the numbers, Cortland."

"If you're upset about losing the case—"

She slapped her hands on his desk and leaned over it. "I don't care about the case. *Fuck* the case. But your brother is my partner and my best friend, and he deserves better than this from you."

Anger had made splotches of color appear under her tan. She hadn't bothered with makeup or jewelry, and she smelled like cigarettes and coffee. And he wanted nothing more than to reach out and grab her by her short brown hair and haul her the rest of the way over the desk.

Realizing that made him rise to his feet and grab his

jacket. "I've got somewhere to go. I'll walk you out to your car."

"Son of a bitch." Slowly she rocked back on her heels. "You know where he is."

And she was too damn perceptive. He found his keys. "I said I'll take care of him."

She blocked his way to the door. *"Where is J. D.?"*

"Go home and get some sleep." His head snapped to the side as her small, knotted fist connected with his nose, nearly breaking it. He caught the second swing and used the momentum to whirl her around and shove her into the wall, where he held her.

It wasn't where he wanted her, but it would have to do. "I could have you busted down to a meter maid for this."

She made a harsh sound. "Beats the typing pool."

Weariness and the blood trickling from his nose made him release her. As soon as he did, she turned and leaned back against the wall.

"Nice move." Her hand went to a reddening mark on her cheekbone. "Maybe you can show me that one sometime."

"Terri—"

She shook her head. "I've got somewhere to be myself. See you, Marshal."

Before he could say another word, she yanked open the door and strode out of his office.

Sable heard the phone ring but didn't move. She didn't think she could even if she wanted to—*did J. D. take off the handcuffs after that last time?*—but then she tested her wrists and found them free. The mattress shifted as he rolled off it and went to the phone.

She yawned and rolled over, burying her face in the pillow. Next time she'd cuff *him* to the bed.

A few minutes later something touched her bare back. "Wake up, sweetheart."

Sable felt weight depress her side of the bed and opened her eyes. "Jean-Del." She rolled over onto her back and stretched, sighing as her muscles sang with a delicious soreness. He was already dressed. "What time is it?"

"Almost dawn." He looked toward the door. "I need you to get up, baby. We've got to move."

She frowned, then propped herself up. "What's wrong?"

"Ronnie's clerk blew the whistle on us. They're coming for us." He handed her the clothes he'd taken from the lost-and-found box. "Get dressed as fast as you can."

"The police?" His nod woke her up the rest of the way, and she began jerking on the old clothes. The jeans were too baggy and the T-shirt was too tight, but she got them on in record time and found her shoes. "They're coming to arrest me?"

"I just need a few hours to straighten things out." He checked his gun before placing it in his shoulder holster, and then came over and put a roll of bills in her hand. "Go over to the Café du Monde and stay there until the tourists start coming out. When they do, take a bus, not a taxi. Go to Hilaire's and stay there."

"I'm not leaving you."

He stroked her cheek with his hand. "I'll catch up." He took a dark blue bandanna from his pocket and folded it in a triangle, then tied it over her hair. "I'm going out through the lobby. There's a side entrance down the other end of the hall—you go out that way." He kissed her brow. "Be careful."

She sat down abruptly on the edge of the bed. "I can't do this."

"You have to." He went to the door and opened it an inch to look out, then held his hand out to her. She went to him. "I'll meet you at Hilaire's as soon as I can." He squeezed her hand in his. "Stay out of sight." He brushed his mouth over hers, then slipped out of the room.

Sable glanced around the edge of the door and saw him talking to a dark-haired coed who had just come out of a room two doors down. The intoxicated girl giggled and nodded, then went with him toward the lobby.

Carefully Sable edged out of the room and headed in the opposite direction, walking toward the side-entrance doors. She could hear sirens growing louder. Sweat trickled down her back as she walked out onto the uneven sidewalk and crossed the street, then walked quickly down the block.

A police car whizzed past her but didn't stop.

Sable walked into the first open bar she came to, where some hard-core partyers were still drinking and dancing to Jelly Roll Morton. She went through the crowd to the other entrance on the opposite side of the building, and saw the street beyond was empty.

From there she could see the front of the Lagniappe Inn, where J. D. and the coed were surrounded by a dozen officers and a man in an NOFD jacket. The latter she recognized as Cort, J. D.'s brother. They were standing toe-to-toe and shouting at each other. That stopped when the coed bent over and threw up.

Darting across the street and keeping her head down, Sable turned her back on J. D. and the police and headed at a fast walk toward Jackson Square.

"His truck isn't here." Lilah sighed as she pulled up

in front of Cecilia and Billy's trailer. "We'd better make this fast anyway."

"I just want my photo albums." Cecilia sat up in back and looked over the front seat. "You can stay in the car."

"No, I'm sticking with you." Lilah smiled at her and picked up the shotgun from the floorboards. "Don't look so scared this is the last time you'll ever have to see this place again."

Cecilia wouldn't feel safe until she left Billy for good, but Lilah was helping a lot. The two of them were going all the way to California, where Lilah said she had a sister who would put them up until they found a place of their own. The sister owned a couple of concession stands on the beach and promised jobs for both of them.

It felt like the weight of the world had been lifted off her shoulders.

As she took out the keys to the trailer, Cecilia's hands shook. "I know it's silly to want a bunch of old pictures, but they're all I have left of my family."

"It's not silly." Lilah followed her inside, then bumped into her back. "What—" She looked past Cecilia, then lifted the shotgun.

Billy jerked it from her hand. "Hello, ladies."

The dodge worked beautifully. With the help of the coed, J. D. was able to decoy the police long enough for Sable to get away from the hotel. Now he rode in the back of his brother's car, mainly to have time to think what his next move should be.

"You'll have to file a statement."

"Terri can do it," J. D. told his brother. "I don't have time for the paperwork."

"You've got plenty." Cort eyed him in the rearview

mirror. "You've been suspended from duty, and the only reason you're not in cuffs is because of me."

J. D. had expected the suspension, and still it pissed him off. "You want me to thank you?"

"I want you to tell me what the hell you think you're doing." When he didn't answer, his brother dragged a hand through his hair. "Jesus Christ, J. D."

J. D. didn't want to think about Sable. The fact that she was out there alone again scared the shit out of him. "Dad talk to you about checking the arson files?"

"Yeah. I was pulling them last night when I got word on you." Cort dragged a hand through his short brown hair. "You're chasing a dead end; no arsonist waits twenty-five years between fires."

That remained to be seen. "Terri come up with anything?"

"Terri's off the case and bordering on suspension herself." He thought for a moment. "You used her place down on the lake to stash the girl, didn't you? Shit."

J. D. stared out the window, watching the buildings go by. When Cort didn't make the turn for the station, he frowned. "You forget where I have to turn in my gun and badge?"

"We're going home. The station is crawling with press, and Mother is frantic."

J. D. didn't want to deal with his mother. "Take me to the restaurant."

Cort glanced back at him. "Dad can't bail you out of this."

"Just do it."

When they arrived at the service entrance to his father's restaurant, J. D. climbed out of Cort's SUV and slammed the door. "Thanks."

"Hey."

He looked back. "What?"

Cort looked as tired as J. D. felt. "I want to help."

"Then go and check the files." J. D. met his brother's gaze. "I need proof that the same perp was behind both fires, Cort—find it for me."

He strode through the back entrance and into the frantic hive of activity in the huge kitchen. His father was at the far end, sorting through crates of vegetables and tossing what didn't meet his standards into a discard bin.

J. D. saw the same lines of strain and exhaustion on his father's face. This case wasn't just tearing his own life apart; it was ripping his family to pieces. "Hey, Dad."

Louie looked up and knocked over a crate of peppers, reaching for his son. "Jean-Del." He took him in a tight embrace, then looked over his shoulder. "Where is Isabel? Is she all right?"

"She's okay—she's waiting for me. Dad, I need a favor." He pulled his father into a storeroom, away from the curious eyes and ears of the staff, and filled him in on what had happened, and then added, "I need you to find Remy Duchesne and talk to him."

"That the man who raised Isabel?" Louie frowned. "Why?"

"He's the only person who knows about the fire when she was a baby. I need to know everything about it, what he remembers, who he thinks might have paid Bud Gantry to set it." J. D. told his father how to get to the Martins'. "They should be able to help you find him."

His father sighed. "You really think he'll talk to me instead of you?"

"You're not sleeping with his daughter."

"Ah. Good point. Here." His father dug out his wallet, removed all the bills from it, and put them in J. D.'s hand. "Don't go home—your mama is on the warpath, and your scalp is number one on her to-skin list."

"Thanks, Dad." He hugged his father, then checked his watch. "I'll keep in touch."

After calling her cousin's store and getting no answer, Sable sat at the table closest to the pay phone outside the Café du Monde. While she waited, she sipped her café au lait and watched a mime pretending to clean an invisible window. Strings of beads hung from the branches of nearly every tree in Jackson Square, like strange Christmas decorations. Their colorful glitter reminded her of the night before.

Jean-Delano. She clutched her coffee between her cold hands. Not knowing what was happening to him made her feel sick.

"Keep up the good work." A street cleaner using a pointed trash stick to pick up napkins, plastic go-cups, and other Mardi Gras debris left on the sidewalk called out to the mime as he passed by. "We got to make everything sparkle, son."

Sable went back to the pay phone and tried to call her cousin again.

This time, Hilaire answered. "Where are you?"

"I'm on my way to you. Are there any police at the store? Has J. D. called you?"

"No. That woman cop called me yesterday, but I didn't tell her anything. J. D. isn't with you?"

"We had to split up. Hil, I need to stay there until he can come and get me, okay?"

"Don't even ask. You want me to come and pick you up?"

"No, I need you to stay there in case J. D. calls. I'm going to take the bus so it'll be a little while." She looked down at herself. "And I really need some clean clothes."

"I'll take care of it. Just be careful."

Sable hung up the phone and threw away her half-empty cup, then stopped to pitch a dollar into the mime's collection basket. When he offered an elaborate bow, she pointed to his invisible wall. "You missed a spot."

With a grin he went back to work with his invisible rag.

She caught a bus running mostly tour groups out to the Atchafalaya Basin, and settled in for the long ride. The hum of the bus's engine nearly made her doze off a few times, but she forced herself to stay awake. As they left the city, her heart seemed to constrict. She didn't want to leave J. D. behind; she never wanted to be parted from him again.

I love you, she mouthed silently as they passed the city limits sign. *Hurry back to me, J. D.*

She had to walk a quarter mile from the stop to Hilaire's store, but it felt good to stretch her legs. The sun had risen high enough to chase off the morning dew and make her take off the trucker's jacket, and when she saw the familiar hand-lettered MARTIN'S COUNTRY STORE sign she picked up her pace.

The store wasn't supposed to open for another hour, but the lights were on and the front door was unlocked. Sable went in, hoping to smell coffee brewing. "Hilaire?"

There were twenty men standing in various spots around the shop. All of them looked at her without smiling. Sable backed toward the door, but before she could run someone seized her from behind. She screamed.

Caine Gantry spun her around. "About time you came home, Isabel."

Elizabet approved of the courtesy the reporter from the *Daily News* showed toward Laure as she interviewed her about Marc's murder. Still, she hovered nearby, ready to offer support for Laure or chastisement for the reporter as might be needed.

"Mrs. LeClare, our affiliate, channel seven, would like to take a statement from you for the noon broadcast. The citizens of New Orleans held your husband in high regard, and I know they would appreciate any words you could offer them. We can do it right now, if you like." The reporter gestured to the photographer, who had also brought in a video camera.

"I never was very good on camera," Laure said slowly, then looked to Elizabet for direction.

Elizabet was torn—her friend obviously didn't like the idea, and under other circumstances she wouldn't have permitted it. Yet she needed her to go on the air in order to condemn Sable Duchesne and her ridiculous claims.

The reporter followed Laure's gaze. "Would Mrs. Gamble like to make a joint statement with you? I know her son is missing—perhaps if she gave us some details, we might be able to help? . . ."

"I would feel better about this, if you're up to it, Elizabet," Laure admitted.

She could do it instead of Laure. This solved her problem perfectly.

"A very brief statement," she said, and came over to sit by Laure as the reporter told the photographer to set up the video camera. Elizabet arranged her skirt and brushed a piece of Laure's hair behind her ear before she gave the reporter a stern look. "There will be no questions, you understand. Laure will address the citizens, and then I will make my statement."

"Yes, ma'am, of course." The reporter, knowing she was getting an exclusive, would have agreed to anything. She nodded to the cameraman, then said to Laure, "Just start speaking whenever you're ready, Mrs. LeClare."

Laure smiled painfully at the camera. "My family and I are very grateful for the outpouring of sympathy and condolence that we have received from our friends here in New Orleans. Marc was a wonderful husband and a great man, and I know you share in our loss. Please keep us in your prayers, and thank you."

The camera turned slightly as the reporter nodded to Elizabet.

"My friend Laure has lost her husband, and the state of Louisiana has lost one of our finest citizens. In times such as these, prayer is our only refuge. My son Lieutenant Jean-Delano Gamble was investigating Marc LeClare's murder and has since disappeared, pursuing a young woman who has claimed to be Marc's daughter. This is simply not true. Isabel Duchesne is an accomplished liar, and this is not the first time she has inflicted herself on innocent people."

Elizabet felt Laure stiffen next to her, but continued on. "Ten years ago this young woman wantonly attacked a group of students at Tulane University, for which she was expelled. You know from the newspapers that she was the only person found at the scene of Marc's murder. Now she has lured my son into the bayou, and to be honest, I fear for his life." She blinked real tears back. "Isabel Duchesne has no respect for others, and whatever lies she tells when she is caught, I hope that the people of the New Orleans will not be deceived by this hateful woman. I personally will not rest until my son is found, and Isabel Duchesne is prosecuted for the crimes she has committed." She nodded to the reporter.

"That was incredible, Mrs. Gamble." The reporter looked ready to faint. "Mrs. LeClare, thank you as well." She glanced back at the photographer. "Let's get it over to the studio."

"I tried to stop them, J. D., but Caine tied me up in the back storeroom." Hilaire was sobbing between the words. "I called you as soon as one of my girls came in and cut me loose."

J. D. looked at the other frightened faces of Hilaire's clerks. He had gotten the call from Sable's cousin a few minutes after leaving Krewe of Louis, and had driven directly to the store to find all the women nearly in hysterics.

"Any of you hear where they were taking her?" No one spoke, but one of the girls looked down at the floor. He went to her. "You, what's your name?"

"Lacelle." She shuffled her feet. "I don't know anything, mister."

"Lacy." Hilaire groaned. "She came in early today— she must have heard me talking to Sable." She came over and grabbed the girl by the shoulder. "You told John, didn't you?"

"I didn't, Hilaire, I—" Lacy looked up into the blonde's furious face and gulped. "But he made me do it. He said they were gonna help her get away from the cops." She shot an accusing look at J. D.

Sable's cousin shook her hard. "J. D.'s been hiding her from the cops, you crazy girl!"

"Hilaire." With effort J. D. clamped down on his own outrage. "Lacy, if Gantry was the one who killed Marc, then he won't help Sable. If he didn't kill him, then he knows who did, and they're both in terrible danger. You have to tell me where they took her."

The girl broke down into tears. "They're not on the bayou, but I don't know where they went. John said Caine would take care of everything."

Hilaire pulled Lacy into her arms. "I've already called a few people I know. Caine's boats are at the dock and he gave all of his men the day off."

"Shit." J. D. needed someone who knew how Gantry thought. "Where is Remy?"

"He went into the city this morning, to see your father."

J. D. called the restaurant and left a message for Louie to meet him at the police station, and then he did the same on Terri's home answering machine. When he finished the calls, he checked his watch. "How long has it been since they left?"

"Three hours." Hilaire released Lacy and touched his arm. "What can I do?"

"Talk to everyone. I have to find out where Caine took her."

"You better come see this, Lieutenant Gamble," one of the girls called from the break room in the back. "Some silver-haired lady is talking about you on TV."

He went back and watched the broadcast on the small black-and-white set, then cursed. "I have to get back to the city and stop this before my mother starts rounding up a lynch mob."

"Good luck, honey," another girl said, making a face at the set. "I know I wouldn't want to take her on."

He went over every aspect of the case in his head on the drive back to the city. Gantry wouldn't have snatched Sable without a good reason—something to do with his arrest, probably. Gut instinct told J. D. the big Cajun wasn't the murderer, and if Sable was right, neither was Remy. He was still at square one as to who had killed Marc.

Reporters and cameramen swamped the front of the police station, so J. D. parked on a side street and went in through the back. Louie met him outside the elevators.

"Where's Mom?"

"Your mother is upstairs, talking to your captain." Louie sighed. "I guess you saw the TV."

"Yeah, I did." He entered the elevator with his father, and then pushed the stop button as soon as the doors closed. "Did you talk to Remy?"

Louie nodded. "He read some letters his wife saved, but he didn't tell Isabel everything. Marc was engaged to someone else when he met Genevieve. His parents came to see her when he broke off the engagement and they scared her into leaving. Marc came back to the bait shop every weekend for the next ten months, begging them to tell him where she went."

"So he was obsessed with her."

"Marc came looking for Sable's mother the day after the fire," Louie told him. "Ginny's neighbors thought he was the one who hired Bud Gantry to set it. They told him she was dead."

"So all these years, he really never knew about her." J. D. hit the start button. "Then Sable shows up out of the blue, and buildings start burning again."

"Cort told me Bud Gantry is dead, that he died a month after he was convicted."

J. D. nodded. "He's dead, but his son is alive."

When they walked out onto the third floor, J. D. saw his mother in the waiting area, with Laure and Moriah Navarre.

"J. D." Moriah saw him first and heaved a sigh of relief.

"Jean-Delano." Elizabet gave her husband an odd look before turning to hug her son and press her smooth cheek against his. "We've been so concerned."

He drew back. "Concerned enough to appear on every news station in town, I understand." He nodded toward the window and the waiting reporters. "The public appeal was quite effective. The tears were a nice touch, too. You haven't done that since I brought home a C on my report card."

She lifted her chin. "I was prepared to do anything to bring you home safely. Now that you're away from that girl, surely you can see—"

For the first time in his life, J. D. turned his back on his mother. "Laure, I'm so sorry about this. You deserved better for you and Marc. Forgive my mother for interfering—she means well."

The widow tried to smile. "You don't have to apologize to me, Jean-Delano."

"Moriah." He took her hand in his. "I know my mother had led you to believe some things about us, but I should have corrected that a long time ago."

Her eyes shimmered but she nodded.

Elizabet threw up her hands. "You are going to let this girl ruin your life? Again?"

"She is my life."

"No. I forbid it. I *forbid* you to have anything to do with her."

"This isn't a C on my report card." J. D. gave his mother a cool look. "I'm in love with Isabel, and as soon as this is over, I'm marrying her. You can make that your next announcement to the press."

"J. D.?" Moriah put a hand on his arm. "That night, before the dance at Tulane, a group of us went over to

Sable's dorm. We'd sent her a message before that, telling her to meet you outside. The boys threw a bucket of swamp water on her. We started the whole thing. Sable was only fighting back when she threw the mud."

"Moriah?"

She turned to his mother. "It's true, and that's not all we did, either." She faced J. D. "We hated her, and we tormented her. We did everything we could think of to make her break up with you. That she endured that as long as she did only shows how much she loved you." Moriah ran from the room, and Laure excused herself to go after her.

"They did that to her?" Elizabet seemed dazed. "I never knew, J. D. I thought—"

"Yeah." J. D. wanted to put his fist through the wall. "So did I."

Louie put an arm around his devastated wife. "Let's go home now, Eliza." He glanced at his son. "Your mother loves you, Jean-Del. She only wanted to protect you."

J. D. would worry about his mother later. He took out his badge and gun as a red-faced Captain Pellerin emerged from his office.

"Gamble." His boss looked ready to detonate. "You've got some explaining to do."

"No, I don't." He handed his gun and badge to the captain. "I quit."

"You bitches thought you'd get away from me," Billy said as he circled around them. He held the shotgun leveled at them and used the back of one hand to wipe the sweat from his forehead. "Guess you weren't as smart as you thought you were."

Cecilia felt the floor of the trailer rock beneath her

feet for a moment, and then something touched her hand. Lilah's fingers, folding around hers. That made her realize what she had to do, and she pushed Lilah's hand back.

"Billy, this is my fault," she said, stepping between her husband and her friend. "I just told Lilah I needed a ride into town. I'm the one you should be mad at. You let her go on out of here and you can do whatever you want."

"CeeCee, don't." The dancer sounded furious. "He isn't going to shoot us."

"You don't think I will, you goddamn dyke?" Billy jabbed the end of the shotgun at her. "Women messing with women." He spat on the floor. "Disgusting bitches, you're going burn in hell for that."

"You narrow minded little asshole, I never touched her!" Lilah shouted. "She's always been faithful to you, God only knows why."

Billy's attention was focused entirely on the dancer now, and Cecilia knew she'd never have another chance. Suddenly all the times Billy had brow-beaten her, scared her, and forced sex on her came rushing through her head. He'd treated her like an animal, and now he thought he could just shoot them?

Never again. I'm never letting him hurt me again. It gave her the courage to pull back her leg and kick her husband in the crotch as hard as she could.

As Billy shrieked and fell to his knees, Lilah grabbed the shotgun and wrestled it away from him. When she aimed the weapon at his head, Cecilia put a hand on her arm.

"No, honey. Don't." She bent over to look into her husband's eyes. "You hear me, Billy Tibbideau? You're not worth the powder and shot to blow you to the devil."

Billy choked and clutched at his crotch with both hands before he curled over and vomited onto the floor.

"Come on, Lilah." Cecilia picked up her photo album and backed away to the trailer's door. "Let's go now."

The dancer hesitated, and then reversed the shotgun. "This is for raping her four nights a week, you bastard." She rammed the stock into the side of Billy's head, which made him topple over into the pool of his own vomit.

"He won't come after us now." Lilah looked at her, completely unrepentant.

"No, I guess he won't."

They walked out of the trailer and Lilah took a minute to stow the shotgun in the trunk of the car. Cecilia waited until she turned around before she rested her hands on her friend's shoulders and leaned in.

Her lips are so soft, she thought as she kissed Lilah. *I hope I'm doing this right.*

When she drew back, Lilah opened her eyes and touched her fingertips to her mouth. "You didn't have to do that."

"I wanted to." Cecilia gave her a shy smile. "You'll have to tell me how to do the other stuff, though. I'm still not sure how it all works when you're both girls."

"Oh, honey." Lilah uttered a shaky laugh and hugged her for a moment before she opened the passenger door. "Come with me and I'll show you everything."

The two women had been gone for nearly an hour when Billy regained consciousness. The vomit covering his face and chest, along with the throbbing agony between his legs, made him puke a second time.

"Fucking bitches." He couldn't get up; she'd kicked

him so hard she'd ruptured him or something. His pants were soggy with his own piss and shit. He rolled over and swallowed against a third surge of bile.

He was down, but he wasn't out. Not yet. As soon as he could, he was going after them. He'd hunt them down and make them pay for what they'd done to him.

Beat them until their bones break, boy, his dead father shouted inside his head. *Screw them until their cunts tear and bleed. Then you skin them alive, an inch at a time.*

The trailer door opened and closed behind him.

He turned his head, saw who it was. "Look what they done to me. I gotta go to the hospital. You gotta take me."

Cold eyes moved over him. "No, Mr. Tibbideau. Our association is finished." A gloved hand reached inside the pocket of an expensive coat.

"You take me or—" his eyes widened when he saw the hand reappear. "No. *No!*"

The gun didn't fire, it hissed. A snake's hiss, which made no sense to him. Neither did the fire in his chest, or the blood pouring from his mouth. The floor rushed up to meet his face, and then everything made perfect sense.

I shoulda listened to you, Daddy, Billy thought as the gun appeared over his face. *You were right.*

The gun hissed two more times.

Chapter Thirteen

Sable strained at the cords around her wrists and ankles again, but Caine had tied her up too tight for her to wiggle free. "Where are you taking me?"

"We're going to go see a friend of mine." He turned off the highway.

"What friend?"

"Did I ever tell you that your mother was the sweetest, kindest woman I ever knew?"

"No." She was cramped and frightened and not sure what Caine was capable of. For now, letting him talk seemed safest. "I didn't know you were friends with her."

"We weren't. She was just kind to me." A faraway look came into his eyes as he stared at the road ahead. "I used to go hang around the bait shop whenever my folks were fighting. Her parents let me sleep there when it was bad at home. She always brought me something to eat and she'd sit and talk to me sometimes. Nobody talked to me except Ginny. I think she was the one who convinced Remy to hire me on."

He sounded as if he'd worshipped her. "I'm sorry, Caine. I didn't know."

"Don't be. Ginny told me about your father and how much she loved him, right before she left. I didn't understand why she had to go, and then she came with you and I did." He glanced at her. "She let me hold you when you were just a tiny little thing. I'd never been around babies, and I'd never seen anything as delicate and helpless as you were."

She swallowed. "Why are you telling me this?"

"Your mama asked me to mail a letter for her a few days after she came back with you. It was addressed to your real daddy. Marc LeClare."

"She wrote to him?"

He ignored the question. "A week after I mailed that letter, my daddy came home and gave my mama a whole bunch of money. He told her she had to say he was home all night, and then he left." Caine paused to pass a slower vehicle. "I followed him to your grandparents' house. I was only thirteen—I didn't understand why he brought the bottles and the gas can. I thought maybe he'd borrowed them from your granddad. Then I watched him fill the bottles with the gas, and I knew what he meant to do."

Her throat constricted. "You watched him set fire to our house."

"I didn't stay and watch after he threw the first bottle in the attic. He was a big man, and I couldn't stop him by myself. I ran down to the dock to get Remy." His hands clenched the steering wheel until his knuckles jutted. "I wasn't fast enough, though. When we came back, my daddy was gone and the whole house was on fire. Remy heard Ginny screaming and ran inside. He broke out a window and handed you to me. You were crying and your hair, your pretty red hair, it was all burned off." His voice broke on the words.

She covered her face with her hand.

"I carried you away from the house, and Remy got your mama out. His clothes were on fire, and his hands and face all black and burned. Other people came, but the roof fell in and no one could get to your grandparents. Your mama came to me, and grabbed you. She was staring at the house and saying his name, over and over."

"Whose name?"

"Marc LeClare." His voice changed. "I went with her to the hospital where they took Remy. I told her everything, about my daddy and what he'd done and the money. She went real quiet, and then she said she should have never written to him, never told him about you."

"Marc didn't know about me." Now she was frightened and confused. "He said he never knew."

"No one on the bayou had any reason to hurt you and Ginny. It could have only been one person."

She shook her head. "No. I don't believe you."

"There was no one else with that kind of money." Caine's voice grew harsh. "Marc LeClare paid my father to burn you and your mother to death. Marc was the one who brought you to that warehouse. He was the one who wanted to kill you."

"You don't know that."

"Yes, I do. We're going to see Billy Tibbideau. Marc hired him to burn down the warehouse with you inside it."

Terri saw her partner exit the elevators and dropped the stack of case files in her hands.

"J. D.!" She ran to him and, uncaring of the disapproving eyes, flung her arms around his neck. "Oh, God, I've been so worried." She drew back and studied him. "You okay? Where have you been? I could just kick your ass right now. Wait." She hugged him again. "Okay, I'll beat the crap out of you tomorrow. What's happening?"

"I quit the force." He helped pick up her files. "Caine Gantry grabbed Sable out on the bayou. He's got her somewhere now."

"Stupid shit for brains." She pressed the heels of her hands against her eyes for a moment. "He won't hurt her, J. D."

"I'm not going to wait and find out."

"I promise, he won't. Caine's my cousin." She grimaced as she met his incredulous stare. "I know, I should have brought that up before, but you had enough on your mind. Caine's been in love with Sable since they were teenagers."

"You know, I didn't need *another* reason to kill him." He looked around and nodded toward a conference room. "Come on, we need to talk."

"Wait." She grabbed a couple of files from her desk.

After Terri filled him in on what little progress Garcia had made on the case, she opened one file. "This is the sheet on Bud Gantry. I can verify that Caine was only thirteen when Sable and her mother were nearly burned to death. He saw his father setting it and ran to get Rèmy that night. Even back then Caine was crazy about Sable."

J. D. related what Remy told his father, and she closed the file. "Okay, so Marc goes to find Ginny the next day and they tell him she's dead. He couldn't have been too broken up about it."

"Why do you say that?"

"This is the background sheet on LeClare." She tapped a section on the front page, then an entry on Bud Gantry's rap sheet. "Look at the dates—his wedding was only three weeks after the fire."

That changed everything, and J. D. went still. "We've got to get into his bank accounts."

"You're no longer working here," she reminded him.

"Run a financial check. Look at all of the LeClares' accounts, personal and business. I'm interested in large lump-sum withdrawals in the last month and twenty-nine years ago."

"You think LeClare tried to kill his own daughter? Twice?"

"Just see what you can find." J. D. checked his watch. "I'm going to see LeClare's attorney, Jacob Pernard."

Terri drove up to her apartment ten hours later. She was tired and her eyes burned from studying printouts of bank records all day. She hadn't been able to find any suspicious withdrawals, and called J. D. to tell him that, but he had only told her to keep searching. He seemed convinced that she'd find something.

All Terri wanted to do was spend ten hours flat on her back, but she'd be lucky if she got five. She kept seeing the look on Cort's face after she'd punched him in the nose.

Felt good, too, she thought as she rubbed the bruised spot on her cheek. *Too bad I didn't break it.*

Standing under the shower until the hot water ran out helped relax her tense muscles, but she'd barely dried off when she heard someone hammering at her front door. Thinking it was J. D., she threw on a robe and ran, only to see Cort Gamble hovering outside her front window.

She unlocked all five dead bolts on her door and pulled it open. "What, are you selling cookies?"

"No." He stared at her oddly for a moment. "May I

come inside?" He sounded as polite as a visiting priest.

She stepped out of his way and then closed the door behind him. "J. D.'s back."

"I know." He looked all around her front room. "This is a small place."

"Not all of us can afford nineteenth-century mansions. I like it." She brushed past him to go into her tiny kitchenette. "Beside, I really only sleep here. Sit down—want a drink?"

He didn't answer her or sit; he only stood in the middle of the room staring at the portrait of Marie Laveau over her sofa and the yellow blessing candles on the shelf beneath it. "You believe in voodoo?"

"No, but some of my family does, and I don't have the heart to throw out the crap they give me." She poured herself a glass of raspberry tea, and after a hesitation, poured a second for him. "So what brings you to my humble, not very architecturally interesting, voodoo-infested abode?"

"I needed to see you." He watched her come from the kitchen and stared at the glass she held out to him. "No, thank you."

This close, she could smell the whiskey on his breath and see the slight glaze over his eyes. Despite his very sober appearance, she wondered if the oh-so-proper Marshal Cortland Gamble might be slightly smashed out of his gourd.

You don't prod a gator with a stick, chère, her mother told her. *Even when it don't look hungry.*

She set the glass down and kept her voice neutral. "What can I do for you, Cort?"

He looked over her shoulder. "Is my brother here?"

"No." She laughed as he went back to have a look

in her bedroom anyway. "Fabio is, though, and he's very tired. Don't wake him up—I wore him out."

Cort returned to the front room. "Where is J. D.?"

"I don't know." He was beginning to worry her now. "Maybe you should go home now, Cortland. Sleep it off."

"Have you slept with him?"

She folded her arms. Here stood the only Gamble she'd ever been interested in, and he thought she was doing it with his brother. There was some kind of sick, twisted message in that. "Fabio? I wish. J. D.? Ah, no, sorry. Department policy, paragraph nine, subsection three: Female detectives will refrain from screwing their partners' brains out at all times."

He didn't like that. "You're always laughing at me."

"What can I say, you're a funny guy."

"No, I'm not." He reached out and touched her shaggy hair. "Why Fabio?" he asked as he fingered the short strands. "Why not me?"

Jesus, he really is smashed. Reasoning with him would be totally useless, so she might as well concentrate on hauling his butt back to the Gamble plantation. "He's richer than you. And nicer. Don't." As he tried to kiss her, she whipped her head to the side.

"I want to."

"I'm getting high enough from the fumes, thanks." She took his arm, trying to steer him toward the sofa. "How about you sit down, let me get dressed, and I'll drive you home."

"I'm not that drunk, Therese."

"You don't want me to make you blow up a funny little balloon, do you?" She gave up on planting him and headed for her bedroom. "Hold on, I'll be right out."

Terri didn't realize he'd followed her in until he

closed the bedroom door and locked it. She was not going to yell at him. He was intoxicated; he didn't know what he was doing.

"I've been dressing myself since I was three, Cort. I don't need help."

"I know what you need." He loomed over her, and brought her hand to the front of his trousers. The ridge tenting them was pretty impressive. He pulled off his shirt. "I'll give it to you."

The temptation was equally daunting—he felt long and thick against her fingers, and lo and behold, the man had the chest of a god. The rest of him had to be as good or better. Terri hadn't had sex since . . . she couldn't remember—it had been that long.

But this wasn't just any guy. This was Cort, and that was broken-heart territory from the borders in.

Carefully she pulled her hand away. "I don't have any paper bags for you to put over your head for when you sneak out of here in the morning."

"I don't sneak and I don't need a bag."

"Go back outside and get a better look at the neighborhood, you'll change your mind real fast."

He turned on the lamp, then came over and tugged at the belt of her robe. She stopped him, and he looked into her eyes. "I need you, Terri."

Maybe he hadn't had sex in a long time. That might explain his choice. "Why now? Why not in 2001, or last Christmas, or next Tuesday?"

"I've tried not to think about you," he told her. "For years, ever since they made you his partner. I can't do it anymore." He untied the belt and parted her robe, then stared down at her.

She knew her breasts were small and she was too thin, and she had to struggle with a terrible urge to jerk her robe shut. "As you can see, I'm built for speed, not display."

"You're . . ." He dragged in an unsteady breath as he cupped her and circled her nipple with his thumb.

She braced herself. "Anorexic? Unappealing? Androgynous?"

"Art. A work of art." He closed his arms around her waist and his mouth over her breast.

The last of her good intentions went straight to Jail, no passing Go, no collecting two hundred dollars. What the hell—she'd have one good reality-based fantasy to masturbate to for the rest of her life.

"This is just sex, right?" When he only moved from one breast to the other, she clenched her hands on his waist. "Uh, safe sex?"

He stood up and stuffed his hand in his jeans pocket, and then slapped several square packets into her palm. "Safe enough?"

She pretended to check them. *He came prepared, bless his stony little heart.* "Latex are good." Though they looked kind of small—or maybe that was like objects reflected in car side mirrors. Next to him, a prizewinning bull would look pretty puny right now.

She placed all but one of them within reach of her bed, then shrugged out of her robe and sat down on the side of the mattress. "Come here."

He walked over to her, but she put her hands on his hips when he would have joined her. "Stay right there." She set the condom aside to work on his jeans, and didn't look at him until he pulled his long legs out of them and kicked them aside. Then she lifted her lashes and stared.

He was, well, *large* didn't quite encompass it. *Gargantuan* might work. Or *lethal weapon.*

Something panicky fluttered in the bottom of her

stomach as she touched him. Smooth, satiny skin over what felt like iron. "I think we might need to sew two together."

He cradled the back of her head, rubbing his fingers against her scalp. "Put it on me."

So her hands shook as she took out the condom, and she fumbled a little. If she'd been thinking clearly, she would have done something sexy like pop the condom in her mouth and roll it down over him with her tongue and lips. Instead she felt like she was playing Pin the Tail on the Donkey—and losing.

His big hand came down and helped her, and together they rolled the thin latex sheath down the wide, thick length of him.

She uttered a shaky laugh. "Houston, I think we're good to go." She crawled backward onto the bed, and he came down after her, blocking out the light with his shoulders, meeting the slight curves of her frame with the heavier, corded perfection of his own.

For some reason she didn't know where to start touching him, so she pretended to fuss with the pillow under her head. He was arranging her legs, placing her feet flat against the bed and bending her knees up on either side of him. She didn't know anything about him as a lover, and worse, she was probably the ugliest woman he'd ever been in bed with. That was a title she could have lived without.

But if I ever hear him say that, I get to kill him.

"Relax." He stroked his palm down the inside of her thigh. "You're all nerves. Tell me what you like."

She didn't need his pity, either. "Could we move on to entrée, please?"

Cort gave her a slow, sexy smile. "Yeah." He curled his hands around her tense thighs and dropped down between them.

"I didn't mean . . . uh . . ." Her back arched as she felt the languid pressure of his tongue laving against her, parting her and tasting her. "Me . . ."

He made himself comfortable, stretching out his body as he feasted on her with his mouth and his tongue. He licked all over her first, like a boy with an ice-cream cone he didn't want to melt, and then he went exploring. By then Terri was panting and twisting under him, trying to move so that he would touch her where she needed it.

When she made a frustrated sound, he lifted his head. "You want me to stop?"

She groped until she found the drawer to her side table, pulled out her spare revolver, and pointed it at his face. "You want to die?"

He only chuckled as he used his fingers to open her. He looked at her for a long moment before lowering his mouth and applying short, wet hard strokes to her clit.

Terri had enough presence of mind to replace her gun before the first spiral of hot delight began uncoiling inside her. He forced her up hard and faster, smashing her through the first climax and into the second, and when she sobbed and twisted he held her pinned and moved her on to the third. Darkness and heat pressed in on her, and by the fourth she was reduced to mindless begging. Only then did he move up and position himself against her.

"Therese." He waited until she opened her dazed eyes, then pressed in. Even with the soaked conditions down there, it was going to be a very narrow fit. She turned her head, but he immediately stopped, halfway lodged inside her. "Don't look away from me."

She felt suddenly, irrationally furious. What did he

want from her? He'd already ruined her for most of the men on the planet; did he have to own her soul?

But Cort didn't know she loved him, and that was one thing he would never get out of her.

She let her lips curve. "Do I have to get the gun again?"

He held her hips down and penetrated her completely with a heavy, forceful push.

All the breath whooshed out of her lungs. *Narrow fit, hell.* She might have to go for some repair work after "I guess not."

He didn't say much, but she wouldn't have heard him. He murmured her name, and watched her eyes as he plowed into her, slow and searching for all the right spots, then concentrating his strokes on them when he found them. They were both covered in sweat—somewhere in the dim recesses of what was left of her mind Terri realized she'd forgotten to turn on the A/C—and their skins made tiny kissing noises as he worked over and inside her.

She wanted to hold on, to come with him, but the unyielding length of him working back and forth inside her was too much. She came with a thin cry, and Cort held himself deep inside her, let her ride it out on him.

He dragged her to the end of the bed, his penis still deep inside her as he loomed over her, his feet braced on the floor, his hands hard on her hips. He never looked away from her face as he started again, harder and faster this time. And even when his thrusts slammed the head of the bed into the wall, and plaster dust drifted down from the gouges the headboard left in it, she never stopped watching his face. His eyes became slits, and then he stiffened and said her name one last time.

She felt every pulse inside her as he came, and counted them silently, the way another woman would pluck petals from a daisy. *He loves me, he loves me not, he loves me . . .*

Terri didn't close her eyes until he collapsed on top of her, and then it was only to hold back the tears she wouldn't let him see.

He loves me not.

Caine drove Sable to a mobile-home park and told her to wait in the truck as he went to the door of a small, shabby-looking trailer. He knocked, then tried the knob and went inside. He emerged a few minutes later looking pale and shaken.

"Caine?" As he put his hand on the steering wheel, she saw a streak of blood on the back of it.

"Don't talk to me."

He drove from there to a small fishing shack he and some of his men used when running his bigger boats on the Mississippi, and this time he brought her inside with him. He wouldn't talk to her or untie her, except when she asked to use the bathroom, and even then he stood watch outside the door, making it an embarrassing business.

"Are you keeping me here?" she asked him as he sorted through the food he'd brought with him, but that only earned her a blank look.

Slowly he seemed to recover from whatever had upset him, and he began to talk to her as he prepared their meal. Mainly he asked her a lot of questions—about Marc, but also about what she remembered of her mother, and why Ginny had been so afraid of people.

"Mama was just shy," Sable insisted as he brought

the pot of gumbo he'd reheated to the table. "She always kept to herself."

"Ginny loved to talk to people. She sold more bait than any girl on the bayou." He spooned some rice into a bowl before adding the rich seafood stew to it. "It was only after the fire that she became that way."

"You think she was afraid of someone." When he didn't reply, she made a frustrated sound. "Caine, Marc wasn't trying to kill me."

He eyed her. "I can prove it."

"Do you know who killed him?"

"I thought I did." He reached behind her and untied her wrists. "I'm not so sure now."

"Who? Was it Billy?"

He thumped the bowl down in front of her. "Eat your gumbo."

That night he made a bed for her with a sleeping bag on one of the wooden bunks, then sat up watching the night through the window. She was so worn-out from worry about what he might do that she drifted off to sleep before she could work out a way to escape him. Then it was morning, and Caine was shaking her and helping her up from the hard bunk.

He untied her again so she could drink her coffee and eat the dish of brown sugar and apple oatmeal he made for her, but when she studied the scalding hot coffee, he tapped her cheek. "You've never been a stupid girl, Isabel. Don't start now."

They left the river and drove back toward the city, joining the long lines of cars doing the same. He made her wear one of his baseball caps over her hair, but otherwise didn't seem to be worried about driving around New Orleans with a known fugitive in his truck. On the contrary, he stopped and parked to watch two different parades, and admired some of the more outlandish costumes. Except for the fact that he wouldn't let her out of the truck, they could have been tourists.

He's biding his time, she decided, *but for what?*

Caine bought an enormous shrimp po'boy from a street vendor, then parked on a tiny side street around the corner and split the sandwich with her.

"This is just so cozy," she grumbled. "We going dancing next?"

He smiled a little. "I used to think about asking you out to a dance. Never mind that I didn't have any money, or even a decent set of clothes to wear. I just wanted to be the one you looked at, the one you smiled for."

She frowned. "When was this?"

"About the time you met that cop, when you were in college." He opened a bottle of soda and handed it to her. "That did hurt, Isabel, but I wanted you to be happy. I sure as hell wasn't good enough for you. So I sat back and watched him take you out."

He was making it sound like he'd had some kind of crush on her instead of her mother, as she'd assumed. "Why didn't you ever . . . ?"

"Tell you? What, and have you laugh at me, feel sorry for me?" He shook his head. "I may come from poor, *chère,* but I've never been short on pride."

"I wouldn't have laughed." She lost her appetite and handed him the rest of her section of the sandwich. They drove around the city for the next several hours, Caine stopping twice to take her into one of the little twenty-four-hour bars to get more drinks and let her use the facilities. She didn't try to run; she knew he'd only chase her down. When she got back into the truck after the second stop, he didn't tie her hands again.

He stopped at another street vendor and bought her a sno-ball mottled brown and white from its topping of chocolate syrup and sweetened condensed milk. "You always loved these when you were a little girl. I never could afford to buy you one back then."

The way he was acting was starting to worry her. "I'm sorry if I hurt you, Caine. I never suspected you cared about me."

"You made me want to be a better man, until that night you came running back from school." He met her gaze. "That's when I found out you were ashamed—not just of me, of all of us. All you wanted to be was like them."

"No, I didn't." But some of the things she'd said that night came back to her, and she cringed a little. "Maybe I was. Caine, I'd just been through the worst experience in my life. The only reason they did that to me was because I was from the bayou, and they weren't."

"What about your charity work? You figure they'll finally forgive you for being Cajun if you're giving handouts to the rest of us?"

Finally she understood why he had been so opposed to the community project. "All I wanted was to help our people, not change or apologize for what we are. I'm proud of our culture."

"We don't need city ways out on the bayou."

"We need better schools and medical care and assistance for people like single mothers and the elderly. We need to help the fishermen get the financing they need to stay in business, and cleanup of illegal dump sites. There are a thousand things we could have for the asking, but no one knows how to file the proper paperwork, or what state agency to contact. I have that knowledge. That's what I want to do—bring our people and the available resources together."

"You can't change the world, Isabel."

"No. But I can try to change the little piece of it that belongs to us." She looked out through the windshield at a young mother pushing a baby stroller over the grass toward the playground. Her toddler son was chewing on one fist and banging the other against the padded frame. "That little boy out there will probably never go hungry. He'll get all the shots he needs, and have his teeth checked, and go to a good school. He won't have to give up his culture for it. Neither do we."

Caine checked his watch and started the engine. "Time to get going."

Chapter Fourteen

Moriah wanted nothing more than to go home and lock herself in her room for a week, but since her mother was determined to find a new dress to wear to the Gambles' gala she forced herself to stay with Laure and keep her company.

"You should go, too, my dear." Laure looked worried. "I know Elizabet is sorry for what happened."

Moriah suspected that Elizabet Gamble would never speak to her again. "It's better that I skip it, now that I no longer have a date."

The older woman looked sympathetic. "Forgive me. I hadn't considered how you must feel about Jean-Delano."

Moriah hadn't been in love with J. D., so her heart would survive, and so would her wounded pride. "I'd much rather be here with you. So what would you like to do this evening? Watch a video? Listen to some music?"

"I think I'll do a little reading." Laure went to the magazine rack and picked out a copy of *Vogue*. "Have you seen the latest fashions for spring?"

Moriah heard the sound of glass shattering at the front of the house. "Is your housekeeper still here?"

"No." Laure rose, alarmed. "I sent everyone home after dinner."

Moriah's heart pounded as she hurried over to the double doors to close and lock them. "Call 911—tell them someone's breaking into the house."

The older woman was already at the desk, holding the receiver to her ear. Slowly she replaced it. "The line is completely dead."

Moriah looked around for anything she could use as a weapon. "Did Marc keep a gun anywhere?"

"No, he hated them." Laure went to the windows, looked out, and uttered a cry. "All of the security people are gone, too. I didn't think I'd need them at night."

Heavy footsteps coming toward the library made Moriah pick up a slender porcelain statue. "Is this priceless?"

"No."

She positioned herself by one side of the door, and flinched as someone kicked it from the other side. "Hide under the desk. Hurry."

Before Laure could move, a second kick drove the door in, and a big, black-haired man came in. Moriah swung the statue at his head only to find it wrenched out of her grip by one of the man's fast, huge hands.

He held on to the statue and yanked someone behind him into the room. "That's no way to say hello, *chère*."

Moriah met Sable Duchesne's shocked brown eyes, and then looked down at the cords binding her wrists. Fear made her move around him, and put herself between him and Laure.

"Who are you?" Moriah tried to sound tough, but he was huge and easily the scariest-looking man she'd ever seen in her life. "What do you want?"

He ran his black gaze over her, then Laure. "You don't want to give me trouble, Goldilocks."

"Moriah." The older woman's voice strangled on her name.

Moriah moved back until she could put her arms around the older woman. "You have no business here. Get out!"

"Caine, please," Sable said. "It's not too late—you can leave right now before anything else happens."

"I do have business here, *chère*." He took a knife from his belt and turned it, letting the light dance over the deadly silver edge.

Moriah couldn't take her eyes off the blade, even when he used it to slash a length of velvet cord from one of the drape tiebacks. She pushed Laure behind her as he approached them, and held out her fists. "I won't let you touch her."

"I don't want her. I want you." He held the knife tip to her throat.

His eyes were so black that she couldn't see the pupils. "I will fight you," she whispered.

"Would you?" He stared at her trembling lips for a moment. "Hold out your arms."

She glanced down at the knife and then lifted her arms. Quickly he looped the cord around them, putting the knife away only once her wrists were bound like Sable's. He left enough cord to pull her toward him with it. "Let's go."

"My parents are rich; they'll pay you whatever you want," Moriah told him. "So you only need me. Let Sable and Laure go."

He paused and smiled at her. "You got some spine on you, girl." He jerked on the cord, yanking her toward the door. "Ms. LeClare, my men are all around this house, so don't you go anywhere. Isabel." He jerked his head toward the ceiling. "Upstairs."

Caine tied the two younger women together and locked them in one of the second-floor bedrooms. He had lied to Laure about having the house surrounded—his men had no idea where he was—but she was still waiting in the library for him when he returned.

"Who are you?" Though she looked ashen, she presented a calm and dignified demeanor, as if he were just a troublesome door-to-door salesman. "What do you want?"

"I want the truth, lady." The fragility of her bones made him careful with his grip on her arm. "Show me where your husband's personal papers are."

She led him out of the library, down the hall, and into a large and beautifully furnished study. "Perhaps if you tell me specifically what you're looking for, I can find it for you."

He released her. "Bank records and personal correspondence."

She went to the desk and opened a drawer. "Marc kept his business accounts at his office." She removed a large clasped envelope. "These are the statements from the last six months."

Caine locked the door to the study and pushed a chair against the knob for good measure. "Open it."

Laure removed the financial statements and set them out on the desk.

"Sit down over there." Caine waited until she lowered herself onto an armchair in front of the desk; then he turned on the lamp and sat down in LeClare's comfortable executive leather chair.

He kept his expression blank, but inside he was still

reeling from finding blood splattered all over the inside of Billy's trailer. Either Billy was dead, or he'd killed Cecilia—or maybe both of them were dead. There had been a lot of blood.

Maybe the wife knows who else was involved. "You saw your husband the day he was murdered, didn't you?"

She lifted her chin. "I'm not going to discuss my husband with you."

"Yes, you are." He began skimming through the documents. "Twenty-nine years ago he paid my father ten thousand dollars to burn down a house. I imagine he had to pay Billy fifty thousand or better to burn his marina and his processing plant. Was there someone else on his payroll?"

She sniffed. "Why in heaven's name would my husband burn his own properties?"

"To blame Cajun fishermen like me for doing it, and get more goddamn laws made against us. Maybe he wanted the insurance money, too." He flipped through to the end of the statements. "I don't see it. Where's the rest of the year?"

"The other records for last year are at our accountant's office. He's preparing our tax return." She half rose from the chair when he jerked open a drawer and began tearing through it. "I'm sorry you're angry, but this will solve nothing. My husband is dead."

"I'm going to prove what he did, and find who he paid to kill Billy Tibbideau." He looked across the desk at her. "And you're going to help me. Come over here."

Moriah listened. "He must have gone back downstairs. I don't hear anything."

"We've got to get loose." Sable tugged experimen-
ᵗly on the short length of cord binding them. They

were both sitting side by side on the floor next to the wall, where Caine had left them tied together by their wrists and ankles. "If you can reach over with me, I think I can untie the one on our legs."

"Okay." The blond girl stretched over with her, and remained still as Sable plucked at the knot. "How did you get involved with that man?"

"He kidnapped me." Sable bit her lip as the stubborn knot eluded her numb fingers. "He hasn't done anything but drag me around the city. I don't think he'll hurt Mrs. LeClare."

"If he does, I'll kill him."

"I'll help you." Finally the knot loosened and she groaned. "Almost there, just another minute." She worked her foot until she was able to tug free of the cord. "Can you stand up?"

"Uh-huh." Moriah tucked her feet under her and braced her back against the wall as she rose. "What'll we do about our hands?"

Sable looked around the room and saw a hand mirror on the dresser. "Over here." She led the younger girl to the dresser and picked up the mirror. It was a beautiful antique, with a heavily ornate, solid silver back. "Seven years' bad luck, you know."

"Do it." Moriah turned her head away as Sable smashed the mirror, then examined the pieces. "That one looks long enough."

Sable gingerly picked up the mirror shard and carefully inserted one jagged end between their wrists. "Hold still. I don't want to cut you." Carefully she began working it against the cord.

Moriah watched with a frown. "I can't believe you're helping me, after what we did to you."

Sable stopped cutting. "What did you do?"

"You don't remember me? I was a member of th

sorority at Tulane," the blond girl said. "I was there that night, outside the dorm." "

I thought your voice sounded familiar." Sable studied her face for a moment. "I remember. You were the one who told them to stop and leave me alone."

"For what good it did." Moriah hunched her shoulders. "I've been carrying around the memory of that night for a long time. If I could take back what we did—"

"What *they* did. You didn't do anything." Sable went back to cutting, then stopped and put down the mirror shard. "Try pulling away from me now."

They strained and twisted, and the cord suddenly broke, freeing their wrists. From there it was just a matter of unpicking each other's knots, which they finished a minute later.

Moriah rubbed her wrists. "We should split up. Do you think you can get past his men outside and get to one of the neighbors' houses?"

"I think he was lying about the men. Wait." Sable sniffed the air. "Do you smell that?"

The other girl breathed in deeply, and her eyes widened. "Dear God, it can't be."

Sable went to the locked door and looked down to see white curls of smoke seeping through the small gap at the bottom. She touched the doorknob and found it cool. "We have to get out of here."

"Watch out." Moriah picked up a heavy floor lamp and used it like a battering ram on the door. Sable grabbed the elongated lamp base from the other side and helped her shove it against the door.

When they broke the lock and the door swung out, clouds of smoke billowed into the room. Pulling up her T-shirt to cover her mouth and nose, Sable moved out into the hall and looked over the landing rail.

Beneath their feet, the LeClare mansion was on fire.

J. D. met Terri outside the station when she got off work. "You look like you've been rode hard and put away wet."

"You have no idea." She rolled her shoulders. "Any word on Gantry or Sable?"

"No, nothing. You have any luck with the records?"

"Marc LeClare kept his books spotless." She walked with him to the parking lot. "He had to, with the campaign contribution auditors looking over his shoulder and so forth. I don't really think I'm going to find anything."

"I don't think you will, either."

She stopped and threw out her arms. "*Now* you tell me?"

"I talked to Marc's attorney this afternoon. Jacob said that Marc had called him the night before he died, to make an appointment to change his will." J. D. stopped beside her car. "Up until then, Laure LeClare was the sole beneficiary. You want to know how much his estate is worth?"

"More zeros than I can count, I imagine. We should talk to her." Terri made a face. "I mean, I should go and type, you should go file for unemployment, and *Garcia* should talk to her."

"I'm still a friend of the family." J. D. eyed her. "You wanted vacation time, right?"

"Yeah." His partner sighed and pulled open her door. "I hate breaking in new partners anyway."

On the way to the LeClare mansion, she pulled out her pack of cigarettes. "J. D., just remember, she's an important lady. You can't just accuse someone like her of bumping off her husband without hard evidence."

"She could have paid someone to do it for her." He

took Terri's lighter and lit the cigarette for her. "Figure it this way: Laure and Marc are engaged; then Marc falls in love with Ginny, gets her pregnant, breaks up with Laure. Ginny disappears, comes back with a kid. She must have tried to contact him, and Laure got wind of it. So she hires someone to kill Ginny and the baby. Marc thinks they're dead, she consoles him, and they get married."

Terri took a deep drag and sighed out the smoke. "Okay, I buy that. So Sable's mom dies, and she finds out Marc's her father, and meets him. Marc is overjoyed; Laure isn't. I don't know, J. D. She came across to me and Cort like she would have welcomed Sable with open arms."

"After all those miscarriages she had, Laure finds out that Ginny gave him the one thing she couldn't— a child. How would you feel in her place?"

Terri thought for a minute. "Pretty pissed."

He nodded. "So then Laure finds out Marc plans to publicly acknowledge his illegitimate daughter. Which will wreck his campaign and ruin her public standing and dignity. They argue. Maybe he tells her he's going to change his will, too, leave half of everything to Sable—a poor Cajun girl with no background and no breeding." His phone rang, and he answered it.

"You'd better get over to the Garden District," Cort said without preamble. "We've got in a call at the Le-Clare mansion. Someone reported seeing Caine Gantry and Isabel going in just before the fire broke out. My trucks are rolling now."

J. D. checked their location. "We're two blocks away." He switched off the phone. "Laure LeClare's house is on fire and Sable and Caine are still inside." He looked and saw the faint outline of black smoke pillowing up ahead.

"Shit." Terri slammed her foot down on the accelerator.

The fire at the old mansion was burning out of control by the time they reached the property, flames lighting up the night sky. J. D. parked as close as he dared and jumped out of the car. He and Terri ran to the first neighbor they saw.

"Did everyone get out?" he shouted over the noise of the approaching sirens.

The frightened woman shook her head. "No one's come out at all."

The house was burning too fast, J. D. realized. By the time the fire crews arrived with the trucks it would be completely engulfed in flames.

As he and Terri ran up the drive, she pointed to a set of French doors on one side leading into a small garden. "We could break those in, use the garden hose."

As she unwound the coil of green hose from the wall clip, J. D. peered inside. The interior was too smoky for him to see much, but he thought he could make out two figures struggling with something. "Spray me down," he told Terri.

She gave the house a wild look. "J. D.—"

"She's in there—do it."

Terri turned on the hose and sprayed him from head to toe. When he was wringing-wet, he picked up a large decorative stone and smashed one of the glass panes of the doors, then reached inside to unlock them.

He crouched over as he hurried into the smoke-filled room, which was like walking into hell. "Sable!"

Someone nearby coughed and cried out, "Here!"

He followed the sound and found Sable and Moriah on their hands and knees, struggling to drag an unconscious Caine Gantry between them.

"We can't find Mrs. LeClare," Sable choked out as he grabbed the big man and slung him over his shoulder.

"Hold on to my jacket." Shifting Caine's dead-weight, he led the two women back toward the French doors. Cort, dressed in protective gear, met them halfway.

Moriah stopped and tried to go back. "I can't leave Laure!"

"We'll get her out—come on." Cort grabbed the women by the waist and hustled them out through the doors.

J. D. followed his brother out into the garden and away from the house. He put Gantry down on the lawn and turned to Sable, who was coughing and covered in soot but evidently not burned. "Where was Laure?"

"In Marc's study." Moriah pointed one reddened hand at the other end of the house, the one that was burning rapidly. Then she fell to her knees, and Terri helped her lie down on the grass.

"We found Caine in the hallway," Sable added when she could take a breath, "but the fire was too hot, and part of the ceiling fell in. We just couldn't get to her."

Cort and J. D. ran back to the house and looked in the windows of the study. The room was ablaze, and they heard the sound of wood giving way.

"Watch out!" Cort lunged at him and barely knocked him out of the way as the upper floors suddenly collapsed. A wall of burning wood fell on top of where they had just been standing.

J. D. looked at the mountain of flaming rubble that had been Marc LeClare's study, and closed his eyes.

*   *   *

At the hospital, Sable stayed with Moriah until she was taken from emergency up to the inpatient ward.

"I'll come to see you in the morning," she told her as she touched her arm. "You rest now, okay?"

Moriah nodded and drifted off as the pain medication they'd given her took effect.

Sable walked out to see J. D. talking to a heavyset, frowning man in a rumpled suit.

"Gantry is in a coma in ICU. He's got second-degree burns and a head wound," J. D. was telling the man. "I'd leave a guard on him anyway." He looked around at Sable. "Excuse me, Captain."

"Hold on, Gamble." The man held out a gun and a badge. "They're yours, if you want them back."

J. D. smiled. "You sure you want me back?"

"No." The captain slapped his arm. "But somebody's got to keep you out of trouble."

Terri and Cort were arguing in low, furious voices about something in the lobby, but abruptly stopped when Sable and J. D. approached them.

"How is Moriah?" Cort asked.

"They're keeping her, but the doctor said she should make a full recovery," Sable told him.

"We're out of here." J. D. looked at his partner. "Can I borrow your wheels?"

"Sure." She gave Cort a sideways glance. "I'm sure your brother will be overjoyed to give me a ride." She handed J. D. her keys.

He was silent as they left the hospital and he negotiated his way through the reveling Mardi Gras crowds. He kept Sable close to him, holding her in the curve of his arm. She rested her cheek against his shoulder and tried not to think of Marc's poor wife, who had died in the fire.

"What will they do to Caine?" she finally asked.

"He has some heavy charges to face—arson, kidnapping, maybe manslaughter." J. D. glanced down at her. "Did you know he was in love with you?"

"I never knew until he told me today." She shook her head. "I don't understand why he set the fire."

"Revenge for you and your mother, maybe." He pulled up into the private garage to his apartment and parked Terri's car in his reserved space. Instead of getting out, he sat and held Sable for a long time. "I almost lost you again. I am never letting you out of my sight for as long as we live."

"That's going to be tough to do. Good thing I'm crazy in love with you." She recalled what his boss had said to him and met his gaze. "But are you sure you want me back?"

"Oh, baby, I want you every way I can have you. In my arms, in my bed, in my life. I want you to stay with me and have my kids and never even think about leaving me again." He trailed his fingers over her soot-stained hair. "I love you, Isabel. I always have, and I always will."

Her heart turned over as he kissed her, and she wound her arms around his neck, feeling as if she had come home after years of emptiness and sorrow.

When he pulled her out of Terri's car and swung her up in his arms, she giggled. "You don't have to carry me around like a caveman."

"Tonight I do." And he carried her into the elevator, and up to his apartment, and straight through to his bed.

It was a long time later that Sable woke up in J. D.'s arms, tired and slightly sore but happier than she had ever been in her life. Her hair was still damp—at some point they had made it into the shower—but she didn't care. She nestled close to him, feeling cold, then went still as someone seized her hair and jerked her head back.

A slight figure loomed over her. "Get up, you little slut," a harsh voice hissed.

Sable released J. D. and climbed back out of the bed, wincing as the intruder's grip nearly tore her scalp. That didn't scare her as much as the smell of gasoline. "What do you want?"

"Justice." The figure held out a red square can and began splashing it on the bed.

"You won't get it this way, Laure," J. D. said softly, and turned on the lamp next to the bed.

Sable stared, horrified, at the woman's hate-contorted face. "Mrs. LeClare? But we thought you were—"

"Dead? Oh, no." Laure smiled. "You see, while that crazy Cajun was setting fire to my house, I made a daring and miraculous escape. But the trauma was too much for me on top of the horrific murder of my poor husband, and it forced me to go into hiding, in fear for my life. In a week or two, I'll recover enough to return and tell the press all the details of my ordeal."

Sable took in a sharp breath. "Caine didn't start the fire. You did."

"I never liked that decrepit old place, but Marc had to have it." She stroked her hand over Sable's hair. "Just like he had to have his daughter. I burned the house, but I can't seem to kill you."

"How many times have you tried?" J. D. asked.

"Three. You think four's a charm with this one?" She yanked Sable's hair. "Look at her. Not a mark on her, just like before. You'd think she was made of asbestos." She glanced at J. D. and held out her arm over the bed. In her fist was a lighter. "Put your hands out where I can see them, Jean-Delano, or I'll set the bed on fire first."

J. D. placed his hands on the edge of the covers. "You

hired Bud Gantry to do your burning for you twenty-nine years ago."

"Of course I did. This slut's mother tried to take Marc away from me." She frowned. "All that trouble—do you know, Bud Gantry tried to blackmail me, when it was his fault he got caught? It's much cheaper to hire someone to kill a man in prison, though. It only cost a thousand dollars and three cartons of cigarettes. Imagine that."

"You hired Billy Tibbideau after Marc told you about Sable."

"He was going to give up everything for her—his campaign, his reputation, our standing in the community; he even threatened to divorce me and leave me penniless if I didn't agree to it. He expected me to swallow all that humiliation because she was his beloved Ginny's little brat."

Sable met her crazy eyes. "You were at the warehouse that morning. Billy didn't kill Marc. You did."

Laure smiled and drew out a strand of dark red hair. "I paid Billy to bring me the pole and set the fire. Marc didn't know I was waiting upstairs for him." She clicked on the lighter. "Unfortunately Billy got there a little early, but he won't be a problem anymore. He has left town—permanently."

"Laure, you need help," J. D. said softly.

"Why? I can burn her by myself. I should have done it the very first time; then she would have never broken your heart, Jean-Delano." Laure applied the flame to a hank of Sable's hair, and chuckled as Sable slapped it out with her hand. "See? No trouble at all."

Sable watched J. D. tense, readying himself to spring. "You can't get away with murder again, not with Caine in a coma."

"Billy's the one who's been trying to kill you. They'll think he finally succeeded." She pushed Sable to her knees. "A shame your mother's not here, J. D. She'd enjoy this as much I do." She clicked on the lighter again and set Sable's hair on fire.

J. D. lunged from the bed, knocking Sable aside and throwing the gasoline-soaked cover over Laure. She screamed as the lighter ignited it and she was covered in a blanket of flame. She fell over, screeching and writhing.

Sable rolled on the floor, away from Laure, burning her hands as she frantically tried to put out her hair. J. D. hauled her up under his arm and ran into the bathroom, where he thrust her under the shower.

Water blinded her, but the heat and the sickening smell of her own hair burning vanished.

He lifted her dripping from the tub and covered her nose and mouth with a wet hand towel before doing the same to his face. "Hold on tight."

J. D. led her back out to the bedroom, where almost everything was burning now. The vague shape of a blackened body lay in the center of the fire roaring up from the bed. The intense heat seared Sable's face; in a few moments the entire room would be filled with flames and smoke.

Sable stumbled through the smoke with J. D. to the front room, where he jerked two coats from a rack before he got her out into the hallway. Fire alarms were ringing and the building's overhead sprinkler system snapped on, and the other tenants hurried out of the apartments as smoke poured into the hall.

As she saw the other people, Sable realized why he had grabbed the coats—they were both still naked.

"It's okay." J. D. paused long enough to wrap her in one coat and pull on the other, then swung her up in his arms. "We're going to be okay now, baby. I promise." He carried her to the emergency stairs.

Epilogue

J. D. waited for Sable outside Caine Gantry's room. The big man had emerged from his coma and was due to be released in a few days. Moriah Navarre had already been released, and was at home resting after dealing with her injuries and the scandal that had rocked New Orleans.

Sable came out, looking fragile but beautiful in her strapless white silk ball gown. She gave J. D. a rueful smile as she rubbed a hand over her short red hair. "He didn't like my new style. He said I look like Anne Heche."

"It'll grow back, and I think you look like Audrey Hepburn." J. D. didn't want to remember how it had felt, watching Laure set fire to Sable's head. "You sure you feel up to going to this?"

His mother had begged them both to come to the Noir et Blanc Gala, and surprisingly Sable had been the one to accept her invitation.

"Absolutely. Your father promised to dance with me, and he says he can waltz way better than you." She slipped her arm through his and admired his black tux. "You can't monopolize me all night, you know, Mr. Bond."

He laughed and led her to the elevators.

After Laure's final murderous attack, J. D. had wanted to keep Sable away from the media, but she had insisted on dealing with the press and the scandal. The Gambles and the Creole community in turn had rallied around her, and now most of Marc's friends and associates had pledged to help her with the Cajun community project.

Sable was grateful for the support but not very impressed by the attention. "I may have LeClare blood," she told J. D., "but I'm not joining the social set. I'm still a Cajun, and I'll always be proud of it."

The gala was in full swing when they reached the Gamble home, and Elizabet herself met them at the door. "I was getting worried," she said as she kissed J. D.'s cheek, then turned to Sable and studied her. "Now, where did you get that dress?"

She glanced down at herself. "I bought it at a new boutique in Metairie. I hope it's all right for tonight."

"It's perfect." Elizabet took her hands and leaned over to add in a murmur, "Take me with you the next time you go shopping there, and I'll show you where I get my shoes."

Sable glanced down at the other woman's elegant black heels, which had sparkling, flirty little toe straps. "Deal."

Sable faced the room with no small amount of trepidation—there were hundreds of men in beautiful black tie, and women in bewildering varieties of white gowns. This time J. D. was at her side, however, and they would face whatever came at them together.

Louie rushed over and with his usual exuberant affection hugged and kissed them both, then hustled them in to introduce them to several family friends. J. D.'s brows rose when he saw Terri in a feminine version of a black tux weaving through the crowd to get to them.

"Jesus, what a crowd. I feel like a transvestite penguin. You clean up nice, partner." She elbowed J. D. and grinned at Sable. "Looking good, too, Red."

Cort appeared and scowled at J. D. before giving Sable a brotherly kiss on the cheek. "I thought you'd never get here. The mayor wants someone to make a speech, and I had to give the last one."

"Oh, no." J. D. noticed how studiously his brother and his partner were avoiding looking at each other, and suppressed a smile. "I've only got one speech to make tonight."

Elizabet took Sable's hand and tugged at his arm. "Now would be the perfect time, Jean-Delano."

He let his mother lead him and Sable out to the garden, where Elizabet called out, "Ladies and gentlemen, if you would join us out here for a moment, my son has something that he would like to announce."

People came out through the French doors into the cool night air, and slowly fell silent as Elizabet stepped to one side. Louie put his arm around her and grinned broadly at his son.

J. D. looked at Sable as he took her hand in his; then he surprised everyone by going down on one knee. "Miss Isabel Duchesne-LeClare, I would be honored if you would consent to be my wife."

Her dark eyes shimmered with tears. "Jean-Delano Gamble, it would be my honor to have you as my husband."

As cheers and applause erupted around them, he took out the diamond ring he had been carrying in his jacket all night, and slipped it on the third finger of her left hand. A sudden boom went off, and colorful fireworks exploded overhead.

"That's the end of Mardi Gras," he said, looking up at the dazzling display before returning his gaze to hers. "Are you sorry the excitement's over?"

"No." She drew his face down to hers. "For you and me, it's just beginning."

Dear Reader,

The great thing about romance readers is our sense of adventure. Look at the wide variety of stories we enjoy reading, from mysteries to fantasy and everything in between. As a writer, I'm just as adventurous. I love writing romantic suspense novels like *Into the Fire*, the story you've just finished reading. But that's not all I write. I've also published many science fiction novels under the name S. L. Viehl.

I'd like to take you on a little adventure right now. Turn the page to read an excerpt from my latest S. L. Viehl novel, *BioRescue*, which comes out in September 2004. The story is science fiction, to be sure, but like my Jessica Hall novels it's also packed with plenty of fun, romance and danger. I had such a great time with this book and I hope you'll enjoy it, too.

All My Best,
Jessica Hall, aka S. L. Viehl

An excerpt from

BioRescue

by S. L. Viehl
Coming in September 2004

In the far future, a young aquatic military pilot defies her people's rigid customs and secretly befriends a land-dwelling war refugee. Yet Jadaira and Shan are unaware of the dangerous forces at work all around them, or the eyes that are constantly watching . . .

Onkar had two reasons for holding on to the encrypted data chips delivered by the quadrant courier. The first was to give him an excuse to return to the grotto. The small body of water was less than ideal for what he had planned—large as he was, he never felt comfortable in such constricted areas—but the opportunity to be alone with Jadaira was irresistible.

The second was why he went to the Trading Center and contracted the services of a footgear peddler, who sometimes did illegal program bootlegging on the side. He had to discover what data was so vital that it ad to be coded for her eyes alone.

Her behavior earlier had been rather odd enough to e him slightly more suspicious than usual. *She is g something from me.* If they were to be together, there could be no secrets between them. He realized he could be over-analyzing the situation; it certainly wouldn't be the first time. *Perhaps it is nothing, and all I must do is be more open and easier with her. Certainly she would approve of that, and it might even prompt her to place more trust in me.*

The front façade of the peddler-programmer's stand seemed to be constructed entirely of the containers in which he packaged his wares. The size and type of the container varied, but all but a few special order items were displayed through the clear rectangular boxes. Behind them was a privacy screen, which concealed him while he attended to his other, much more lucrative business, and it was there that Onkar paced as he waited.

After several minutes without results, Onkar checked his wristcom. "This is taking too long."

"Keep your flightsuit on, Lieutenant." The bootlegger sucked some air in through his teeth as official-looking data began filling his screen. "These chips have TS-5 level clearance codes. You sure you want to know what's on them?"

TS-5? Now he had to know. "Yes."

"Your court martial." The bootlegger rapidly tapped his keyboard before he blanked out his display and inserted a data storage chip.

"Why did you shut down the screen?" Onkar demanded.

"If they catch you and you implicate me, I can honestly state that I never saw what was on them. Saves me from spending my best years hacking out minerals in some penal colony mine." He finished copying the data, and exchanged both sets of chips for the agreed upon credits. "Nice doing business with you, L tenant. Come back if you ever get tired of those fluke boots."

Onkar left the Trading Center and went straight back to Dair's puddle in the forest. He was hot and irritable and his hide was flaking, but as he made his way through the trees, he heard her voice. The pure joy in the ringing sound of it sank into him like waspnetter venom and made him forget everything except being near her again. He began unfastening his flightsuit as he drew near, wanting nothing more than to dive in the cool water and hear her speak to him with such pleasure. He was so eager that he nearly stepped out onto the bank before he realized she was no longer alone.

"You're doing fine, don't stiffen your neck." Dair had the Skartesh pilot in the water with her. He was bare-chested, floating face-up, and she had her arms around the center of his body. "Loosen your muscles and let the water support your head."

Onkar drew back into the shadows.

Shan did not seem as happy as Jadaira. "I will sink as soon as you let go of me."

If he does not, Onkar thought, *I can arrange it. Easily.*

"No, you won't. Try to relax." Dair stroked the furry surface of the Skartesh's hair-covered, heaving chest with her hand. "Don't fight the water, try to be a part of it."

She had never touched Onkar like that. In fact, she had gone to great lengths to avoid touching him at all.

"How does one become part of liquid?" Shan asked her.

His recessed eyes narrowed to slits. *I could show you.*

"You already are." She moved him in a slow circle ᴏund her. "If I were to cut you, you wouldn't bleed ᴅ." She hesitated. "You wouldn't, would you?"

Onkar's teeth ached as he thought of the many satisfying ways in which he could open the Skartesh's veins.

"No." Shan made a low, rumbling sound and brought up one paw to rest over her hand. "You are trying to distract me."

"Yes, and I'm having a very hard time of it."

Rage continued to seethe inside Onkar, burning away every other emotion as he watched them. Soon he felt as if there was nothing left in him but the heat of fury; not since ranging alone in the outer currents had he felt so empty.

Jadaira had always claimed that she would never mate, and here she was, alone with this male who had done nothing but pursue her since he had arrived on-planet. If she had not made her choice, she soon would.

Let her play with the mouth-breather now, he decided as he curled his fin around the encrypted chips. *It will keep her occupied while I do what is necessary. And when she brings him into my water, then I will show her what— and how—he bleeds.*